FIVE
LITTLE
INDIANS

FIVE
LITTLE
INDIANS

MICHELLE
GOOD

HARPER PERENNIAL

Five Little Indians

Copyright © 2020 by Michelle Good.
All rights reserved.

Published by Harper Perennial, an imprint of HarperCollins Publishers Ltd

First edition

This is a work of fiction. Any resemblances to places or people,
living or dead, is purely coincidental.

HarperCollins books may be purchased for educational, business
or sales promotional use through our Special Markets Department.

HarperCollins Publishers Ltd
Bay Adelaide Centre, East Tower
22 Adelaide Street West, 41st Floor
Toronto, Ontario, Canada
M5H 4E3

www.harpercollins.ca

"Starwalker" written by Buffy Sainte-Marie, published by Caleb Music (SOCAN).
Used with permission.

Library and Archives Canada Cataloguing in Publication

Title: Five little indians / Michelle Good.
Names: Good, Michelle, author.
Identifiers: Canadiana (print) 20200178903 | Canadiana (ebook) 20200178911 |
ISBN 9781443459181 (softcover) | ISBN 9781443459198 (ebook)
Classification: LCC PS8613.O62 F58 2020 | DDC C813/.6—dc23

Printed and bound in the United States of America

LSC/H 1 2 3 4 5 6 7 8 9 10

For the Boy, Jay Daniel Good.
My devoted son,
the reflection of the self I saw in your eyes was,
and is, my lifeline.

and

For every terrified child taken.

PROLOGUE

‑‑‑‑‑‑‑><‑‑‑‑‑‑‑

Clara stood behind Mariah's cabin, the late summer warmth rising from the soil. She looked down the hill and watched Mariah's helpers readying the sweat lodge. She turned and headed toward the cabin door, a silvery glimmer distracting her. She looked east and saw the beginnings of the many trails she and Mariah had walked so many years ago. She thought she saw her dog, now long dead, a ghostly image running ahead of her as he had done then. She made her way toward the beginning of the trail she and Mariah had often walked to set snares, a faint tinkling rising on the breeze from the grove around the lodge. She walked, oblivious to time, only turning back when the sun was high and the birch leaves shimmered all around her.

It was just after noon when she got back to the cabin. Kendra stood in the doorway, looking this way and that, smiling, when her eyes fell on Clara.

"I was wondering where you went. You okay?"

"Lot of memories out there." Clara reached out and hugged the young woman. Kendra was as close as she came to having a child, the daughter of her closest and oldest friend. The women entered the cabin to find Mariah preparing her smudge bowl.

"Come here, you two."

Clara and Kendra sat with Mariah as she lit her smudge, a special combination of many different medicines. As she prayed in her soft Cree, Clara leaned over and took Kendra's hand. They prayed in silence as Mariah prepared an offering for the ancients. They opened their eyes, relaxed, an air of peace beautifying the simple cabin. The truck would be here soon. Clara leaned over to Mariah.

"Kendra's a doctor, you know. First Indian doctor in Canada."

Kendra corrected her. "Aboriginal."

Clara rolled her eyes. "Native. Aboriginal. Whatever. Call me Indian till they get it right in the Indian Act."

Mariah put her hand over Clara's. "Now. No politics here."

"Mariah's a doctor too." Clara nodded, looking at Kendra. "She sure fixed me up."

Kendra shrugged, her discomfort plain.

Clara laughed and squeezed the young woman's hand. "Mariah's got a whole different kind of science. She learned it here. Didn't need no fancy school."

The three women fell silent, waiting. Before too long the truck pulled up. The driver climbed out, waving at the women as they walked out to meet him.

Mariah nodded and pointed. "There's some helpers by the lodge. You'll need them." The driver headed around back of the cabin and the women went inside, Clara making tea for the newly arrived.

Vera, the driver's wife, pulled up a chair to the kitchen table. "Did you find a place?"

Mariah nodded. "Not too far from the lodge."

Clara had just poured the tea when Mariah nodded toward the

window. "Here come the helpers." She rose as the men joined them in the cabin.

One of them turned to Mariah. "You ready?"

She nodded, gathering up her bundle. "You men carry her down. We'll follow."

They all gathered around the pickup. The men pulled the casket from the truck bed. They walked round the cabin in the direction of the sun before making their way down the hill to the open place in the earth prepared for her.

They gathered in a circle around the open grave. The men gently placed the casket in the raw earth. Clara wept.

It had taken a dedicated researcher to find Lily's remains, and even then it was almost impossible to get the Church to give her up. "We found you, Lily. We brought you home," Clara whispered. Kendra put an arm around her. "I couldn't leave you there after what they did to you. We finally got to go home. You and me both."

Mariah prayed and the helpers followed with their deep voices, the hand drums filling the air around them with a deep sense of both peace and anticipation. When they finished their honour song, Mariah led the group to the sweat lodge, entering first and then inviting them all in, Kendra first to sit beside her and Clara next to Kendra. They all sat in a circle as the helpers brought in the white-hot rocks, filling the pit before them. Mariah began her prayers, placing the sage and cedar on the stones, the magical scent of the medicines rising, filling the lodge.

Clara leaned over and took Kendra's hand. "Doc." She smiled. "Get ready for some doctoring."

The helpers closed the door.

1

KENNY

>-----<

Kenny took one backward glance, the tiller firm in his hand. Today, the clouds swirled at sea level, the shifting mists like a painter's brush, all but obliterating the island. The Mission School might not have been there at all, a bad dream, it was lost so completely in the deep coastal fog. The first time he'd seen the Mission, he was six years old, crammed into a boat with a dozen or so little kids, the steeple piercing the clouds as though it floated above them all, unhinged from the earth. Back then, he'd sat there, numb, as the boat docked, overcome with a feeling he didn't understand. Now, he was too familiar with that feeling. Being totally helpless was his daily fare at the Mission. Being used to the feeling made it no easier.

He reached into his pocket, double-checking, and pulled out a small piece of paper. It had been folded and folded again into a small, dusty square. He thought of Lucy, risking a beating to pass him that note, that day in the dining hall. He read it again, as he had over and over in the past weeks. *Yor brave.* His determination rose every time he read it, as did his humiliation, remembering he had been wearing a purple-flowered dress, his head shaved, with a sign around his neck, *I am a runaway*, in bold red letters, when she'd slipped him the note. Brother had just exposed his bare ass to all the kids gathered in the dining hall and beat him and beat him with his paddle, determined to make him cry, furious when he couldn't.

A chill overtook him even though the sun had burned through the morning mist. He reached up and touched his still-shorn head, his hair barely starting to grow back. Brother was none too gentle with the electric shears, the scars like raised rivulets across his scalp from being shorn the last time he'd run away. That time, the RCMP had intercepted him, not three miles off the school's dock, the engine on the punt dying and leaving him afloat. Easy pickings. He couldn't stop thinking of Howie, no matter how hard he tried, the boy lying there in his bed, bleeding and beaten. Even as he filled his mind with images of his mom, home, the smokehouse, he could not. Images of Howie followed him like a cold wind as the punt skimmed easily across the quiet sea.

Just that morning, a brilliant morning, Kenny had opened his eyes astonished that, once again, Brother hadn't come for him in the night. He got out of bed with the rest of the boys and washed and dressed in preparation for the morning prayer. Looking to the next bed, he noticed Howie still sleeping. Kenny stood between the door and Howie's bed, trying to hide him from Sister, who was busy at the end of the dorm with a bedwetter.

"Psst, Wilfred, wake Howie up before Sister sees him."

Wilfred nudged him, urging him to wake up. Howie remained motionless in his bed. Wilfred looked at Kenny and shrugged. He poked a little harder at Howie. Still nothing.

Kenny leaned over the boy. "Howie, wake up. Sister is going to see you."

Wilfred nudged Kenny. "Too late."

Sister came striding through the rows of beds, her robes rustling, veil flying behind her like some menacing black bird. She ripped Howie's covers off, grabbed his mattress and rolled him out of bed onto the floor. Howie lay there motionless, the bloodstained pillow and sheets on top of his still body. Sister shrieked and ran out to the hallway, calling for Brother. Brother John came running, picked up the small boy and, with long strides, was out of the dorm in seconds. Sister scooped up the bloodied linens. Howie had not moved once, his head lolling over Brother's arm. The boys looked at each other and congregated at the window.

Wilfred came up beside Kenny at the window. "He had a big black eye. Brother came for him last night."

The boys stayed at the window, watching. Finally, Brother John and Sister appeared below the window. Sister stayed on the steps as Brother carried Howie down to the dock.

"They will take him to the hospital." Wilfred didn't sound too sure.

"Will they?" Kenny and Wilfred were the last two boys at the window. "It should have been me." Kenny choked out the words, struggling not to cry.

Wilfred moved closer to his friend. "It should have been no one."

The boys, washed and dressed, milled about confused, not knowing what else to do. Finally, like homing pigeons, they formed the chapel lineup and waited. Sister Mary appeared at the door and for once the bedwetters got a reprieve. "You're late for Mass. Move!" The boys headed for the chapel, quiet and tense.

Our Father.

In the dining hall, Kenny saw Lucy, still wearing her *I am a liar* sign. He ignored Sister and walked straight over to the girls' side. He whispered to Lucy, "You are strong too." He noticed the scrapes on her head, now healed to little scab trails.

The girls giggled. Lucy looked up at him and took hold of one of his hands. It seemed forever they stood there, motionless and quiet, the other kids wide-eyed, waiting for Sister to notice and give them both a licking. But she didn't, by some miracle.

Kenny pulled his hand away and nodded at Lucy. "Remember that."

After chores, during free time, Kenny put on an extra pair of socks and pulled his only sweater on over his shirt, grabbed his jacket and headed to the playground. There was no one around but kids. He slipped through the salmonberry bushes to the dock trail. The punt, its new motor shining and bigger than the old one, bobbed in the lapping waves. He figured they must be right tired of chasing after him since, this time, the punt was tethered to the dock with a length of chain and a shiny new lock. The sky was a thin blue, the last days of summer. *Maybe the sockeye are running.* He thought of his uncle gearing up to sail to the fishing grounds. *Maybe if I could make it to Port McNeill, someone would take me home.* He sat at the end of the wharf, feet dangling inches above the water. He thought of Howie, small and bloodied. He thought of Lucy, shorn and scabby. He thought of Wilfred, alone in the dorm without him. He thought of that big cop who'd dragged him back to the school the last time—the one who wouldn't believe him about what Brother was doing. He thought of his mom. A long, low sob fell out of him and the tears flowed. He felt like he was crumbling. He steadied himself, placing his hands on his knees.

With no tears left, he stood slowly, walked back up the dock and down to the beach. He chose a rock so big he had to carry it with both hands, smashed the lock off the chain, then tossed the lock and chain into the quiet water, watching it sink like some weird shimmering snake. Kenny knew he was the last thing on anyone's mind. He jumped into the punt, gunned the new engine, and the punt bounce-skimmed across the quiet bay.

The tide and the weather favoured him. For hours he chugged along, trusting his sense of due north. When the sun was high at midday, an orca breached not twenty feet from the punt. He gasped, both terrified and astonished at its sleek white-and-black beauty. Not long after, he could see the shoreline and prayed it was Port McNeill. He guided the punt in close, passing a large dock with at least a dozen commercial fishing boats tethered in their slips.

He cut the engine and the punt rode the waves effortlessly to shore. Kenny gauged the depth of the sea water and jumped over the side. The cold water dragged on his jeans as he hauled the punt ashore and secured it tightly to a waterlogged cedar long dead and errant from some logger's boom. Chilled almost numb from his long day on the water, he gathered shards of driftwood for a small fire, water squeaking with every step of his soaked sneakers. Just as he didn't dare dock the punt at the main harbour, knowing the Port McNeill detachment would be watching for him, he now decided against a fire. He pressed his hands under his armpits, craving what heat was left in his body. His body warmed a little as he climbed the sandy bank, anxious to get back to the docks. When he was little, his uncle talked about Port McNeill. He just might be here.

With less than a hundred yards behind him, Kenny ran back, untied the punt and pushed it back into the water. *Let them think I drowned.* Once again, he reached the crest of the hill. Not far off, the main road, a grey-black ribbon, wound toward the harbour. He thought of that cop who didn't believe him, and rather than risk capture again, he walked along the craggy shoreline. Just as the last light of dusk seeped into the blackening sea, he stepped onto the docks and made his way to the far end, away from junctures, searching out areas where the fewest people might be. The throaty calls of the owls warming up for the nightly hunt got him thinking of bears and coyotes hungry for the day's remains from the boats, and he wandered back in the direction he'd come from, craving some kind of shelter. He saw a skiff moored to a large fishing boat, rolling gently in the water. He loosened the ropes that lashed its cover in place, pulled the skiff parallel to the dock and tumbled in. He tightened the ropes as best he could from the inside, hoping no one would be looking too closely. He thought for sure he would never sleep. The chill and his chattering teeth would keep him awake. Eventually, though, the toll of the day won out and sleep overtook him.

Kenny awoke, slightly nauseous and sweltering in the small space of the skiff. He punched open the edge of the canvas and the morning air rushed in, cool, like a fast-running stream. As his stomach growled, he lay there, wishing he'd brought his only other pair of pants. The long, damp cruise had left his clothes clammy and ripe with the smell of the sea. Involuntary shivering had awoken him throughout the night, but the morning sun soon turned the damp interior of the skiff into a stuffy, steamy hot box. He took in another deep breath of the cool fresh air.

His thoughts of dry clothes and something to eat left him as soon as he heard the sound of boots on the dock's wooden walkway, signalling someone's approach. He closed his eyes, hoping whoever it was would just carry on by, but the footsteps stopped. Expert hands loosened the knots securing the canvas cover. Kenny curled up, waiting for the fisherman to throw off the canvas, poised, ready to jump and run. When he did, the sunlight was surprisingly blinding.

"What the hell?" The startled fisherman dropped the canvas and took a step backwards, staggering just a little.

Kenny jumped out of the boat half-blinded by the sun, and if he hadn't tripped, he'd have made it. As he tried to recover his footing, the fisherman grabbed him by the shoulder.

"Kid! What the hell are you doing in my skiff?" He held Kenny firmly by the shoulder.

Kenny struggled for a moment then sighed and stood still. "I just fell asleep."

"Where's your family?"

Kenny shrugged.

"Well, I better take you to the detachment."

"No, no! I'm looking for my uncle. He said I could work on his boat. He's supposed to be here."

The fisherman loosened his grip on Kenny's shoulder but stood between him and the town side of the dock. Kenny looked up at him for the first time, surprised. This guy could even be his uncle, with that shining black, rod-straight hair, gumboots, fisherman's sweater and suspenders.

"Work on his boat?" He shook his head and laughed. "How old are you? Twelve?"

Kenny squared his shoulders and tried to seem tall. "What? Twelve? Heck no, I just turned sixteen. I can work."

"Sixteen?" He laughed again. "You sure as hell ain't no sixteen. What's your uncle's name? Shouldn't you be in school?"

"Clifford. Clifford Bart. He has a big purse seiner." Kenny stood a little taller, trying not to look scared at the thought of being sent back to the school.

"I know Clifford." The fisherman looked at Kenny, as if for the first time taking in the clothes, the immediately identifiable Indian School issue. "Just saw him yesterday. Didn't say a word about you."

"Musta forgot."

"Let's go find him. See what he has to say about all this."

"Oh, umm, all right." Kenny smiled up at the fisherman, his heart pounding.

"He's probably on his boat."

"You could just point the way." Kenny smiled as though his pants were dry and he had real leather shoes or even gumboots. "I can find him."

"No trouble." The fisherman placed a hand, softly this time, on Kenny's shoulder and steered him toward the far end of the dock. "This way."

Kenny hadn't seen so many grown-up Indians since he was taken to the Mission. Both men and women worked the boats, checking the rigging, readying their nets. The sun shone off their slick black hair, tied back or cut short, as they greeted the fisherman and looked curiously at Kenny. A tall, muscular woman straightened, removed one work glove and wiped wisps of hair from her face.

"Who you got there, Mack? Long-lost love child?" She pulled her glove back on, laughing and elbowing her crew mate.

Mack the fisherman looked up at her, shielding his eyes from the sun. "You seen Clifford this morning?"

"Yeah, he's getting ready to pull anchor. Heading back to Simpson. Sockeye are thick at the mouth of the Skeena, I hear."

"Well, boy, you're in luck."

Kenny couldn't tell if he meant it or if Mack knew how surprised Clifford would be to see him. The pair walked past three more boats and Kenny figured this one must be it. Had to be. The last slip.

Mack stopped at the prow, looked up and called out, "Clifford! Clifford! You up there?"

"Yeah, yeah. I'm busy here." Each word seemed louder, punctuated by firm steps on the deck, as the speaker made his way from the stern. A large, exasperated dark man leaned over the prow. "Whaddya want? Oh, hi, Mack."

The fisherman nudged Kenny a little toward the boat. "Your new help is here."

Kenny looked up, barely recognizing his mother's brother. "Uncle Clifford!"

"What?" Clifford raised a gloved hand to shield his eyes from the sun. "Who are you?"

"It's me, Kenny. Bella's my mom."

"What? I'll be right down." Clifford was on the dock in no time, agile and fast for such a big man.

"I found him stowed away on my skiff. Says he works for you. Sixteen, he says."

Mack chuckled. Kenny looked up at him and didn't think Mack found it funny at all.

"Well, he's all yours now, Clifford. I'm heading up Simpson way too." He waved over his shoulder without looking back. "Maybe see you in Rupert."

Kenny sat on the deck. "I can help you. I can work for you. Help you for getting me home."

"Kenny, you're just too young. You can't work for me. C'mon, let me get you some dry clothes."

Kenny followed him below deck and changed into the clothes, rolling up the ankles and sleeves, trying for a better fit.

"I work all the time. I'm strong. I can do it. Just give me a chance."

"You're supposed to be in school. They could throw me in jail just for having you on the boat. I just can't risk it. I'm going to have to take you back."

Kenny followed him back above deck and sat on the deck next to some rigging. "I can't go back. I just can't." Panic rose in him, thinking of Clifford delivering him back to the Mission.

Kenny stood up, Clifford's clothes hanging off him. He threw off his uncle's shirt, exposing the rainbow of red, purple and yellowing bruises. Ashamed of the tears he couldn't hold back, he turned and gripped the railing. He pinched himself hard, willing the tears to stop. *Uncle won't want a crybaby.* His ribs, exposed from too little to eat, were punctuated by the marks, old and new, of Brother's handiwork. Choking back the tears, he turned to his uncle. "Please. Please don't take me back."

Kenny flinched and pulled away when Clifford reached out to put his arm around his shoulders.

"Who did this to you, Kenny?"

"Brother. He hates us. They all hate us."

"But why would he do this?"

Kenny shrugged and looked at his feet. "He does other things too. He hurts me."

Clifford stepped back from Kenny and looked away. "He's supposed to be taking care of you."

Kenny shrugged again. "There's never enough to eat."

"You know, me and your mom, we never had to go to the Indian School. Your grandfather made sure of that. He would take us out on his fishing boat every fall for a few days when they were coming to collect the kids. Never wrote our names down anywhere so the government didn't have us on their list." Clifford picked up the shirt and wrapped it around Kenny's shoulders. "We knew it was no good, but not this."

"Why didn't Mom come see me? You could have brought her on the boat." Kenny looked away, feeling the tears pressing at his eyes again.

"We did. The year they took you, we went down during the halibut season. We docked right there at the school. The principal—don't remember his name—"

"Father Levesque."

"Yeah, that's right. He wouldn't let us see you. He said he would send us a letter saying when we could see you and if we came back before then, he would call the police. Your mom never got a letter."

"So you just gave up?" Kenny broke down, sitting in a puddle of khaki, sobbing.

Clifford put his arms around him and rocked him gently. "No, Kenny. Your mom wrote that school every day. She walked to town every day to mail her letters, asking about you. She even wrote to the Indian agent in Terrace. She wrote you letters, too. Sent you money. Even presents at Christmas. That principal never wrote back either."

Kenny rubbed his eyes with the heels of his hands. "I never got any letters, Uncle. Not one. Nothing." The tears started again. "Please don't take me back. Please."

Clifford stood and turned his back to Kenny, taking his work gloves out of his back pocket. "I'm heading up to Simpson tomorrow to pick up a crew. The sockeye are running. We'll be fishing outside of Rupert within a day or two."

"So, I can work for you?" Kenny leapt up, grabbing on to the waist of the too-large pants to keep from losing them. "Okay, what do you want me to do? Just show me once. I'll do a good job."

Clifford laughed. "You are too young! Maybe next year, when you're fourteen, I'll take you out. Show you the ropes. I'm gonna take you to Simpson. To your mom."

"Really?" The thought of his mom worried him. He'd been gone such a long time.

"Yeah, really. If that priest wants you back at that school, he can come get you himself." Clifford stood and pointed below deck. "Come on. Let's get you fed up and then we are out of here."

Like a jackrabbit suddenly free from the trap, Kenny ran a full circle around the deck, laughing at the top of his lungs, running finally into his uncle, hugging him for dear life. "You'll see. I'll help you."

Clifford hugged him back. "Now look at me, Kenny. It's been rough for your mom. You were all she had after your dad died. When they took you . . . Well, it's been rough."

Kenny looked at him, wondering what this could mean. Just as he was going to ask, the crew started climbing aboard and the fishing boat came to life.

A day later, after a refuel at Port Hardy and fish and chips for Kenny, the fishing boat docked at Port Simpson. The men rushed through their work, anxious to secure the boat and carry on with their evening pursuits.

"Five a.m. sharp!" Clifford called out after them as they disappeared into the late afternoon. "The rest of the crew will be here, and we'll be pulling anchor right away. Don't be late if you expect a pay packet."

Kenny stood next to Clifford, afraid for reasons he couldn't figure out.

"Come on, I'll walk you to Bella's. Do you remember the way?"

Kenny felt small and unsure. The tall, narrow two-storey houses, built chockablock in a long crescent above the beach, looked smaller now, like faded ghosts of the brightly painted houses of his memory. He inched closer to Clifford. "I used to think of it all the time at school. Sister would get mad at me for daydreaming."

Clifford put his arm around Kenny's shoulder. "Must feel a little strange, eh?"

"Yeah." Kenny didn't understand the sinking feeling in his stomach. The village was eerily quiet, with only the occasional cry of a baby from deep inside one of the ghost houses. They walked by the empty playground. The rusted chains of the swings hung motionless, the canvas seats long rotted away. The slide lay on its side and the sandbox was overgrown with sedge grass and dandelions. Not a single child played on the sunny beach, in front of the houses or on the walkway.

"Do you remember?" Clifford pointed to a faded moss-green house, the last house above the beach.

The house looked so much smaller and sadder than Kenny remembered, with the roof starting to sag in the middle. Kenny ran to the front door, leaving Clifford behind. He struggled with the door, but it was locked. He turned and looked at his uncle, confused.

"Why is it locked?"

"Well, I guess she's not home."

A sudden exhaustion overtook Kenny. His knees felt weak. A small, weather-beaten three-legged stool sat beside the front door. He remembered it from all those years ago. His mom would sit him there while she got her gear ready for the smokehouse. The stool looked so small now, and no longer the bright blue it was then. He sat down, his elbows on his knees, his head in his hands.

"Where is she?"

Clifford craned his neck to peer through the window and then looked away quickly. Just as he did, a couple stepped out of the house next door.

"Oh, hi, Clifford." The couple smiled and walked toward them. "Who is this?"

"Do you remember Kenny?" Clifford motioned to Kenny to stand and shake hands.

"Kenny!" The young woman threw her arms around him. "You're all grown up."

Kenny normally would have been overcome with pride that someone recognized he wasn't a kid anymore, but he was tired from the last couple of days and all he wanted was his mom.

"Do you know where she is?" He stared up at the sturdy, dark-haired woman.

"Lots of goings-on here last night," she said, then hugged Kenny. Catching Clifford's eye, she raised one eyebrow. "I saw her heading for the pebble beach just before dawn. I think she was headed to her smokehouse."

A rush of memories washed over Kenny, welling in his chest so much as to be painful. The salmon, like red ribbons, hanging, cured by breeze and smoke. His mother, singing to him in the old language, smiling and putting him to work, carrying the little load of kindling he was strong enough for. *Mom.* Kenny ran, his feet remembering a long-ago path. He forgot Clifford, the pretty dark-haired lady and her quiet man. He forgot the boat, the school, the long, cold escape. He felt as though his feet weren't even touching the ground until he ran through the seagrasses at the end of the trail and his feet fell against the heavy layers of small stones that made the ground both solid and malleable. He ran in an awkward stagger, his feet sinking inches into the layers of pebbles with each stride. He saw the smokehouse and was sure he could smell the slow alder smoke, just like that day seven years ago.

Breathless, he ran into the smokehouse and was stunned to find it empty and cold. No fire, no salmon hanging, no mom. He looked around at the broken-down smokehouse as a cold breeze blew through the door. The plank walls looked like a toothless monster, the sea visible through gaps left without repair. A pile of ancient alder firewood stood rotting in one corner. The firepit lay bare of even ash, leaving just a circle of cold stones.

Mom. This time he heard his own voice and a rustle from the front of the smokehouse in response. Kenny walked slowly and quietly toward the sound. There she sat, on their favourite driftwood seat, huddled over, her arms wrapped around herself in an empty embrace. She rocked slightly back and forth, and he could hear his lullaby, practically a whisper.

"Mom." His own voice was a whisper too. She didn't respond, just sat there, her back to him, gently rocking. He cleared his throat. "Mom."

She turned, looking at him over her shoulder as though not expecting to see him at all. Her eyes, narrow and swollen, shot open and she tried to stand so quickly she slipped off the smooth driftwood.

"Kenny!" she cried, and scrambled to her feet. Kenny ran, colliding into her and wrapping his arms around her, the two of them a jumble on the pebbles.

"Mom!"

"My boy!"

In an instant, the years of terror and hunger shook through him like a riptide and Kenny sobbed in his mother's arms.

Bella ran her fingers through his salt-crusted hair and wept with him. "Kenny. My boy." Her voice was strangely harsh, not at all the soft, singing sound of his memory.

Kenny caught his breath and they sat together on their driftwood seat, their arms still around each other. She looked older, shots of grey evenly sprinkling her black, black hair. He rested his head against her chest and closed his eyes, the warmth of her arm around him like medicine. "I love you, Mom. I was so lonely for you."

"I thought I would die without you." She kissed him on the top of his head. It was then that he smelled it for the first time—that sickly sweet smell. Just how Brother would smell when he came for him in the night. He looked up at her with a question in his eyes. She had never smelled like that before.

Just then, before he could say anything, Clifford emerged from the smokehouse, a little out of breath.

"Boy, can you ever run! Bella, you okay?" Clifford sat cross-legged on the pebbles in front of them and told the story of Kenny's escape, about seeing him for the first time on the docks at Port McNeill and barely recognizing him, and the sail home. All the while, Bella and Kenny clung to each other as if at any second they might be ripped apart.

Bella looked at Clifford, terror in her eyes. "Are they going to come for him again?"

Clifford looked down and shook his head. "I just don't know, Bella. He left the punt he escaped in adrift. We can just hope they think he drowned. Give up. Too much trouble, maybe."

Bella stood shakily. Kenny wondered if it was the pebbles. She ran her hand through his hair. "Let's go home, son. You must be hungry."

Clifford laughed. "Oh, he's always ready for a meal, this one."

Kenny smiled at his mom.

As the three of them walked back through the smokehouse, Kenny looked up at his mom and asked, "How come no fish, Mom? I dreamt about it."

His mother looked away and replied in her soft, rough voice, "Oh, I haven't made fish in quite a while. No one to feed but me."

"I'm home now, Mom. Clifford will bring some sockeye and we'll fix up the smokehouse and make some together. Okay, Mom?"

Bella smiled and squeezed him. "Okay, my boy."

The three of them walked back along the trail, slower this time, and soon arrived at the house. Bella fished in her pocket for her key, then hesitated as she put it in the lock. She looked at Kenny.

"Things are different, son."

Kenny followed her inside, and his heart sank as the cozy home of his memory dissolved into the shambles before him. The once-immaculate living room was strewn with empty wine and beer bottles and overflowing ashtrays. Plates of half-eaten food were stacked precariously on the counters and filling the sink. The place stank of stale booze, old food and rotting garbage left under the sink too long. Bella threw the discarded clothes off her armchair and looked away, silent.

Kenny looked up at Clifford. "What happened here?"

Clifford looked away too. "I told you, it's been hard on your mom."

Kenny left them there in the fetid mess and went to what had been his bedroom. Everything from his toys to the pictures on the walls were as they had been before he was taken, and the room was impeccably clean. He sat on the bed and looked around. His mother came to the doorway and stood in front of him.

"You kept it for me."

"Yes, Boy. It was the only thing I cared about."

"I'm a hard worker, Mom. We'll fix it together."

"That he is, Bella," said Clifford, who was now standing in the doorway too. "He works like he's doing it to save his life."

Bella smiled. "You were always such a good boy, Kenny."

"Well, I gotta head back to the boat, Bella. You need anything?"

"Okay, Cliff. No, I got everything I need, right here."

"Me too!" Kenny jumped up and ran to Clifford, hugging him tight. "Thank you, Uncle."

Clifford put his hand on Kenny's head. "You take care, boy. If you need me, check with the dock master, he can tell you if I'm coming in and he can get a message to me." He looked at Bella. "I'm heading out for sockeye in the morning. I'll bring you a bin-full for smoking." He paused. "If you're up for it."

Kenny nodded, looking from one to the other, a little confused.

"I'll be up for it, Clifford." Bella straightened her back and smoothed her hair.

Over the course of the evening, Kenny and Bella scrubbed that sad little house from top to bottom. They dragged boxes and bags of bottles out to the back of the house to be sold back tomorrow. They hauled six full bags of garbage to the burn bin and got the fire going, making trips back and forth, adding more and more debris. Kenny washed the floors while Bella washed the dishes and drank glass after glass of cold water. After a couple of hours, they took a break.

"You hungry, my boy?" Kenny nodded as Bella rifled through the pantry cupboard. "Not much here, but I can patch something together. Tomorrow we'll take those bottles in, and I have a few dollars left from my widow cheque. We'll go shopping."

"Shopping?" Kenny had almost forgotten what it was like to wander the aisles of the little grocery store in Port Simpson. "Guess I'm too big to ride in the buggy now, eh, Mom?" The two of them burst out laughing both at the memory of little Kenny in the buggy reaching and pointing for items on the shelf and at the idea of big Kenny stuffed into the little seat.

"Maybe just a little." Bella laughed as she turned to making supper for her boy.

That night they dined on mac and cheese, fried baloney, and fry bread slathered with margarine with the meal and with huckleberry jam for dessert. A feast to Kenny, who, stuffed to the gills, collapsed on the couch next to his mom and rested his head on her shoulder. They sat together, wordless, until Kenny's head started drooping as he fell asleep then jerked up as he tried to stay awake, only to droop again.

"Son," his mother whispered. "You're exhausted. Come on, let me tuck you in."

Kenny mumbled through his sleepiness as his mother walked him to his room. He stripped down to his shorts and climbed beneath the fresh sheets. Bella tucked him in, kissed him on his forehead and sat at the edge of the bed until he drifted off to sleep. But he woke again and watched her as she walked softly out of his room and into the kitchen. She lit a small candle and reached for a clean ashtray, a water glass and then the half-empty bottle of wine that she'd hidden in the pantry cupboard. She sat at the kitchen table, lit her smoke and took a long draw. Inhaling deeply, leaning back, looking up, she exhaled a long, slow plume of smoke into the dark reaches of the rafters. She toyed with the empty water glass and looked at the ruby liquid in the deep-green glass. She smoked and sang his lullaby.

The first few months were like a dream. Kenny and his mother rose with the birds and most days headed to the smokehouse, taking a lunch with them along with the tools they would need. Even more than the house, the smokehouse was like a wound each of them carried, a brutal reminder of the day Kenny was taken. The day the first fire was lit in the smokehouse was like a rebirth. Bella's expert fillet knife glinted in the sun, the red salmon ribbons hanging and waving gently in the breeze above the smoke. For Kenny, this was home.

They fell into an easy routine, tending the smokehouse, carefully preserving half-smoked salmon, managing a simple life. On Sundays they would stay home all day with the curtains closed, just in case the visiting priest got wind of Kenny's return. Neither of them spoke of their years apart, and over time the truth of their separation grew between them, like a silent wound, untended and festering. Kenny started spending more time at the docks, visiting the fishermen and making friends. Every now and then Clifford or Mack would give him some work. Kenny would carefully count his pay, folding the bills neatly in three and slipping them into an old, slim tobacco tin he'd rescued from the junk heap. Bella started spending less time at the smokehouse, more time at the kitchen table, smoking and gazing out the window. Sometimes she wouldn't even hear Kenny when he came in from a day of wandering. He would slip into the chair beside her and marvel at the two-inch ash at the end of her smoke.

"Mom?" Kenny said, moving the tray under her precarious ash. "What's wrong, Mom?"

Her eyes looked as though she was rising from some perilous place deep inside her. "Oh, don't worry, boy. Everything's okay." She stubbed the already-dead cigarette in the ashtray and instinctively wiped her hands on her apron. "Are you ready for your lunch?"

"Mom, it's suppertime."

His mother looked out the window at the changing afternoon light. "Well, so it is. Go wash up. I'll cook."

They ate in silence these days, words growing more and more awkward between them. Kenny would wash the dishes, Bella would dry. But on this day, she reached for her sweater instead. "I'm going for a walk."

Kenny reached for the towel to wipe the suds off his hands. "I'll come."

"No, that's okay. I won't be long. Just finish up there."

It was long after dark when she finally returned. Kenny lay in his bed, still and quiet, watching. She lit a candle on the kitchen table, pulled the bottle from her purse and set it on the table. She looked at it for what seemed like forever before slowly twisting the cap off and taking a long draw. Kenny turned his back to the open door and closed his eyes.

The following morning, his mother was gone. The coffee pot was cold. The ashtray had been emptied, the bottle was gone, but a wave of sadness rolled over Kenny just the same. He took his jacket off the hook by the door, slipped it on, and walked to the docks and filled his day with odd jobs, adding a few bills to his tobacco tin. Late afternoon, he headed to the smokehouse. It felt as if his mother's heart was pulling him there. The racks were empty, but the wonderful smell of smoked fish still permeated the building from their last batch. He found his mother sitting on their driftwood seat, gazing out to sea. Without a word, he sat beside her and took her hand. Wordless, they sat pressed together for what seemed like hours.

Finally, he whispered, "What's the matter, Mom? Aren't you glad I'm home?"

She looked at him and tried to speak but could find no words. Kenny reached for her hands and held them in his. They sat, mute, watching the sun begin its lazy descent into the sea.

"I just don't know what to do." Bella squeezed Kenny's hand. "It's like most of me is gone and I can't get it back."

"Clifford has some work for me. He's heading to Rupert. Gonna take me with him."

"You like working with him. That's good."

"I'll be back on Saturday."

"Okay, boy."

Kenny stood, hugged his mom and headed for the docks, strangely relieved by the idea of heading out on the boat.

It was New Year's Eve on Saturday, and the sun had just set as Kenny walked up the path to the house. A box of empty beer bottles sat on the small painted stool next to a damp bag of garbage. Kenny opened the door and saw some woman he didn't know sleeping in his mother's armchair. Bella sat at the table, a glass of wine in her hand, and a man and a woman argued about who had made the last booze run. His mother looked up just as Kenny slipped back out the door.

He spent the night in the net shed next to the dock. The following morning was bright and clear. Chilled and hungry, he walked to the last slip, where he knew he'd find Mack hard at work, getting ready to head south.

"Hey, Happy New Year, kid! It's 1967. Wonder what craziness the world will cook up this year."

"Yeah, same to you," Kenny replied. "You got any work?"

"You lookin'?"

"Yup. As much as you got." Kenny felt for his tobacco tin in his shirt pocket.

Mack beckoned him aboard. Kenny carefully counted out ones

and fives from his tobacco tin and passed Mack twenty bucks. "Give that to my mother next time you see her, okay?"

Mack folded the bills carefully, then put his hand on Kenny's shoulder for a moment before they turned to ready the boat for sea.

2

LUCY

Y ou." Sister Mary loomed over the senior girls at breakfast, pointing to Lucy. "Back to the dorm. I will be there presently."

Lucy waited until Sister was gone. She looked at the girls she shared her meals with and shrugged her shoulders. "Now what?"

Edna, Lucy's closest friend since Maisie's departure, spoke up with a catch in her throat. "I told you. It's your birthday tomorrow. You're gonna leave."

The following day was Lucy's sixteenth birthday. It was well known to the inmates at the Mission that they were supposed to be allowed to leave the school when they turned sixteen. But it didn't always happen that way. Since they were cut off from the Mainland, it was not as if the students could just walk away. They needed aid and permission. Sometimes, especially in the cases of orphaned children with no one to raise questions, they would be kept at the Mission for years after they hit the age of freedom. At sixteen, their status quietly changed. They became the voiceless ghosts, paid a few dollars in return for long days as scullery maids and labourers—mid-century indentured servants. Lucy fully expected she would be the next pitiful graduate scrubbing the huge pots and pans encrusted with old porridge or stew. She was resigned, wondering what else she would do anyway.

Lucy sat on her cot, hands in her lap, trying to ignore the fear rising in her as she waited for Sister. She ran her hand through her hair, her fingertips homing in on the raised scars from the razor. Finally, she could hear the reports of Sister's hard leather heels announcing her approach. She counted them and sat on her hands so they wouldn't shake. She looked to the window at the low-hanging clouds, hoping for the best.

Sister stopped at the end of Lucy's cot, the clicking of her rosary beads carrying on an extra beat after the footfalls stopped. She placed a small cardboard suitcase on the cot.

"You're leaving tomorrow. Pack your things. The boatman will be picking you up at the dock at three."

Lucy reached for the suitcase. "Where am I going?" Lucy almost smiled at how short Sister had become over the years. She remembered Sister looming over her with the razor ten long years ago, when Lucy stood before her, fresh off the boat, seasick and terrified. She had seemed like a giantess then.

"We have a ticket for you to Vancouver."

"But I don't have any family there. What am I to do there?"

"You have no family anywhere as far as we can tell. What you do or where you go once you get there is no longer my concern. We will give you the address for the welfare office." She looked down her nose and sniffed. "Bring your suitcase down to lunch. New girls are arriving tomorrow, so strip your bed in the morning. Go to the laundry and make it up again with clean linen. You will leave after the noon meal at some point. Now go to class." Sister turned away from Lucy, the crackling of her regalia fading, the dorm sinking back into silence.

Lucy placed the suitcase on the floor at her feet and sat once again on the bed, numb with the notion of freedom. She reached into the small metal locker beside her bed and retrieved the small pink envelope. Maisie had promised she would write when she left last year, and she had. Once. Lucy pulled the single sheet from the envelope and once again took comfort from her friend's words. *When they let you out, come find me. I have a job and you can stay with me.* Lucy tucked the letter into the suitcase and slipped it under the cot.

A strange lightness filled her as she walked to the classroom. She looked at the worn black-and-white floor tile, the thickly painted windowsills, the warped glass of the old panes, the giant crucifix on the chapel door. It seemed impossible that she would not see them again after today. Lucy slipped quietly into her place in the classroom.

"Well?" In the next desk, Edna stole a glance at Lucy.

"I'm leaving tomorrow."

"Told you." Edna's eyes welled with tears. She caught them before they fell.

"Eyes front, Edna, or you will be in the corner again with your friend the dunce cap."

"Yes, Sister." Edna waited until the teacher turned once again to the blackboard. "Tomorrow?"

Lucy whispered. "Yes. Vancouver."

Edna's mouth fell open. "Are you going to see Maisie?"

Lucy nodded toward the front of the class and Sister's broad hips shimmying to the rhythm of her chalk as it moved along the blackboard. Lucy pressed a finger to her lips. "Let's talk at lunch."

Edna had a talent for gossip, although she was a little iffy on the facts most times. All the senior girls would know Lucy's news long before she had a chance to tell them. When the lunch bell rang, she felt the trance take hold again as she took it all in with new eyes. Never again would she wash those stairs or dust the banisters or clean Father's rooms. She smiled as she walked into the dining hall, the rest of her dorm mates there, huddled around Edna at their table.

"Lucy! Hurry up!" Edna beckoned her friend, announcing for the rest of the girls at the table, "See, I told you it was true." All eyes were on Lucy as she took her place at the table, waiting for confirmation.

"Yes, it's true." Lucy looked at them in their brown leotards and school skirts, all the same, like a chain of dolls cut from brown paper. "Sister says I'm going to Vancouver."

"Are you going to stay with Maisie?"

"Did she ever write again?" The girls all spoke at once, peppering Lucy with questions.

"I only got one letter from her, but she told me to come see her, so I will."

Edna looked at her friend, the excitement draining from her face. She burst into tears. "You'll forget about us too."

Lucy grabbed her friend's hand. "Wipe your tears, Edna. How could I ever forget you?" The girls laughed. "You're getting out next year too, right?"

Edna nodded, wiping her face. "Yeah, can't keep me any longer than that."

"Well, you can come see me then too."

"Let's have a party tonight." Edna had that look about her, the one that Lucy knew meant she had trouble in mind. "Fresh baking tonight for the nuns. I may have to take a trip to the kitchen after lights out."

Lucy shook her head and smiled. "Edna, you are a fine thief."

The girls choked back their laughter as Sister approached to silence them, stopping short and turning away as the girls sank into silence.

Edna rolled her eyes. "Why should they get all that while we starve?"

The girls nodded silently, slurping the thin soup that was their daily fare, happy for a chunk of potato, ecstatic for a piece of the gristle or fat that passed for meat.

That night, the girls lay in their beds feigning sleep, waiting. Lucy lay on her side and watched Edna place her ear against Sister's door, listening for the familiar snoring. She smiled at her friend as Edna moved silently toward the stairs, pillowcase in hand. Lucy counted, a habit she had never slipped out of since that first day in the classroom when Sister had hit her over and over with her pointer stick because she didn't know her letters. Now she counted everything, especially when she was nervous, which seemed to be more and more often. She counted the cots in the dorm, the desks in the classroom, the tables in the dining hall, the panes in the windows, the seconds it took for the clouds to cover the moon. It calmed her. Tonight, she counted the seconds it took for Edna to return to the dorm, one thousand, two thousand, three thousand, four. It was as if Edna would not come back if she didn't count. Five thousand, six thousand, seven thousand. Finally, she returned, looking like a wiry hobo with her pillowcase slung over her shoulder, bulging with the promise of a good feed.

The girls slipped out of their beds and tiptoed to their place under the glowing red exit sign. There, in the red darkness, they gathered round as Edna rolled open the pillowcase to reveal the booty. Oatmeal cookies, cinnamon buns, butter tarts, shortbread. Edna handed each girl a treat, saving Lucy for last. Lucy reached for hers, but Edna pulled it back.

"Wait a minute, Lucy." Edna felt around in the bottom of the bag. "Don't look!"

Lucy dutifully covered her eyes, wondering what her friend was up to now.

"Okay, open 'em!"

Lucy moved her hands from her eyes and there before her was a single pink candle sticking out of the cinnamon bun. Edna reached once more into the bag, fished out a kitchen match, struck it with her thumbnail and set the candle aflame. The girls sang the birthday song in whispered tones and then pushed the bun toward Lucy.

"Make a wish!" Edna held the bun out for Lucy to blow out the candle. "Make it a good one, I only got one match." The girls giggled quietly, tugging at Lucy's pyjama sleeve, urging her to make a wish.

Lucy closed her eyes and blew out the candle.

"Well?" Edna raised her eyebrows.

"I can't tell you! Or it won't come true."

Edna started chanting in whispered tones, "Lucy and Kenny, sittin' in a tree."

The other girls giggled behind their hands and joined in. "K–I–S–S–I–N–G!"

Lucy blushed and nudged Edna. "Geez, you! Cut it out."

The girls finished their treats and snuck back to bed. Lucy counted as each of them fell into the deep breathing of sleep. Sleep did not come to her, though. Instead, she watched the night fade into the brooding grey clouds of a coastal morning. While the other girls still slept, she slid the cardboard suitcase out from under her bed and flipped it open. She opened her locker and emptied it of her things, packing them for her trip. She closed the lid of the suitcase over her bobby pins, a change of clothes, her hairbrush, a toothbrush and the pink envelope. Lucy dressed and sat on her bed, the tears rising as she watched her friends sleep, wondering if she would ever see them again. They had been together forever. She turned to look to the other side of the dorm and caught Edna in the next bed looking at her.

"Don't cry, Lucy. You're free. Be happy."

"I will write, Edna, I promise. And more than once, too."

"I know you will." Edna stood up by the side of her bed, reached into her locker and pulled out a small cloth purse made of odd pieces of fabric sewn together. "I made this. I collected scraps when we were mending the boys' clothes. I thought I might need a purse when I left. You take it, okay?"

Lucy took the bag, tears getting the best of her. The two girls hugged each other, the pale-yellow moonlight melting into darkness as the clouds covered the moon.

The mist sat low on Arrowhead Bay as Lucy followed Sister Mary down the hill toward the dock. She turned, looking up. Edna and the girls were crowded together by the dining hall window. Lucy stopped and waved, wishing she didn't have to leave them, for a moment wanting to race back to the dining hall. Edna pushed the window open and stuck her head out.

"See you next year, Lucy!"

Lucy waved and turned once again toward the dock. Sister was well ahead now. Lucy quickened her step to catch up, willing herself not to look back. She caught up with Sister, the boatman stubbing out his cigarette when he saw them approach. Sister Mary handed Lucy a slip of paper.

"This is your voucher for the bus ticket." She nodded toward the boatman. "He will take you to the bus depot. Give it to the ticket girl and they will give you a proper ticket."

"Thank you, Sister."

"Now don't forget your prayers."

"Yes, Sister."

Sister Mary handed her a small envelope. "It's a prayer card. Saint Christopher. For your travels. Now go." She turned her attention to the boatman. "Take her directly to the bus depot." Without another word, Sister Mary turned back to the school, her rosary chattering,

her heels beating that sharp, familiar rhythm on the wooden dock.
The boatman helped Lucy on board and gunned the engines. Halfway across the bay, she could see the Mission rising above the rainforest. She wondered if Edna was in the corner with the dunce cap.
She tucked the envelope in her purse.

The morning fog had all but evaporated under the sun's efforts
at spring. Everything seemed so bright to Lucy. Even the air seemed
fresher, the water a deep blue rather than the persistent grey she saw
from the windows of the Mission. The brightly coloured houses that
speckled the hillside above the bay seemed to be welcoming Lucy as
the boatman skilfully docked the boat. He helped her step down to
the dock, the short trip across the bay at an end.

"There's the bus depot." He pointed. "Over there."

Lucy squinted toward the corrugated iron building. "The one with
the dog sign on top?"

"Yep. You going to Vancouver?"

"Yes." Lucy nodded, wondering what it mattered to him.

"Well, go down to East Hastings. Lots of your kind there."

"Thanks for the ride." Lucy turned from the boat and walked
toward the small depot. The smells of the village made her hungry
and nauseous at the same time. The ripe smell of the boatman choked
her. The aroma from the fish and chip stand at the end of the wharf
wafted past her and she wondered how good it would taste. Even
the brackish water under the dock seemed beautiful to Lucy with its
rainbow circles of leaked diesel fuel.

She opened the door to the depot. A blue cloud of cigarette smoke
hung in the air, combining with the stale smell of old magazines and
dirty ashtrays. The bored-looking woman in the wicket put down
her True Crime paperback, took Lucy's voucher and replaced it with
a ticket.

"Will this get me onto the ferry?"

"Well, it says so, doesn't it?" The clerk spat her words at Lucy like sunflower seed hulls.

"Thank you." Lucy averted her eyes, an Indian School habit, turned and went back outside. The listing wooden bench in front of the depot was grey with years of erosion by the sea air. She wrapped her thin cotton sweater around herself and gazed out across Arrowhead Bay. The girls would be cleaning the dorm right now. She looked at the parked bus and marvelled at the size of it. She could hardly wait to write a letter to Edna to tell her about this boat on wheels. She crossed her ankles, sat back and realized that she had not counted a single thing all morning.

"Tickets, tickets," the bus driver called out as he opened the bus door. A middle-aged couple and a large man in a red-checkered woollen jacket were the only other passengers boarding the bus.

Lucy handed over her ticket. "What time will it be when we get to Vancouver?"

"Ten thirty tonight."

Lucy climbed the narrow, ridged steps to the seating area on the bus. The bus driver directed her with a turn of his head to the back of the bus. The dock was still visible but not the Mission. It was as though it no longer existed. Lucy gripped the seat as the engines roared to life. Panic overtook her as the bus pulled out and headed toward the highway. Gripping the seat tighter, she desperately looked for something in the landscape to focus on. She counted the fence posts. The rhythm of the counting soothed her and she relaxed back into her seat.

The windows of the bus were so dirty, all Lucy could see clearly in the window was her own reflection. She considered herself. The image gazing back at her seemed so small—brown and plain but for her thick, luxuriant black hair in its regulation style. Lucy touched her hair, curled and sprayed so as not to look like Indian hair, but not teased so as to be stylish.

She reached into her purse for her comb, her hand brushing up against the envelope Sister Mary had given her. Alone in the back of the bus, Lucy opened it and pulled out the card. A muscular Saint Christopher carrying the Christ child looked back at her, the prayer embossed underneath the image: *O Lord, we humbly ask You to give Your Almighty protection to all travellers. Accept our fervent and sincere prayers that through Your great power and unfaltering spirit, those who travel may reach their destination safe and sound.* Behind the card she found five well-worn five-dollar bills. Lucy tucked the bills back into the envelope and carefully placed it in her new purse. An impermeable darkness filled her in the face of this appalling kindness. She ran her hand through her hair, her fingers outlining the raised and rugged scars from Sister's favourite punishment. Punishment for what? For nothing. For being a little kid. Lucy wept as her mind turned to the second time she lost her hair to Sister Mary. She could still feel Sister's hard fingers gripping her shoulder even though many years had passed since then.

Sister hadn't believed her when she tried to tell her about what happened with Father. Instead, Sister dragged her down the hallway to the girls' bathroom. Beyond the tub room was another room that all the girls saw at least once. It was here they lost their hair, emerging under a cloud of green powder when they first arrived at the school. It was here that Sister wielded her favourite weapon.

"Sit."

Lucy sat on the stool and closed her eyes as the buzz of the electric shaver hummed against her ears and grated along her scalp. She winced, gritting her teeth, willing herself not to cry, but Sister caught the tear.

"Do you think I want to do this? You give me no choice."

Lucy swallowed her tears and sat, numb, watching her hair, like raven feathers, falling to the floor. Sister stepped back and looked at her handiwork. She put the razor away and crossed her arms.

"Now, clean up this mess."

Lucy looked around for a broom, but there was none.

"Come on, I haven't got all day, clean this up."

Lucy lowered herself to her hands and knees and gathered her hair into a pile. Sister kicked the wastebasket toward her, rosary beads clicking. Lucy placed handful after handful of her hair in the basket. Finally done, she stood in front of Sister, who directed her out of the bathroom and toward the staircase. Sister reached into her pocket and produced a toothbrush, a damp rag and a bar of soap. "Clean them. I will be back in half an hour, and if these are not gleaming, you will go without dinner."

Sister's echoing footsteps faded as Lucy sat on the top stair, running her fingers over her head, the scrapes and abrasions leaving pink impressions on her fingers. Wiping the blood on the inside of her dress so no one would see, she leaned into her job. The day's grit lifted from the metal grips at the edge of each stair and she swept it up with her cloth. She scrubbed and wiped, her shaved head throbbing. There was a rhythm in the movements of her work and she started counting each movement until the rhythm possessed her, obliterating all else. It was almost peaceful.

The echoes announced Sister's return. She looked at Lucy's work and shook her head.

"Stand up."

Lucy stood and looked at the grass stains on her shoes, afraid she would cry again. Sister lowered the cardboard sign over her head. *I am a liar.* She pointed her toward the dining hall. They walked, Lucy's head throbbing again. Sister stopped her in the entrance to the dining hall. Lucy's face burned in embarrassment as she stood in front of the whole school, thinking of her naked head and red-lettered sign.

Sister blew three loud blasts on her whistle and the room, crowded with whispering children, fell silent. All eyes turned to Lucy. Sister's face was a grim mask of satisfaction as she directed Lucy to her seat among the junior girls. Lucy looked up briefly and caught Kenny's eye for a split second before he turned away. She looked again, but he was talking to Wilfred as if nothing was wrong, as if his own red-lettered sign, *I am a runaway*, was not hanging around his neck, resting on his purple-flowered dress.

The scream of air brakes roused Lucy from her reverie as the bus stopped for a roadside passenger. She wiped her eyes on her sleeve and returned the envelope to her purse. *I was nine. Where was your kindness then?* The new passenger staggered to his seat as the bus pulled back onto the highway. The rocking of the bus lulled her to sleep as she clutched her suitcase.

When she awoke, Lucy found herself alone on the dark bus. She had slept the whole trip. Rubbing her eyes, she strained to look out the window and saw that the bus was parked with a lot of other cars. The rocking told her they must be on the ferry. She checked in her purse again to make sure her money was safe, hesitated for a second and then tossed the prayer card on the bus floor. The ferry whistle blew and the captain's voice boomed, "All drivers and bus passengers please return to the car deck. We will be docking at Horseshoe Bay in ten minutes."

Lucy wondered if this was Vancouver. The other passengers boarded, and before long the bus engine rumbled to life. Wide awake now, Lucy pressed her face against the window, astounded by the lights, the endless flow of traffic, stores and malls and gas stations, things entirely new to her. Her life in the outside world ended abruptly when she was five years old.

Finally, the bus slowed. The air brakes howled and the bus slid into its bay at the terminal. The passengers collected their items and moved to the front door. Lucy approached the bus driver.

"Is this Vancouver?"

He looked at her like she was some kind of alien. "Uh, yeah."

Lucy pulled the pink envelope from her purse and showed the return address to the bus driver. "Do you know how I can get to this place?"

"Catch the number 47 bus."

"Okay, where do I get a ticket? And where do I get on that bus?"

The bus driver looked down at her, weary and indifferent. "You have to go through the terminal. Right across the street is a sign and a bench. Wait there. You pay the driver when you get on the bus."

Lucy picked up her suitcase and her purse and walked into the terminal. She sat for a moment on one of the hard plastic chairs and wondered why they were all attached to each other. People swarmed around the crowded depot as though they were a solid mass, undulating up and down the length of the room. A vague smell of urine permeated the air, blending with cigarette smoke and diesel fumes. She had never seen so many strangers in one place—men and women, girls and boys all together, sipping soda at the diner or standing in line together. The tension rose in her, a certainty rising in the back of her mind that Sister would swoop in, meting out punishment left and right. She was fascinated by the ease with which boys spoke to girls, without fear, without sneaking. A light-headed feeling propelled her from the fetid room and to the empty bench at the bus stop. She was thankful for the street light that cast a bluish halo around the bench. A familiar panic rose in her as the darkness deepened and the strange noises of the city hummed around her. She thought to count the cars whizzing by, but they were moving so fast it agitated her further.

Finally, a trolley bus hissed to a stop in front of her. She jumped as the folding doors slapped open, grasped the rail and stepped up into the bus. She fished in her purse and pulled out one of the flaccid bills and handed it to the driver, who peevishly pointed to the sign on his cash box.

"Exact change only, kid."

"But this is all I have."

"Well, you'll have to get off, get some change and wait for the next one."

"Hold on, hold on." A man at the back of the bus stood and made his way toward Lucy and the driver. "Young lady, I happen to have an extra quarter in my pocket. Here you go, driver."

Lucy watched, fascinated, as the coin worked its way through the cogs of the fare box. She looked up to the man. The bus lurched forward, throwing her off balance. Grasping for the pole, she steadied herself and looked up to the man. "Thank you, but you didn't have to do that. I have money."

"No problem, honey. We all need a little help sometimes. My name's Walt. What's yours?"

"Lucy."

"Well, Juicy Lucy, you can come and sit with me. Where are you headed?"

Blushing, Lucy sat on the green vinyl bench seat beside Walt and pulled Maisie's pink envelope from her purse. Pointing to the address, she asked Walt, "Do you know where this is?"

"Why, sure I do. It's not too far from my place. Do you want me to take you there?"

"Sure!" Lucy wondered if the Saint Christopher prayer card had anything to do with this and thought how horrified Sister would be to see her talking to a man. Shyness overtook her and she turned to face the window, watching the strange sights of the city go by.

The bus moved past homes and the occasional store and into the downtown core. Cresting the small incline at Main and Hastings, Lucy was dumbstruck by the cascading neon signs flashing and blinking. Two Indian men swaggered down the sidewalk, their arms around a woman who walked between them. A woman in a zebra-print skirt swatted her male companion with her clutch purse. A group of young men passed a bottle between them at the entrance to an alley. A pair of policemen held a man in a huge cowboy hat against a wall, one of them running his hands over his clothing. Exhausted by the strange sights and the long trip, Lucy turned to Walt.

"Are we almost there?"

"We get off at the next stop." Walt winked at her as he pulled the bell string. The two exited the bus from the front.

The bus driver touched Lucy's elbow, his eyes never leaving Walt. "You be careful down here, girl."

"Mind your own business, man." Walt took Lucy by the hand and gently pulled her off the bus. "Let's go, kid."

Lucy stepped down from the bus and immediately placed her hand over her nose and mouth. The pavement along the storefronts and alleyways released its unique and acrid smell, a stupefying fog of urine, vomit and car exhaust. "Why does it smell so bad?"

"That's the city for you." Walt laughed and took Lucy by the elbow. "Come on. That address you're looking for is down this way." They walked another block. "Let me see that envelope again."

Lucy fished the envelope out of her purse and showed it once again to Walt. "You see the number?" Lucy pointed to the corner of the envelope. "1617 is the number."

"Yeah, should be right here. Here we are." They stood in front of a pawnshop displaying used toasters, guitars and baseball cards in the window. Next to the door was a panel of four buzzers with the numbers for the suites upstairs.

Lucy looked at the buttons. "What are these for?"

"They ring a bell in the apartments upstairs." Walt looked again at the envelope.

"Okay. Apartment 104." He turned his back to Lucy, blocking the buzzer panel as he pressed one.

A woman's voice crackled through the speaker. "Yes?"

Lucy jumped forward, putting her face close to the speaker. "Maisie? It's me, Lucy."

Irritated, the voice replied, "Wrong apartment. No Maisie here."

Lucy stood dumbstruck. She had not for a moment thought she would not be able to find Maisie. She looked at Walt. "Are you sure this is the right place?"

"Yeah, it's the right place. She must have moved."

"What am I going to do now?" Lucy felt the panic rising.

"Stay with me and my old lady. You can look for your friend tomorrow."

"You live with your mother?"

Walt laughed and put his arm around her shoulder. "No, Lucy. It's just a nickname for my girlfriend. Come on. Let's get you to my place. You must be starved."

"Are you sure your girlfriend won't mind?"

"Na, she does what I say."

Lucy and Walt walked the six blocks to his building and climbed the three flights of stairs to his apartment. Walt unlocked the door and the pair walked into the dark silence.

"Wait here for a minute, Lucy. Nope, she's not here. Must be working late again. Come on in, Lucy. You want a sandwich?"

Her grumbling stomach answered for her. She sat at the table while Walt mined the fridge for something to eat, looking around with a mixture of curiosity and nervousness. There were clothes, bottles and glasses scattered around the apartment. Ashtrays overflowed onto the coffee table and dirty dishes were stacked next to the sink. It looked as though the floor hadn't been washed in months. Lucy shuddered a little, wondering what Sister Mary would think of a place like this.

"Here you go." Walt put a peanut butter sandwich and a glass of water in front of Lucy and joined her at the table. "So, Lucy, you ever been on a date?"

Lucy blushed and put down her sandwich, thinking of the Harlequin romance Edna had brought back to the Mission when she came back from summer holidays. "No. I just got out of the Indian School."

Walt smiled. "Well, would you like to go on a date? I know a guy who would just love you."

Lucy blushed. "But it's so late."

Walt put his hand on hers. "How about you just meet him tonight, and then maybe tomorrow, after you find your friend, you can go on a date. I'll call him and he can come over here for a little visit."

"Well, okay."

"Why don't you go freshen up. Bathroom is down the hall."

Lucy practically ran for the bathroom, afraid she'd pee her pants, her embarrassment having stood in the way of telling him she had to go. The relief bordered on pleasure as she emptied her bursting bladder. She wondered who Walt was talking to and then realized he must be on the phone. At the Indian School the only phone was in Father's office. She tried not to listen, but Walt's voice trickled through the thin walls.

"Absolutely, she is as fresh as they come. Yes, yes. Thirty bucks. Take it or leave it."

Lucy wondered what he was talking about. She washed her hands and was startled by her reflection in the mirror. She patted her well-sprayed hair back into place and returned to her half-eaten sandwich. Walt made a weak effort at tidying the cluttered living room but stopped short of any real cleaning. He picked up Lucy's suitcase.

"You can sleep in our room tonight. You must be tired."

"But won't your girlfriend mind?"

Walt threw a clean sheet over the bed and grabbed a blanket

from the closet and smiled at Lucy. "Don't worry about it." A heavy knock on the door caught Walt's attention. "Come on, that must be your date."

Lucy sat on the couch, on edge and confused. Walt opened the door and the man who entered the room was at least twice her age. His pot-belly stuck out beneath his too-small T-shirt and what he lacked for hair on his head was made up for on that swath of pale belly. She could have sworn she saw money pass between the two men when they shook hands.

"Lucy, this is my friend Pete. Pete, Lucy." Pete stared at Lucy and smiled.

"Why don't you two go on down to the bedroom. You can have a little privacy there. Get to know each other a bit." Walt took Lucy by the hand and pointed down the hall. Pete followed her.

Panic rose in her as she felt him so close behind her. She entered the bedroom and before she could turn around, she heard the door close and felt one of his arms wrapped around her, the other groping between her legs. She turned and pushed him away. "What are you doing?"

"You're gonna make me happy, little girl. Now, take your blouse off nice and slow. Let me see those fresh little titties."

"No!" Lucy felt the terror rising as Pete bore down on her again, grabbed her and threw her down on the bed, his mouth all over hers, stale and stinking of cigarettes. He fumbled under her blouse and grabbed her breasts.

"Wait! I need to go to the bathroom. You don't want me to pee the bed!"

He laughed and let her up. "Okay, honey, you go freshen up. I'll be right here when you get back." Pete lay down on the bed, his arms crossed under his head.

Lucy opened her suitcase. "Gotta get my toothbrush." She turned her back to Pete, stuffed her purse in the suitcase, rose with her back still to the bed, the suitcase in front of her so he couldn't see it, and slipped out the bedroom door, closed it and tiptoed down the hall. She peeked around the corner and saw Walt sitting at the kitchen table talking on the phone.

"Yeah, I got thirty bucks for her. I'll let Pete take her home and we can party when you get home."

Lucy made a run for the door just as Walt caught sight of her.

"Hey, you little bitch, get back here." Walt jumped up from the table and ran for the door.

Lucy leapt down the stairs two by two, her suitcase bouncing against the wall. She burst out onto the street and ran back in the direction they had come from. She didn't stop until she was once again in front of the building where Maisie was supposed to be living. She dropped her suitcase and leaned over with her hands on her knees, trying to catch her breath. She looked around to see if Walt was after her, but the street was empty. She thought of Pete and his hairy belly, leaned over once again and puked into the hedge, the stench of digesting peanut butter filling her nostrils. Lucy leaned against the pawnshop door and tried to clear her head. *What now?*

After a few minutes, she heard the apartment door open. She turned to see an older woman in a purple hat leaving the building. She caught the door before it closed and snuck inside. She faced the stairway but noticed a crawl space to one side of the stairs. She opened the wooden door and saw a swinging light bulb with a chain hanging from it. She pulled the chain and the space filled with light. She crawled in on her hands and knees and closed the door behind her. Crouching in her hiding spot, she sensed the city swirling around her, sirens wailing in the night. The front door clicked open and shut twice, and each time Lucy cringed, certain she would be discovered by someone else wanting to hurt her.

She tried to think of anything else, but her mind kept returning to the Mission. She thought of Kenny. Father Levesque had told them he had drowned, but none of the kids believed it. He was their hero. The one who got away. She felt her heart contract as she remembered their mostly silent moments of connection. She would never forget the day they brought him back from one of his many attempts to escape. He stood next to Brother in front of all the kids in the dining hall, his head down, hands behind his back. The purple-flowered dress Brother had made him wear hung down to his ankles. His head had been shorn and Lucy could see the bloody trails left by the careless razor. Brother beat him that day until he collapsed on the floor. But he never uttered one cry, his defiance all he had left. The next day, after breakfast, in spite of the terrible risk, Lucy managed to slip Kenny a note, stopping in front of him and pretending to tie her shoe. He in turn slipped it into his shoe. She would have been next for a beating and shorn head if she'd been caught talking to a boy. After that day they would look for each other, careful not to draw attention. A smile, a nod, it was enough to make the days bearable.

Finally, the heat of the light bulb in the tiny space and her cramping legs forced Lucy from her hiding place. She crawled out, stretched her legs and sat on the bottom step, too afraid to face the city streets. She watched the dark brighten into day from her step. Too tired to worry anymore, she didn't even try to hide when she heard someone coming down the stairs. A tall, thin woman walked past Lucy and turned to face her, one hand on the door.

"Who are you?"

Lucy pulled the pink envelope out of her purse. "I'm looking for my friend, Maisie. She sent me a letter and it says she lives here. I was here last night, but it wasn't her who answered the buzzer."

"Was that you who buzzed my apartment last night? Maisie lives here, but you buzzed 106 instead of 104."

Lucy almost cried thinking of Walt and how he tricked her.

"Come on, I'll take you to Maisie's."

Lucy followed her up the stairs, nervous that this might be another trick. The woman knocked at the door at the top of the stairs. Maisie, in a turquoise bathrobe and fluffy bunny slippers, answered the door. Lucy burst into tears.

"Maisie!" She ran to her friend and threw her arms around her, sobbing, her words a cascade of gibberish as she tried to tell her friend what had happened.

Maisie's arms wrapped around Lucy as she waved and called out her thanks to the tall woman. "She's my school friend."

She guided Lucy into the apartment, one arm on each elbow. "Lucy, calm down. Come inside. I'll make tea."

3

MAISIE

>------<

Lucy threw her arms around me so tight I almost lost my balance as I opened the door, gripping my housecoat around me. The words fell out of her mouth like alphabet soup, a garbled, sobbing mess.

"Lucy! Get in here. When did you get into town?" I pulled myself free of her. She felt feverish and looked like she'd slept in her clothes.

"Maisie, thank God I found you." Lucy hugged me again, this time so hard I stepped right out of my bunny slippers. She took a deep breath and the sobs became more like hiccups than heaving gasps.

"When did you get here? What the heck is going on? Come on, sit down. You're safe now. I'll put the kettle on."

Last night's clothes and a fake leather paddle strewn in the hallway to the bedroom seemed to fill the whole apartment. I scooped them up on my way to the kitchen and tossed them through the bedroom door.

"I thought he was nice. He brought me here when I showed him your letter."

"Who? Who did you think was nice? I was out last night."

"I thought he was just helping me." She wiped her eyes on her sleeve.

"Lucy, who are you talking about?" I poked my head through the kitchen pass-through.

"He said his name was Walt."

I slid the teapot and two mugs through the pass-through and walked around to the living room. "Walt?" I raised my hand above my head. "About this tall? Brown hair, skinny?"

"Yeah, he doesn't live far from here."

I sat down beside her. "Lucy, he's a pimp. Hangs around the Manitou, where I work. He's a creep, always trying to pimp the working girls."

"What do you mean, 'pimp'?" She looked at me and I wondered if I had seemed like such a child when I first hit the city.

"Men who make women have sex for money, then take their money from them."

Lucy sat so still, frozen almost, looking at her feet. "He tried to. This ugly, stinking man came and tried to touch me."

"Did he hurt you?" I thought of Walt and his junkie friends. I looked at Lucy and thought I could kill that bastard without batting an eye.

"He tried, but I ran away."

"Drink your tea. It will calm you. Why didn't you write me to say you were coming? I would have picked you up at the bus."

"No time. Sister just came to me one day and the next afternoon I was on the bus."

"Assholes." I saw the shock in her eyes. "Ah, don't look at me like that. Sister isn't hiding around the corner here."

Lucy looked around as if expecting to see Sister jump out of the closet or something. I poked her in the ribs.

"Remember the time Sister Mary was yelling at us in the dormitory? That time you forgot your laundry downstairs?"

"Like I could forget." Lucy wiped her face on her sleeve and smiled.

"She was so mad, calling you lazy and stupid. And then, when she turned, her habit was stuck up in her bloomers."

For the first time since crashing through my door, Lucy laughed. "Yeah, and she was stomping out of the dorm all high and mighty with her old baggy bloomers sticking out." Lucy put her mug on the coffee table for fear it would spill, her body shaking with laughter.

I pushed harder, trying to distract her from the night before. "Remember? We all laughed so hard and she turned on us like an old bear. Didn't know what was going on. We all shut up, though. Could hardly hold it in, but she was going for her strap." I reached for my king-sized extra-long cigs. I laughed too, and the memories started flowing between us of the Mission and Sister, and Father, half-deaf and always where you didn't want him to be.

Lucy inhaled sharply. "You smoke now?"

I laughed. "Like I said, Sister ain't lookin' around these corners. These are *my* corners." I lit the smoke and inhaled deeply, blowing smoke rings to impress her.

"Wow." Lucy took in the apartment like she had just arrived. "You live here alone?"

"Yeah, pretty cheap rent."

"Rent?"

"Yeah, I pay the owner every month so I can live here. That's what rent is." Lucy blushed and I knew she felt stupid. "Hey, how would you know? No rent at the Mission."

I pinched her arm, like we used to when Sister hit us. We pinched ourselves harder and harder so we knew we could take the pain. She smiled at me, with her sad Lucy eyes. I remembered watching her sitting with the little girls but always by herself. Quiet. Always alone. Almost invisible. She pinched me back.

"You can stay here, Lucy. Don't worry. You gotta sleep on the couch, though. Come to the Manitou with me tomorrow and we'll make Harlan hire you."

"We?"

"Yeah, me and Clara and Liz. You remember Clara? She was in my dorm at school."

"A little. We were never in the same dorm."

"Harlan can't live without us. No one else would work in that dive for what he pays."

Lucy smiled, the excitement clear on her face. My heart sank looking at her, so happy at the prospect of a shitty job with a shitty boss always trying to put his hands on us. But who else would hire a kid like her, fresh out of Indian School? At least at the Manitou, I could watch out for her.

"You must be exhausted. My boyfriend will be here pretty soon. Go wash your face and have a sleep on the couch, if you want. I'll get you some towels and a blanket."

Lucy looked at me and raised her eyebrows. "A boyfriend?" Even the word seemed to make her nervous.

"Yes, Lucy, people have jobs and boyfriends and apartments in the real world. Not like being locked up in Indian School." I walked to the hall closet and pulled out a couple towels and a blanket and handed them to her. "The bathroom is just down the hall, make yourself at home." The intercom sounded. "That will be Jimmy."

I buzzed him up and left the door ajar so he wouldn't have to knock. I turned my back to the door, picked up the empty teacups and slid them through the pass-through. The ceramic mugs clattered against the uneven tile, like the endless clicking of Sister's rosary beads, slapping against the stiff folds of her rustling habit.

"Fucking bitch." I slid the mugs toward the sink. I hadn't thought of her in so long.

"Who's a bitch?" Jimmy sidled up beside me and put his arm around my shoulder.

"Oh, never mind!" I smiled at him, pushing his hand away as he reached for my boob.

"Aw, Maisie, when am I even gonna get to second base with you?" He shook his head a little, his long braids sliding across his chest. "You know I love you, girl."

"Sshhhhh! My friend from the Mission is here. She showed up

this morning. They just put her on a bus. No notice, no nothing. Walt got his hooks into her. Luckily, she got away from him."

"Well, at least kiss me!" He pulled me to him, teasing me, pressing me against the wall.

I kissed him lightly. "Yeah? Well, when I see a ring, we will know what's what." I looked up into his teasing eyes. He loved me. I knew it. But I wouldn't let him touch me. I just couldn't. How could he love me then?

Lucy stepped out of the bathroom just as Jimmy planted a kiss on my forehead. She hesitated and watched.

"You're such a goody two-shoes." Jimmy smiled at me. "So, what did you do last night? I came over, but no answer."

"Aw, nothin'. Harlan worked us to death at the Manitou yesterday. I just came home, had a hot bath and fell asleep. Didn't even budge till Lucy was at the door this morning."

Lucy looked at me, puzzled, and I gave her the Indian School "keep quiet" look. She did.

"So, this must be Lucy. Hi, I'm Jim."

"Hi." Lucy turned away, not meeting his eyes.

"Don't worry, kiddo, I won't tell Sister you were talking to a boy."

I thought of the fences between the girls and the boys at the Mission, the line dividing us in the classroom, the dining hall, the chapel. I remembered how long it took me to get used to talking to boys any time I wanted, and pinched Lucy. We laughed again. It was like a new world to be with each other again, free of the constant watching eye of Sister Mary. It was both exciting and strange to know that we didn't have to sneak to talk with each other or use our secret sign language.

Jim shook his head at us. His parents moved, taking him across the line to the States before the priest could come for him, so he didn't know what it was like. His parents told him about it, because they had gone to one of the Indian Schools, but he didn't really understand. How could anyone?

"Come on, ladies, I will take you to the Only for soup."

Lucy laughed. "Ladies." She looked at me and blushed. "What's an only?"

"Restaurant in Chinatown. Best soup ever!" I grabbed her sweater and tossed it to her, threw mine over my shoulder, and we headed out. Jim held my hand for a minute, then I pulled it away. He held on to my shirttail instead.

We slid into our favourite booth at the Only, next to the front door and the big windows that gave the best view of the drama playing out in the street. The spicy smells of the Chinese food were still foreign to me even though Jimmy and I came here at least once a week. It really was the best soup ever, and so cheap. It cost less to eat soup here than to make it.

Lucy scanned the menu with a look of panic on her face.

"I'll order for you, Lucy. Don't worry."

Lucy put the menu down, relaxed and focused her attention on the busy street outside. "The Manitou's just around the corner." I pointed east in the direction of the motel. "It's not far to walk from the apartment."

Lucy suddenly ducked down in her seat below the sill. She looked at me, fear in her eyes, pointing toward the window. I looked out just as Walt was sauntering by. I felt the blood rush to my head, the sounds of the restaurant muted by the pounding in my ears. I jumped to my feet. Jimmy tried to grab me, but I was already out the door.

"Walt, you fucking piece of shit. What the fuck you doing going after my friend?" I strode toward him, tying my hair back as I walked. "Come here, you scrawny fucker. I am going to kick your ass."

Walt backed away from me. "What the hell are you talking about, Maisie?"

I grabbed him by his shirt collar. "Don't fuckin' lie, you. She told me. She showed you my letter. You knew she was my friend and you were gonna do her in anyway." I wound up as if I was gonna punch him and when he pulled his hands up to protect his face, I kicked him square in the balls. He went down like a sack of potatoes. I jumped on him to finish him, but Jimmy pulled me off. "Fuck off, Jimmy. This fucker deserves every bit of it."

Walt lay curled in a ball, clutching his groin, moaning and crying, as Jimmy pulled me away. I spat on him. "You pig. Next time you want to hurt a kid, you come see me."

Jimmy put his arm around me, but I pushed it away, my heart racing. He grabbed my shirttail and nudged me back toward the Only. Lucy stood in the doorway, her mouth hanging open. "Fuck him, eh Lucy. You don't mess with Indian School girls." I grabbed her arm and we headed back to our booth, but one of the Chinese cooks stood in our way.

"You go now. No trouble here. Go on." He waved his hands at us, his gory apron barely white, his face a picture of exasperation. "You go!"

"No trouble here." I slid past him and sat down at the booth and started eating my soup. "Just gonna finish my soup."

"No trouble!" He waggled his finger at me.

I was tempted to bite it off, but instead I showed him my teeth. "No trouble, just soup." I glanced over the top of my spoon just in time to see Walt limping around the corner. I looked square at Lucy. "You can't take no shit."

The next morning, I nudged Lucy awake. The ripple imprints from the corduroy couch cushions striped her cheek, her hair a flat mess on the side she slept on, wild on the side she didn't. She looked at me, half-awake and confused.

"Good morning, sleepyhead." I stirred the boiling water into the instant coffee crystals. "Do you like coffee?"

"I don't know. I'll try it." She watched me pour the sugar and canned milk and did the same.

We drank our coffee together, both of us quiet. I was sure she was thinking about the dining hall too: the watery porridge, the cold toast, and if that wasn't bad enough, Sister watching over us like some circling vulture. Indian School seemed like a hundred years ago, but with Lucy in my living room, it seemed like yesterday. Even though it made my stomach tighten when I looked at her and thought of Father, I couldn't help but think that, in spite of it all, we were here. We made it. I reached over and hugged her. She giggled.

"So, do you have anything else to wear other than those Indian School clothes?" I knew she didn't. "Come on, let's get you dolled up." I lent her my new bell-bottom jeans, but she said no to my best Stones T-shirt. She didn't like the tongue.

"Come on, I'll take you to the Two Jays. A buck and a half gets you two eggs, toast, hash browns and coffee. Then we'll go get Harlan to hire you. You're gonna have to make some money." I felt the pressure building, the need to get out. As much as I wanted her there, her presence seemed to suck the air right out of the place. Being close was just too close. Those crowded dorms weren't easy to forget. I didn't want her to feel unwelcome, but I had needs. "Before you know it, you'll be able to get your own place." I watched her tense up and knew she couldn't even imagine it. "Hey, it was not even a year ago I left the Mission, and I got my own place. You can do it too, girl."

Lucy ate the runny eggs, wiping up every speck of yolk with her toast. There was something so sad about her and that yellow, dripping toast. Probably hadn't had an egg in years. I paid and we walked to the Manitou. Not many people stayed overnight there, but we changed every bed, every morning. The hookers rented the rooms by the hour. They paid extra for a supply of clean sheets, just in case the john cared. They made up the bed themselves, leaving us a pile of stinking sheets in the morning. Me and the girls, we cleaned up after them. Harlan took a cut from the whores and paid us less than minimum wage, in cash, so we didn't have to get bank accounts and face the stiff smiles of the blond tellers at the bank on the corner.

I stepped into the lobby, holding the door open for Lucy, who followed me inside, a smile frozen on her face. Harlan sat behind the counter, paging through his magazine, flipping his toothpick from one side of his mouth to the other.

"Good morning, Harlan." I put on my best phony singsong voice.

"Get to work. You're late and every room in the house is dirty."

"Aw, Harlan, don't be like that. Look, I brought more help."

Harlan looked up from his magazine, ready to tell me to get the hell out of the lobby. He didn't like Indians in the lobby. Then his eyes fell on Lucy. He looked her up and down.

"And what do we have here?"

"This is Lucy." I felt sick to my stomach, like a pimp myself. "We went to school together and she's looking for work. You're always saying how you need good help. Well, Lucy here is the best damn cleaner you could find."

"You got a boyfriend, Lucy?"

She blushed and rolled her eyes. "No."

"Good. You're hired. Pull your shirt tighter around yourself. Let me get an idea what size uniform you need."

Lucy started to pull the T-shirt tight around her body. I pushed her hands away. "Cut it out, Harlan, she's a kid."

"Well, get her a smock and get to work." He went back to his magazine, looking up to watch Lucy walk by on our way to the supply room.

I took Lucy into the supply room, the sudden darkness after the morning sun blinding us. I walked past her to the smocks and picked out the least worn one for her. Clara sat on the overturned milk crate, head in her hands, hungover again. Liz slapped piles of thin sheets onto her cart, and if looks could kill, Clara would have been pushing up daisies.

"Girls, this is Lucy. Clara, you left the Mission the year after Lucy arrived. Do you remember her?"

Clara looked up, bleary-eyed. "No. Maybe. I don't know." She put her head back in her hands.

"Hi, Lucy." Liz waved at her. "Glad you're here. Oh yeah, I remember you. You and that Kenny were always sneaking looks at each other in the dining hall."

Lucy blushed. "Yeah. Kenny."

"Maybe you can pick up Clara's slack."

"Aw, fuck you, Liz. I always get my rooms done."

"Cut it out, you two, geez! Clara, go get a goddamn cola from the lobby and take a pill. Get yourself cured up and get on with it. I am not gonna listen to you two argue all day about who is doing what."

Clara grumbled her way out the door toward the lobby. Liz shook her head and pushed her loaded trolley out of the supply room.

I took Lucy to her cart and showed her how to fill it up. "Come with me when I do my first room. I'll show you what we do and then you can carry on with yours."

I gave her a room list, trying not to let my irritation show, but I was getting so wound up. I'd wanted to go out last night but couldn't think of an excuse to tell her. Tonight, she'd be on her own. *I gotta get out.*

"Okay, Lucy. Let's get to it." We pushed our carts toward Room 15.

"I'll do a good job, Maisie. You know, we really are good cleaners." Lucy smiled at me.

"Yeah, Sister made sure of that with her toothbrush and her strap, the bitch." That's what they schooled us to be. Maids. All I could think about was getting away.

"Yeah. The bitch." Lucy tried the word on her tongue, and I could see she liked it. "That old bitch." We laughed and pinched each other.

We got home from work starving and I knew she couldn't cook, so I showed her how to cook eggs. When I got out of the Mission, I lived on chips and pop for three weeks until Jimmy showed me how to cook eggs. Now I could cook spaghetti and meatballs, meat loaf and even fancy omelettes. That was about the only thing I remembered about my mom: she made really good spaghetti. She used to let me stand on a chair by the stove and stir the sauce. That was before school.

When they let me out of the Mission School, Sister travelled with me all the way to Vancouver and put me on a boat that was supposed to take me home. There were seven of us girls from the Mission School and another twelve boys and girls from other Indian Schools who joined up with us to catch the boat and head back up north to our coastal village. Ten years had passed since they'd dragged me away from my mom, kicking and screaming, and it was the last time I'd seen her or my dad. When we got to our village, tired, cold and hungry, we were herded off the boat in single file. Standing on the beach at the end of the dock were a group of men and women, milling around and looking to the dock as we walked toward them. For a moment the two groups just stood there—kids on the dock, parents on the sand. Then a boy from one of the other schools broke and ran, calling out for his dad. The rest of us ran too, right into that crowd of grown-ups who were supposed to be our parents. We were all pretty much as tall as them now and everyone was looking at everyone else, looking for something familiar, something to recognize. I didn't know what to do, so I just stood there, hoping one of them was my mom and that she would recognize me. I couldn't pick her out in the crowd. A woman approached me, gently asking if I was Sally. No. Not me. Finally, I noticed a woman, her hair wrapped tight in a pale-blue scarf, standing at the edge of the group looking straight at me. I knew. It was my mom. Arms open, she ran for me, crying.

My mom took me home and gave me tasty things to eat. My dad was out fishing, she said, but would be back in the morning. She said they weren't really sure I would be there that day. The house was smaller than in my memory, but familiar, and the whole evening I just wanted to cry as I took it all in, the place I had been dreaming about for ten years. My dad came home the next morning and held me so tight. He smelled of woodsmoke and fish, and that primal smell tumbled me back in time to a thin memory of me and my mom meeting him at the dock, him tossing me in the air, me laughing so hard my belly hurt. He would carry me home like I weighed nothing, my face in the crook of his neck, rough sea salt rubbing off on my face. They told me that after I was taken, no one told them where I was. They still didn't know which school I'd been sent to. I couldn't help but wonder if they'd tried to find out. They must have. But the angry question kept rising in me anyway, and their constant affection began to disgust me.

I lasted a month. No matter how hard I tried, this place, their house, was no longer home, and these people, though kind and loving, were like strangers pretending to be family. I hitched a ride on a trawler to Prince Rupert and took a bus to Vancouver, with the hundred dollars my dad pressed into my hand as my mother stood by, crying.

Not so long ago I was at the Balmoral and met a girl from up there. After the expected ritual sharing of who your aunties and uncles are, she told me she was sorry about my mom. I didn't know, but she didn't need to say more. I had so many dreams at the Indian School about going home to her. Dreams about sleeping safe in my own room, playing on the beach at ease and without fear, and cooking with her. What I so desperately needed was to be standing on that stool by the stove, carefully stirring under her watchful eye like when I was little. To be little again, living without fear and brutality—no one gets that back. All that's left is a craving, insatiable empty place.

"That's not so hard, is it?" Lucy said, so proud of her first-ever creation, a plate of scrambled eggs and some toast.

"Nope," I said with a mouthful of toast. "Most stuff is not too hard to cook. You'll get used to it." I eased the rising pressure by thinking of my nighttime clothes waiting for me under my bed. "Jimmy and I are gonna go to a movie tonight. You okay to stay here by yourself? You can lock the door behind me."

"Yeah, I'll be okay. Long as I can leave the window open."

"Why do you need to leave the window open? It's pouring out there."

"I don't know. It just makes me feel better sometimes. Been like that since I had to clean Father's rooms. It was so stuffy in there." She looked away from me.

I used to have to clean Father's rooms too. He stopped picking me when I started fighting. That's when he chose Lucy. I knew she remembered that day on the playground too, but neither of us ever spoke of it. I'd sat on the ground and went limp, refusing to go with him, Sister whipping my legs with a switch, grabbing my arms, like that would make me stand up. I wouldn't. So he took Lucy instead.

"Yeah, sure, leave the window open." I got up and headed for the bedroom. "Just put a towel on the sill if it starts pouring in. I'm gonna get ready."

I stood in front of my vanity mirror and brushed the hairspray out of my hair, styling it straight and plain with a small barrette to keep it out of my eyes. Just the way Jimmy liked it, simple and soft.

He called my hairspray "chemical garbage." I put barely any mascara on and a touch of light-blue eyeshadow. The ice-pink lipstick looked even lighter against my skin. I liked my handiwork reflected in the mirror. Jimmy's girl. I opened the other drawer of the vanity and pulled out my large cosmetic bag, unzipped it and made sure everything was there: black eyeliner and mascara, lash curler, hairspray, green eyeshadow, fire-engine-red lipstick, garter belt, fishnet stockings, a chocolate finger candy bar in its bright-red wrapper. I pulled the clothing bag out from under the bed and picked out the see-through lace top, the black lace bra, the green miniskirt and my over-the-knee black boots. I managed to fit it all in my big zip hobo-style purse. I slipped into my jacket, slid the bag over my shoulder and looked in the mirror. Nothing suspicious. Nice girl. I closed the door softly and headed to the living room.

"Okay, Luce, I'm outta here." She sat looking at the snow on my little television set. "Here, just wiggle the rabbit ears and you'll get a show."

"Rabbit ears! Yeah, I guess they do look like rabbit ears." Lucy gave me a hug. "You look pretty."

"I won't be too late. Eat whatever you want. Bye-bye." I pulled the door shut and it felt like I could breathe again.

I took the stairs two at a time and headed out the door toward the bus stop. Off to the Kingsway area, away from where people might know me. The bus driver ignored me as I dropped my quarter in the fare box, waving off the transfer. I took up my place in the back-corner seat and watched Main Street unfold into its gritty early evening. The dealers were out in force, the hookers hanging on their arms, hoping for a straight trade. I held my bag closer.

I rang the bell to get off across the street from the Knight and Day. Always open, no cover. I slipped through the tinted glass doors and headed for the ladies' room. I pulled out reams of paper towel and headed for the last cubicle. I hung my bag on the hook on the back of the cubicle door, placed the paper towel carefully on the floor and unzipped the bag. I put the boots on the back of the toilet, took off my jeans and underwear, and slipped into the garter belt, the stockings and the miniskirt. I slipped the boots up over my knees, pulled my Jonathan Livingston Seagull T-shirt off, and slipped into the black bra and the see-through lace blouse. I pulled the cosmetic bag out and stuffed my clothes in. The third sink was under a light fixture. Good for applying my makeup. I applied the eyeliner and mascara and curled my eyelashes. The red lipstick rolled on smooth and creamy, and in the mirror, Jimmy's girl was gone. I sauntered into the coffee shop, chose a table by the window and lit up a smoke.

"Fries and gravy and an orange pop." The red-headed waitress pursed her lips as she took my order. Fuck her too. I lit a smoke and watched the night fall on the Kingsway stroll. The neon signs turned on, red and blue, blinking and twinkling. The dealers sold, the junkies creeping into the alleys, anxious and alone. The hookers smiled and cocked their hips as the johns strolled by, picking and choosing. When the johns passed them over, their smiles faded into grim stares, blank and removed. I nibbled the fries between drags on my smoke and sips of my soda. I waited and watched.

It was full-on dark, the ashtray full, the gravy congealed, the ice melted, before he finally walked by, looking and not looking at me. I rose, paid my bill and walked. The Old Man. He was waiting at the bus stop bench but stood and started walking when he saw me emerge through the restaurant doors. I followed him to the parking lot. Our routine. The blue dumpsters sat in a three-walled cinder-block enclave. This was where we met. We both knew the routine. No words needed.

I handed him the red package. He put his hand on the back of my neck and turned me to face the wall. I smelled his old man smell and stared at the age spots, the white hairs on his knuckles, just like Father. He braced himself against the wall. I heard his zipper as he pulled up my skirt. He stuck it in me, hard and deep, each thrust with all his weight bashing me against the wall. His breath, short and foul.

"Say it," I told him again. "Say it or I never will come here again."

"Slut. Savage. Filth. Stupid. Cunt. Whore. Slut. Savage."

These were Father's words. They took the rhythm of his thrusts. And I couldn't breathe without this. I didn't exist without this.

He grunted his finish and pulled out of me. I turned, faced him and spat on him. He pulled two tens from his shirt pocket, stuck them in my bra and handed me the red package. A candy bar. Just like Father.

"Fuck off." I pushed him away, pulled my skirt down and walked back to the front of the building. I sat on the empty bus stop bench, crossed my legs and pulled out my smokes. The cigarette hung out of my mouth as I torched the bills and lit my smoke with them. I inhaled deeply, tilted my chin up and exhaled slowly, my body collapsing like a spent balloon. I peeled back the red foil and ate the whole candy bar, bite after bite. I finished my smoke, stubbed it out under the toe of my boot and headed back to the ladies' room at the Knight and Day, where I transformed again, changing back into my other costume.

Lucy was on her feet before I even got the key out of the lock. "I was so worried about you! Jimmy was here looking for you."

"Yeah. He must have gone to the wrong theatre. I waited and waited, and when he didn't get there, I just went to the show by myself."

"He didn't say anything about a show."

"That's Jimmy. I'll see him tomorrow. I'm kinda tired now, though. I'm going to have a bath and then go to bed. You should sleep too. Work tomorrow. See you in the morning."

"Well, okay."

I could feel her eyes, her questions following me all the way down the hall, but pretended I didn't. "Good night!" Oh, my phony sing-song is getting good.

The steam billowed out of the bathroom as I made my way to the bedroom wrapped in my towel. The lights were off in the living room, so I closed the door quietly without another word to her. I stood in front of my vanity mirror, wrapped in my towel, in my bunny slippers. I reached for my jewellery box, opened it and pulled out my penknife. I let the towel drop and drew the knife along the flesh two inches below my collarbone. The blood pearled pretty red against my brown skin and rolled over the row of scars below this latest drawing. I looked at my face, clean of makeup, clean of pain. Then, I could see Jimmy's girl.

The following morning, Lucy pushed the bedroom door open, her face twisted with panic. "Someone's pounding at the door!"

"Well, open it, geez. I'm going back to sleep." I rolled over and closed my eyes, my body aching from the night before. I could feel Lucy's fear and indecision lingering in the doorway. My irritation rose even though I tried to stuff it down. "Lucy, one day you will not be staying here and you will have to deal with these things on your own." I regretted my words the moment they rose in the air. Her constant presence was like a barbed lump in my throat.

The pounding on the door resumed, louder, more insistent. I rolled out of bed and forced a smile at her.

"I'm sorry, Maisie, it scares me." Lucy looked like she might cry.

"It's okay, girl. I got it." I pulled my housecoat on, zipped it to the neck and headed for the door.

"Maisie! Open the damn door."

Jimmy. Wonder how you got past the security door this time.

I slid the chain lock open and turned the deadbolt. Before I could even reach for the doorknob, he pushed the door open. Lucy ran for the kitchen and stuck her head through the pass-through, safe but able to watch the goings-on. I turned away from him, casual, like it was any other morning.

"Where the hell were you last night?" Jimmy grabbed my shoulder and swung me around to face him. "I was here. Did she tell you?" He tilted his head in Lucy's direction.

"Yeah, she told me." I pushed him off me. "What the fuck is your problem?"

"You told me you were staying home. So, I come see you and this one"—he pointed at Lucy—"tells me you were at the movies with *me*."

"You said to meet you at the Vogue. I went. You didn't show up, so I went by myself." I could feel the rage rising.

"You're lying, Maisie. You said you were staying home."

"Fuck you, Jimmy. I told you I was staying home tonight, not last night. And besides"—I waggled my left ring finger in his face— "you see a ring on this finger? Maybe then you can start bossing me around."

"Maisie." He reached for my shoulder again.

I ducked. "Don't." I could hear Lucy crying in the kitchen. "You told me to meet you at the theatre."

"No, I didn't."

"Are you telling me I'm lying? Get the fuck out of here." I could hear myself screaming inside, *Jimmy, Jimmy, Jimmy, forgive me.* "Who fuckin' needs you."

"Yeah, Maisie, I know." He looked like he might cry. "Nothing or no one. Right? Isn't that what you say?"

"Fuckin' straight. Leave me alone." I headed down the hall for the bedroom, scowling at Lucy as I passed the kitchen entrance. She stood there frozen, like a wounded bird hoping the cat will just disappear. I slammed the door, locked it behind me and stood in front of the vanity mirror.

I could hear them talking, their voices a mumble from behind the door. I unzipped my housecoat and let it fall to the floor, slipped my nightie over my head and tossed it. I watched in the mirror as I pressed the scabbed line just below my collarbone. Fresh from last night's drawing, the blood pearled again, red and brilliant against my brown skin. The second-day pain was not the same. No piercing with the knife. It was duller, but still sharp enough to make me feel clean. I looked at my face and pressed the wound; the pain sharpened a little and the tension eased. I could see Jimmy's girl in the mirror again. I pulled a tissue from the box, daubed the ruby droplets and placed the tissue carefully under the pantyhose box in the basket so no one would see. I sat on the bed and dressed, straining to hear what those two were talking about. I knew I had to find a way to get Lucy to stay quiet when I went out. I pulled on my jeans and T-shirt, brushed my hair and pinned it back with a small barrette the shape of a bow. The kind Jimmy liked. I opened the bedroom door and walked into the living room. Lucy sat on the couch, a stricken look on her face, Jimmy next to her looking like a beat-down dog.

"I'm sorry, Jimmy." I put my hand on his shoulder and he looked up at me, puzzled and hurt. "I musta got it all mixed up."

"Yeah, I guess it just got mixed up." He stood and looked down at me for a long moment. With a deep sigh, he leaned over and kissed me on the forehead.

"Lucy and I have a day off tomorrow. Why don't we show her the seawall? Let's hit the park and make a day of it." I looked at Lucy and smiled. She exhaled like she'd been holding her breath all this time. "Lucy, you will love it there. We'll pack a lunch tonight and we can head out early in the morning." If it weren't for the ache between my legs, I might even have convinced myself I had been at the movies the night before.

Jimmy held my hand as we sat on the bus. Lucy sat on the single seat across from us and looked out the window, her face a picture of wonderment at the city sights. I smiled, thinking of my first days in the city, remembering how it had been so frightening and awesome at once. I nudged Jimmy.

"Was I like that when I first got here?"

"You were just like that." He put his arm around my shoulder and squeezed. "Like an old woman and a little kid at the same time."

I smiled at him, the panic rising in me. I knew he loved me, but he wouldn't if he knew. I slipped out from under his arm.

"Hey, Lucy, that's English Bay where all the hippies hang out." She was gawking out the bus window at the wildly dressed and under-dressed collection of free spirits on the beach.

She reached over, nudged me and whispered, "Those girls aren't wearing bras!"

I laughed at her. "Lucy, freedom comes in many forms."

"Or lack of forms," Jimmy added, looking all innocent.

I reached up and pulled the bell. "Guys—that's all you think of, innit?"

"What?!" He laughed and shrugged his shoulders as we got off the bus at the corner of Denman and Davie.

"Come on." I stuck my arm through Lucy's. "We'll walk to the park from here."

I smiled at the look of disbelief on her face as she took in the sights of the sidewalk vendors and their wares, ranging from silver puzzle rings to happy-face T-shirts, trade bead bracelets and *huarache* sandals. Wafts of patchouli oil rose from the naked arms of the hippie girls swirling around their stands in their exotic Indian print cotton skirts. Young men, barefoot and shirtless, with hair longer even than the women, played guitars and bongo drums, some singing, some extending their hats for spare change. Lucy turned to me, her eyes wide, speechless. Instead of words, she laughed her tumbling laugh.

"It's a long way from the Mission, isn't it?" I wondered how long it would take her to adjust.

"Can you imagine Sister here? She would go crazy."

Jimmy sighed. "God, do you ever stop talking smack about that woman? I'm sure she was just doing her job."

Lucy and I looked at each other. "Yeah, right," Lucy half whispered as the exuberance of the day drained from her face. "If her job was to try to kill us."

"Jimmy, you don't know what you're talking about. You didn't have to go there or any place like it either." I punched him in the shoulder.

"Really?" Lucy turned to look at Jimmy like he was some strange creature. "How come? I thought all Indians had to go or the parents would go to jail. That's what they always said."

"Jimmy's parents took him across the line to Seattle before the priest could get him. He went to school with all the little white kids in Seattle. Didn't you, Jimmy?"

He got that sullen look. "Yeah. So? I still think she couldn't have been that bad."

"Oh really? Maybe you should ask your mom and dad how good it was. So good they had to run away with you so you wouldn't go through it."

"I told you, Maisie, they never talk about it."

"I wonder why! Lucy, show him your ear." Lucy pulled her hair away, exposing the angry red scar. "Come on, Lucy." I grabbed her arm again and we fast-walked, leaving Jimmy to follow.

"Don't be so hard on him, Maisie. How could he know?"

"Well, he could just believe us. Why would we lie? He says he loves me but won't believe me about it? I can't handle that." A jittery feeling rose in me as we practically jogged toward the entrance to Stanley Park. Jimmy, looking confused, hurried behind us.

Lucy was more entertaining than the park that day, amazed at the whales in the aquarium and laughing herself silly riding the kiddie train through the zoo. She had me and Jimmy laughing too. Our stomachs hurt with her imitations of the monkeys outside the monkey house. I thought of myself fresh out of the Mission, and couldn't believe I had seemed as much like a child as she did.

I reached for Jimmy's hand as we headed home. He looked at me, all hurt.

"I know I didn't have to go, Maisie, but you don't have to hold it against me like that."

I pulled my hand away. "I don't hold it against you, Jimmy, but you gotta realize. Shit happened there. Shit you don't even wanna know about. You weren't there. So why do you have to pretend you might know something about it? You don't. That girl and me, we know. Things you would never believe."

Lucy caught up to us after dawdling behind, talking to a vendor. I gave Jimmy my best shut-up look and hoped he would. He didn't.

"Lucy, what was the worst thing that happened to you? At least you're alive, here, free like anyone else."

Lucy froze on the spot, her face a picture of panic.

I turned to Jimmy. "Just shut up about it now. Why would anyone wanna talk about it?" I looked back at Lucy and saw the little girl again, always quiet, always alone, always walking off the playground with Father. I thought she was going to cry. "Why don't you just fuck right off, Jimmy. Grab a goddamn brain. Go home!"

We left him standing there, his mouth hanging open, and headed for the bus stop on our own. I could see the anger flash in his eyes as he turned and strode away in the opposite direction.

"I'm sorry, Maisie."

"Shit, Lucy, don't be sorry. He was being a complete dick. I don't know why he practically stands up for those assholes at the Mission. Come on, here's our bus."

We settled into our seats and I looked at her. I wanted to tell her that I had cleaned Father's rooms too, that I knew when he plucked her off the playground that day what would happen to her. I wanted to say I was sorry. Instead, I pinched her and we laughed, remembering how we never let Sister win. She would never get the satisfaction of seeing us cry.

I left Lucy alone again that night. This time I didn't even bother coming up with a story, I just said I had to go out. I grabbed my special bag and headed for the Kingsway bus, ready for the transformation again. When I first got out of the Mission, I only had to go out maybe once a month, sometimes once every two months even, and I would be fine. That unbearable panic and urge to scream that I could barely suppress would ease. But now, it seemed like every day all day, it was all I could think of. The last few months the Old Man had given me something to smoke. Called it horse. Said I'd like it, and I did. Made it hard to remember and easy to forget the disgust I felt for him, for myself, for my need to do it again and again, like it might make it all go away.

Tonight, he was waiting for me at the Knight and Day. He had never seen me not dressed in the slut clothes. I think the good-girl clothes freaked him out. This was new.

"Go get dressed. I have something special for you."

I slipped into the ladies' room at the Knight and Day and into the far cubicle. I made the transformation, hastily applied the green eyeshadow and screaming red lipstick, the thick black mascara and eyeliner, the pink powder against brown skin. I stepped outside and he was in his usual place on the bench, waiting for me. He stood and sauntered down the alley to the three-walled cinder-block enclosure for the dumpsters. I followed, wondering why the routine had changed. I turned the corner and saw someone was with him.

"Fuck you, I'm outta here." I glared at him, sucking spit into my mouth, ready to baptize him Kingsway-style.

"Wait. This is Steve. He has something for you. I paid for it, for you. You will love it. It's horse, but better. You'll see."

"After. I'll do it after." I handed him the red package. I couldn't wait anymore.

"And him watch?" His false teeth slipped as he leered at me. He grabbed me, turned me and pushed me against the wall, and pulled up my skirt. "This one likes to be told who she is. Won't do it otherwise."

The other guy laughed, nervous arousal in his voice. I heard the Old Man's zipper and felt him push into me, his hand on the cinder block beside my head, dirty fingernails and long white hair on his saggy arms. He thrust.

"Say it. Or this will be the last time. Say it," I growled at him.

Over and over the ugly words rang in my ears, reminding me of who I was. Just like Father. He finished and I turned to him. He stuffed the two tens in my bra and looked at Steve. The two shook their heads and laughed. I spit in his face. "Give it to me, asshole." He wiped the spittle away and laughed again, handing me the candy bar.

"Now, my little Pocahontas, Steve here has something special for you. Sit down here against the wall and wait for a little piece of heaven."

I wondered how that peaceful feeling could be any better than when I smoked the junk he usually brought me, but I wanted it. The spike didn't scare me as I watched Steve draw the liquid into it from the spoon. The needle slid in, he drew back blood and then he pressed the plunger in all the way. The peace. No pain. No jitters. I puked and then slumped into the euphoria. I barely registered their laughter.

"Come on, my Indian princess, let's get you outta here." The Old Man pulled me up by one arm and Steve grabbed the other. Between them they dragged me down the alley, back to Kingsway, and propped me up on the bus stop bench.

"Meet me here tomorrow if you want more." Steve lifted the two tens from my bra, laughed and sauntered down Kingsway with the Old Man.

I could barely move, the pleasure was so deep. I must have nodded off, because the next thing I knew it was dark and I was being dragged into the back of a police cruiser.

"Get your hands off me!" I pushed at the cop as he tried to bend me into the back seat. "What did I do? Get the hell away from me."

"Soliciting. Loitering. Get in the goddamned car." He shoved me and I fell in headfirst, face down on the seat. He laughed. "Nice ass."

I remembered I was still in those clothes. "My bag. Where's my bag?"

"What bag?" He slammed the door and walked around to the driver's side.

"The one with my clothes. My jeans. My T-shirt."

He sat behind the wheel like he didn't hear me, gunned the engine and drove away. I looked out the window and watched my bag, sitting at the edge of the bench, disappear. It got smaller and smaller as the car pulled away. I thought of the blue barrette, the college-girl jeans, the wallet with the only picture I had of my mom. The car turned a corner and I lost sight of the bag, and with it my life as something other than what Father made me. It slipped out of me, gone, like it never existed.

They let me out the next morning with a promise to appear. Smelling of puke and craving a bath, I walked from 222 Main all the way to the far side of Chinatown. The cheap patent leather boots chafed at the soft flesh behind my knees and I could feel the blisters forming on my toes. I sat down on a bus stop bench, pulled them off and massaged my feet. I looked up just in time to see a woman, an early riser no doubt, walking her dog before heading off to some office. I saw her look away when I looked up at her. She crossed the street, suddenly interested in the store window displays of embroidered hankies and silk coin purses. I carried on in my stocking feet, carrying my boots. No bag, no bus fare, no keys. I prayed Lucy would be there to let me in. I picked up the pace, hoping I could catch her before she left for work at the Manitou.

I caught sight of myself in the window of the Army & Navy store, stopped dead in my tracks, the boots dropping from my hand and clattering against the pavement. There were mascara trails running down my cheeks. There was a large hole in my stockings, runs bubbling over my flesh. I licked my fingers and rubbed my face as clean as possible. My hair was a matted mess. I pulled my fingers through my knotted hair, trying to perform some kind of magic. I struggled with it. What had been teased before was a rat's nest now. I stepped closer to get a better angle on the mess and was confronted with my own face, my eyes swollen and framed with smeared makeup. I waved off the hankie offered by a working girl making her way home after a long night. It seemed a long time that I stood there, looking at that woman in the window.

I turned away and headed toward Chinatown and the apartment, leaving the boots on the ground, not hurrying anymore. There was no sense of relief or familiarity as I reached my block. Nothing. I couldn't feel anything except my hurting feet. Even the sound of the buzzer seemed disconnected from the act of pressing it. Standing in place, I lifted one foot off the ground after the other, the balls of my feet raw from the cement and gravel.

"Hello?" Lucy's tentative voice crackled through the intercom.

"Lucy! It's me, buzz me up." My voice came out as sharp as the bursting blisters that I would have to explain. My mind raced. I looked at my clothes, the stink worsened by the moist drizzle of the Vancouver morning. I felt the leftover puke loosening in my hair.

"Maisie! Where have you been?"

"Jesus, Lucy, just buzz me up." Finally, the familiar buzz and click, and I pushed through the door.

Lucy stood in the open doorway at the top of the stairs. I couldn't help but notice she was wearing my bunny slippers. Her mouth fell open when she caught sight of me, and she held her hand up as though to stop me.

"Maisie, no . . ."

I pushed past her into the apartment just as Jimmy rose from the couch and turned to look at me.

"When you didn't come home, I phoned him. I didn't know what to do." Lucy started crying.

"Oh," he said. "Now I understand." He reached for his jacket and eased by me toward the open door.

"Jimmy, no, wait. Let me explain."

He recoiled from my outstretched hand. "Explain what? That you're a whore?" He stepped farther away from me, his face filled with disgust. "You stink."

"Jimmy." I thought I would vomit, the tears I never cried rising, choking out of me in wrenching sobs. "Jimmy."

"Fuck off, Maisie. Don't ever call me. What was with all that good-girl stuff anyway? How many johns were you fucking or sucking or whatever you do when you wouldn't even let me touch you?"

I couldn't bear it. He would never understand. My chance of being Jimmy's girl was gone before I even left the Mission. The rage ran up my spine in uncontrollable waves. I watched him go, his broad shoulders filling out his fancy leather coat. I ran after him through the doorway and pushed him with all my strength. He staggered, catching himself on the railing.

"Fuck off, Jimmy, you piece of shit. Too good for everyone, eh? Fuck off and die!" I turned back into the apartment and slammed the door, his stunned face the last Jimmy expression I would see.

I turned on Lucy. "Get the fuck out of my slippers." She kicked them off her feet with a look of terror on her face as though she had never seen me before. Maybe she hadn't. I grabbed the slippers, ran into the kitchen and threw them out the window. I ran into the bedroom and pulled the drawers open and started pitching the pretty things out the bedroom window. "Fuck it. Fuck it all."

Lucy came running into the bedroom. She grabbed my arm as I started throwing my shoes and sandals out the window. "Maisie, stop."

I turned on her, the tears a flood now. "Why? Why should I stop? Look at me. This is what I am. Who would ever want me? No one. Get me a fucking cigarette." Lucy ran into the living room and brought back a pack of smokes, matches and an ashtray. I slumped down on the bed, lit a smoke and inhaled deeply.

"Maisie, you were always the strong one. You always found a way to make us laugh."

"Yeah, and who takes care of me? Fuck this, Lucy. I give up. I just don't care about anything anymore." I caught my reflection in the vanity mirror and wiped my stained face on the corner of my pillowcase. "What does it matter, anyway?" I picked up the ashtray and headed for the kitchen, plugged in the kettle and pulled the instant coffee out of the cupboard. "You better get to work, Lucy, or Harlan will dock your pay. Tell him I have the flu."

"You gonna be okay, Maisie? I'll be home right after work."

"Just go, Lucy. We been through worse than this, innit."

Lucy left me with my coffee, closing the door quietly behind her. I sipped and smoked and thought about Jimmy and the poison that would always set me apart from the Jimmies of the world. I stubbed the life out of my smoke and headed for the bathroom. I drew a hot, steamy bath, undressed and threw those shameful clothes in the garbage. I submerged myself in the soothing, soapy water and closed my eyes. I thought of the little picture of my mom in my wallet, abandoned on a Kingsway bench, and wept. I thought of her and how she would take me walking with her on the rocky shore, looking for shells and listening to the seagulls. I thought of the one birthday party I remembered, my mom and dad so happy. I thought of the strangers I went home to. There was no violence, no rage to the tears that melted into the bubble bath.

I sat in front of the vanity mirror, looking at the reflection, this stranger. I looked close into my own eyes and saw a truth there I knew I would never be rid of. I towel-dried my hair and pinned it back with one blue barrette. I slipped into a pair of jeans and the old checkered work shirt Jimmy had lent me a while back. I left my face naked, stuck my Indian Card and my last fifty bucks in my back pocket, my smokes and lighter in the front pocket, and headed out the door, not bothering to lock it behind me.

I walked, my feet still sore from those stupid boots but bearable in my runners. I found myself down at Victory Square, sat on one of the benches and smoked. I watched the winos and the hookers wander through, looking for a drink or a john. I watched the straights leaving their offices, walking in a hurry, looking directly through the people who made this place their own, vanishing them into thin air with their indifference. I smoked some more, flicking the lit remains at their heels, making them look at me.

As late afternoon bled into evening, I walked across the square to the pay phone and called the Old Man. Could he send Steve to Victory Square. Tell him I want my own rig, too. Not a problem, he told me. I didn't think it would be. I walked back to my bench and pulled the second-last smoke from my pack and waited. It wasn't long. Steve ambled across the park and sat down beside me.

"Give it to me." I pulled the money from my pocket but held it tight.

"I'll shoot you up. Come on. We'll sit behind that hedge."

"Fuck that. I want the rig and the horse. I got the money. Give it to me and leave me alone."

"No need to give me the money, honey. You can work it off with that nice ass of yours."

"Whatever. Just give me the stuff and leave me alone. I want enough for tomorrow too. Give me four packets. You'll get your payback later."

"Okay, but no funny stuff. I'll be looking for you."

"No doubt." I watched him saunter away, his long-fingered hand wiping his limp hair out of his eyes.

The park, a study in darkness, was richly golden, briefly glorified in the light of transition from day to dusk. I stood to greet a nameless, toothless woman, her black hair shot with grey. Weariness etched the lines of her face as she pulled her laundry cart packed high with all she owned. She smiled at me, confused, as I pressed the fifty into her palm, hugged her and gave her my last smoke. I felt her eyes on me as I wandered over to the short rock wall. I slipped between the wall and the boxwood hedge where no one could see me. I sat there and emptied all four packets into the spoon. I slid my left arm out of Jimmy's sleeve and tightened the tubing.

I looked, one last time, at the skyline.

4

KENNY

The packed dirt floor of the pickers' shack seemed darker than usual, even with the thin shafts of light pressing their way through the gaps in the raw plank siding. Kenny didn't need a watch to know how late he was. Instead of the early morning clatter and chatter that filled the air around the shacks, there was a heavy silence broken only by the sound of the rain in the trees.

"Shit." Kenny rolled out of bed and dressed quickly, shirt unbuttoned, boots tightly laced. He took a long draw of water from the barrel outside the front door, the spillage from the dipper cold on his chest. He filled the dipper once more and splashed water on his face, gasping at the chill. He could see the other pickers in the trees already, almost like fruit themselves. Kenny ran across the meadow, the lazy rain the promise of a cold day in the trees. The bone-deep warmth of the August sun was now completely replaced by an early September chill. His head throbbed with every stride.

"You're late." The foreman stood leaning alongside an apple bin. Kenny would not have seen him had he not called out.

"Sorry, boss." Kenny slowed his pace to a walk, stopping in front of the foreman.

"And you stink, too." The foreman took a step away from Kenny. "Gonna have to dock your pay."

The sickly sweet smell of last night's cinnamon whisky rose from his skin, and he looked away. "Long night, boss, but you know I'm never late. One chance. Please. I need the money."

"You gotta do the job to get paid. What is it with you people? You're your own worst enemy." The foreman turned to walk away, shaking his head. "There're ten guys just like you lined up for that job. Get to work or get lost."

Kenny watched him walk away into the orchard. The foreman's fresh khakis felt, for some reason, like a further insult. He shook his head and wandered over to a row of trees with the fewest pickers. Yesterday's ladders remained in place. He looked for an empty one in the least populated row. The closest picker was old Rosa, the Mexican *mamacita* of the camp. She was a small, quiet woman, deceptively strong. "Small mercies," he muttered to himself, thankful for at least a couple hours of peace and quiet as he picked in the orchard. He grabbed his bucket and climbed to a good picking level.

"Hey, Kenny! Guess we're picking together today."

"Shit." It was Wilfred. He'd been a newcomer on the orchard circuit, showing up in the pickers' camp during the plum season, and stayed on right through peaches, pears and now, the last crop of the year, apples. Kenny kept his own company, but Wilfred was always friendly when their paths crossed. "Not today," Kenny muttered to himself.

"Let's kick the shit out of this row, Ken. Bet you we can get it done before lunch break. Double that by the end of the day. Maybe even get a bonus for extra bins."

Kenny sighed, wishing only for a quiet morning to get over his hangover. Wilfred's exuberance was like salt in the wound. But since Wilfred was not going anywhere, and with a shrunken pay packet fresh in his mind, Kenny relented. "All right, man, let's do it."

Silent for the most part, stopping only at the hottest part of the day to strip off a shirt or for a hastily downed drink of water, the two young men picked into the late afternoon, the occasional careless insult the only words between them.

Kenny felt better and better with the exertion, and easily kept up with Wilfred's pace, even though Wilfred was a much taller and bigger man. It seemed like no time had passed when the end-of-day siren rang. The sun sat poised to slip behind the stalwart hills, set perfectly to protect Washington's primary crop, the apples of the Wenatchee valley. Kenny and Wilfred walked to the foreman's shack to collect their daily pay packet.

The whistle finally blew, and Wilfred fell into line behind Kenny, waiting their turn with the paymaster. Storm clouds gathered, the wind giving them force, readying themselves for a full-on downpour. The young men raised the collars of their jean jackets.

"Well, we should get a bonus. We filled two extra bins beyond the quota." Wilfred rubbed his hands together. "You want to go for a beer with me? That was some thirsty work."

"Hmmph." Kenny kicked a casualty McIntosh missed by some picker's hand. It split in three pieces, white flesh lush, juice spraying in its wake. "You might be getting a bonus. I might be just breaking even."

"Late, huh?"

"Once. I ain't never been late. Not once, till today. You think that greedy fucker would give me a break?"

Wilfred laughed. "What does he care about you? It's all just money."

"Yeah, I guess. Trying to save. Hard to do when the thirst is on ya."

"What are you saving for? A car?"

"Naw. The bus is good enough for me. Or this." Kenny stuck his thumb out in an exaggerated hitchhiker's pose.

Wilfred laughed. "What, then?"

"Probably never happen, but one day I would like my own little place. Someplace no one can tell me what to do."

"Yeah. No bells."

"Bells?" Kenny looked closer at Wilfred.

Wilfred walked a little slower, as if to claim his time as his own. "Indian School. When I get sick of people telling me what to do, I think of those bells. Man, if you didn't get where you were supposed to be when those bells rang, shit, there was hell to pay."

Kenny stopped next to the truck where the day's bins were being loaded. He looked at Wilfred as though seeing him for the first time. The seconds felt like hours as the familiarity of a long-ago face emerged.

"What school?" Kenny tried to sound casual, but Wilfred was now giving him a funny look too.

"Kenny? Are you *that* Kenny?"

"Arrowhead Bay?" Kenny knew it before Wilfred could answer.

"Kenny!" Wilfred charged his old friend, laughing and shoving playfully like in those old days at the Mission.

"Holy shit, Wilfred, man, it's been years since I saw you. You sure bulked up. With all that long hair, no wonder I didn't recognize you. You ain't that little boy no more!"

"They told us you drowned."

"Naw, I made it. All the way home."

"We talked about you for years. At night, after Brother went to sleep. We imagined you free while we ran for those bells."

"Yeah, well, we're back in the same place again, aren't we?" Kenny motioned toward the foreman, his khakis still spotless, blowing on a whistle and yelling for everyone to hurry up. "Come on. Better get this done or he'll keep it himself." Kenny nudged Wilfred. "I'll join you for that beer, for sure."

"Hey, you shorted me." Kenny had already started to walk away, counting the bills in his pay envelope.

"Two basket penalty. You know the rules. You were late." The foreman picked up an apple from his makeshift table, took a bite, wiped the juice from his chin and set it back down on the table, rifling again through the pay envelopes.

A rush of rage ran up Kenny's spine like a monster, pressing against him for release. Kenny turned to face the foreman. "Yeah, but me and Wilfred, we picked two whole extra bins above quota. Where is the bonus for that?"

"You know the rules. No bonus unless you meet quota. After the penalty, you didn't reach quota. No bonus."

"What?" Kenny could feel the monster rising even closer to the surface.

"You heard me. You know the rules. If you don't like it, move on. Lots of guys are happy to follow the rules."

"*Once.*" The monster writhed. "I been working in this orchard for three seasons. I always pick more than the quota. Once. Just once I'm late, and you take from me like this?"

"Move on." The foreman waved him aside. "The line is backing up."

Kenny took a step closer to the foreman instead. The orchard seemed to disappear. All he could see was this impeccably dressed man standing next to his little table with the basket of pay packets. The rage buzzed in his ears, his focus now entirely on the apple— round, red, fresh. The voices around him were muted and distant. Another colour seemed to bleed into the apple and in a second Kenny was sure it had transformed into an orange, horribly familiar. The bright-blue label pasted on the wooden crate of oranges Brother always kept in his room filled his eyes as though he were there, here, now. The smell of Brother filled his nostrils, the foreman's hand waving him off now Brother's fat, pale hand, handing him an orange every time, counting on his hunger. And then, in a heartbeat, it was raining money, notes floating like feathers around him, and it was like he had been thrown back to earth, hard and fast, the foreman lying under him, his lip and nose pouring blood. The workers swirled around them, yelling and grabbing at the money that had taken flight after Kenny kicked the table sky-high. Someone was pulling on his shoulder. Wilfred.

"Kenny! For chrissakes, snap out of it."

Kenny looked around him, almost as dazed as the semi-conscious foreman flat out under him. He looked at the bloodied face and his own fist and jumped up, surprised as anyone else to find himself assaulting the boss.

Kenny staggered back from the melee. Pickers were still scrambling for the bills that had flown and fallen from the air like snowflakes. Arguments were breaking out among them, one faction saying to return the money and let it be recounted, the other ready to run for it. Rosa walked quietly over to Kenny, took his lacerated fist in her hand and gently pulled his fingers open. She placed four crumpled ten-dollar bills she'd harvested from the money storm in his hand and looked up at him.

"Go. Now. He will call the police. Go."

Her gentleness brought Kenny back to earth. He knew she was right. "Wilfred, I'm outta here. You coming?"

Rosa pulled a blue cotton handkerchief from her pocket and walked toward the foreman where he sat on the ground dazed, surveying the chaos. She reached to clean up his face, but he brushed her arm away and staggered to his feet. "Where is he? Someone hold him while I call the police. There's fifty bucks in it for you." Just then he seemed to realize what had happened to the payroll. "You all bring that money back!"

The crowd of workers dissipated, everyone fading into the orchard. Soon it was just the foreman wandering around the clearing, grasping at the few bills still left on the ground, Rosa walking behind him, handkerchief outstretched.

Kenny and Wilfred ran back to the pickers' shacks and bundled up their few possessions. Kenny kicked the door open as he left, the legs of his extra pair of jeans hanging out of his sleeping bag. The door hung off its last remaining hinge, crying out a rusty complaint as the wind threatened to finish it. "Hurry up!" He looked over his shoulder as he ran, Wilfred trying to catch up.

"Head for the creek. We can hide there for a day or two." Wilfred tried to tighten his bundle of blankets and clothes as they ran.

Red willows grew all along the banks of this nameless creek, a tributary of the mighty Wenatchee River. It was not unusual to find the deserted camps of the many itinerant workers who took refuge along her banks while moving through the picking season. During the down times, between hiring for the different crops, the pickers would just fish and snare for a few days, and laze alongside the easy-running creek, happy even for a few days with family, or a few days alone. When Kenny and Wilfred ran to her banks, the occasional leaf had already begun to turn and they felt the chill of fall in the evening. They found a good spot, a camp that looked long abandoned. Someone had taken the time to dig a bit of a firepit and surround it with stones from the creek rather than just making fire on flat ground. The fugitives threw their belongings down and dropped onto their respective piles of blankets and clothes, breathless and wary.

"Man, you went nuts!" Wilfred shook his head, laughing.

"Well, fuck him. Geez, a guy should get paid what he's owed. This's why I want a place away from people. No bullshit." Kenny shook his head. "Now what the hell am I gonna do? No pay and no doubt he's blacklisted me. I won't get any more work this year, around here anyway."

"Well, I wouldn't worry about the pay part of it." Wilfred started emptying his pockets. He pulled a big wad of crumpled bills from his jeans pocket and then reached for his jacket pockets.

Kenny did a double take and laughed. "What the hell, man!"

"It was raining money. Thought I best get our share." Smiling, Wilfred handed a couple of wads to Kenny. "Come on, let's count it."

They counted, making neat piles of the ones and fives, tens and twenties. Kenny pulled out the forty Rosa had given him and added it to the pile.

"Remind you of anything?" Kenny nudged Wilfred with his elbow and smiled.

Wilfred looked up and burst out laughing. "Yeah, the raids. Man, we sure made out. The staff leftovers. They had such good food. My mouth is watering just thinking about it."

Kenny nodded. "Yep. Between the raids and the fiddleheads in the bush, we survived. Okay, I got two hundred and twenty-seven dollars in this pile."

Wilfred laid down the last of his bills. "One hundred and ninety-three. We're rich!"

Kenny massaged his scraped knuckles. "Well, we got enough to lay low for a couple of days while we figure out what to do." He handed his pile of bills to Wilfred, who quietly counted and divided the total in two, handing Kenny half.

Wilfred stood and stretched. "I'm going to walk into town and get some food and a few supplies. See if I can steal some ass-wipe from the café." They both laughed. "They won't be looking for me. I'll see ya in a couple of hours."

"Sounds good." Kenny took his boots off and stretched out on his sleeping bag, arms crossed behind his head. He closed his eyes as Wilfred headed for town.

He slept longer than planned, the sun already behind the horizon when the knock and shuffle of Wilfred making a fire woke him. Kenny had dreamed of her again, as he often had in the years since he'd left the Mission: Lucy and her almost smile, passing him a note and then she was gone.

"What happened to her?"

"Oh, you're finally awake there!" Wilfred stacked the firewood. "Everyone in town is talking about the crazy Indian in the apple orchards. I think the cops are lookin' for you."

"They'll get bored soon enough." Kenny sat up and flexed his skinned knuckles.

"What happened to who?"

"Your sister. Lucy."

"You still sweet on my little sister?"

Kenny blushed. "Just wondering." He thought of how much Wilfred had changed since he'd last seen him and wondered how different Lucy would be.

Wilfred fanned the little flames until they wrapped themselves around the dry twigs and branches, burning hot and smokeless. He pulled out a can of beans and stabbed it with his hunting knife, neatly working his way around the edge to open the can. "She's in Vancouver. I heard she's working at some fleabag hotel." He placed the can of beans in the fire, its ragged lid still attached, setting it at an angle to protect the contents from floating ash. "She's single, I think. You know, I never really knew her well. She was just a toddler when I was taken. They whipped my ass when I tried to talk to her when they brought her to the Mission. They didn't care she was my sister."

They sat at the fire, watching the beans rise and bubble. Kenny turned to his friend. "And whatever happened to Howie after he escaped? Did you ever hear from him? I wonder if he's still down the States."

"Nope, never saw him again, but I heard he had to leave the States because he didn't have proper paperwork or something. I ran into some of the guys from the school and they said they heard he was back in Arrowhead Bay trying to get his papers fixed and he ran into Brother. Kicked his ass. Beat him to a pulp. Heard he almost died. I don't know if Howie escaped or got thrown in the can."

"I felt so sorry for that kid. He was so small and terrified all the time. I think Brother would have killed him if he hadn't escaped."

"Yeah. I remember that morning. I thought he was already dead, he was so limp, and all that blood."

Wilfred used two twigs to pull the can out of the coals and set it between himself and Kenny. He pulled two small forks from his shirt pocket and handed one to Kenny, smiling. "Nabbed them from the café along with the TP."

Kenny laughed. "Some things don't change, eh? Still making raids to get by." The friends took turns taking forkfuls of beans from the can, as the hesitant dusk turned into night, the full moon casting a pale reflection on the creek. "Don't know what I'm gonna do now."

"You ever worked the logging camps on the island?" Wilfred took the last bite of beans and rinsed out the can in the creek. "Pretty good coin if you can get on. Lots of jobs, but you kinda have to know someone."

Kenny nodded thoughtfully. "Naw. Never had enough money for the gear. This guy once told me you can make enough money in the logging season to live well for the year."

"Well, you burned your bridges here. Might as well go. I know a guy. I'll give you his number. He might be able to get you on."

"What about you?"

"No cops lookin' for me." Wilfred laughed. "I'll find another apple orchard. Finish out the season."

The young men spent the rest of the night catching up and drinking tea made in the bean can with tea bags also lifted from the hapless café. The next morning, they bundled up their few possessions and stood, now at a loss for words, as the day pulled them in different directions.

"Man, it was good to run into you, Kenny." Wilfred reached into his jeans pocket and pulled out a small piece of paper. "Here, this is that guy's number. Pretty sure he'll get you workin'. Tell him I said hi. I was his lead hand for a while. Oh, and this is the place Lucy was working. If she's still there."

"Thanks, man. You gonna head back toward town?"

"Might as well. Maybe the competition is hiring."

Kenny looked in the other direction. "Well, I think I'm gonna follow the creek for a while. Stay off the road. Head for the border."

Wilfred held his hand out to his friend. "Good plan."

With nothing left to say, they shook hands. Wilfred headed south, Kenny north, looking over his shoulder once, waving to his friend.

Kenny walked along the meandering creek, enjoying the sound of it when it narrowed and quickened, the peace of it when it widened and slowed, deeper and quieter, the rusty-coloured stones casting a sparkling copper tone on the crystalline water. There was a bitter sweetness in seeing his old friend. He was happy to share their tricky survival memories; it was the other ones, the ones that slipped in through the silences, that he was relieved to lose in his usual solitude.

The collar of Kenny's jean jacket did nothing against the wild coastal rain so heavy he could barely see in front of him. He walked quickly to catch shelter under the huge, bright sign announcing the Manitou Motel to anyone within a block's radius. He stood under the sign, watching as the maids rolled their trollies to the rooms. He wondered what Lucy would look like now. The cigarette drowned instantly when he threw it on the ground. He headed through the lobby door. The man behind the desk lowered his magazine and looked Kenny up and down without saying a word.

Kenny cleared his throat. "Ah, I'm looking for an old friend of mine. Heard she was working here. Lucy. You know her?"

"Maybe I do, maybe I don't." The manager worked a toothpick with his tongue.

"Aw, come on, man, I'm just looking for my friend. Is she here?"

"Not now."

"But she works here? She'll be back?"

"Maybe. You never know with these Indian chicks."

Kenny looked down at his knuckles, which were just starting to heal, then at Harlan's sneering face. The anger rose, but he swallowed, hard. "Well." He cleared his throat. "Can you tell her I was here looking for her? My name's Kenny."

"If I don't forget. Now move on. I have real customers to deal with."

Kenny looked around the empty lobby, turned and left, the blood ringing in his ears.

Before the door closed behind him, Harlan called out, "Hey, I think she lives above Chong Li's. Just down the block."

Kenny let him think he hadn't heard. With darkness deepening, he walked through the rain to the entrance to Chinatown and Chong Li's grocery. He looked up and figured there was only one apartment there. The rain slowed to a drizzle and Kenny stood, across the street from the grocery, wondering if she would even remember him. He thought of her, head shaven, eyes downcast, that horrible sign around her neck, and he couldn't stand still any longer. He walked down the alley and headed for the Balmoral for a beer. As he rounded the corner and looked back, he thought he caught sight of two women in the corner of his eye, but when he looked again, he saw nothing. He shrugged and carried on.

5

LUCY

------>-<------

There was a time of day, just past three, when the Manitou Motel didn't look like a crime scene. Swept clean of grimy evidence, its early 1950s facade seemed almost family friendly. Lucy liked the Manitou in the afternoon, buffed up and almost shiny for a few hours, before nightfall and the inevitable onslaught of customers rendered it unrecognizable, again, under a layer of empty bottles, overflowing ashtrays and mangled linens. She nodded in satisfaction, the beds neatly made, the bathroom porcelain gleaming, the towels artfully folded, as though by some magic she wouldn't be wading through the fetid mess again the next morning. Daydreaming, Lucy walked straight into Clara as they both reached for the door to the linen closet.

"Hey!" Clara bumped her with a swing of her hip and held the door for her. They shrugged off their smocks and punched their time cards by rote, the sudden darkness of the windowless room no longer a hindrance to their practised hands. Tired and ready to leave the Manitou to its ghosts, they sauntered into the sunlight.

"It's your big day tomorrow, Lucy, right?"

"Yep."

"You scared?"

"Nope. I'm going to pass that test. It's not the same as if you go right through high school. But it's kinda the same as grade twelve. What would Sister think now?" She waved her hand as though swatting a fly.

"Yeah, she'd probably faint, the old bitch." The two girls snickered at the thought of Sister Mary fainting dead away at the news of her success. "You know what day it is today?"

Clara shook her head. "You mean other than Thursday? What?"

"Two years today since Maisie died."

The girls walked in silence, finding no words.

Lucy turned to her friend as they approached Chong Li's. "Hey, you want to come up for a cola? Just got some new 45s. 'Ruby Tuesday' too."

"Nah, I can't. I promised Liz I'd meet her at Woolworth's."

"I sure hope she shows up tomorrow. She promised she would cover for me."

"Yeah, but you know Liz and her promises. She better show, because I sure don't want to be doing all those extra rooms."

Lucy touched her friend's shoulder. "I'll come straight back to the Manitou after the test, and if she doesn't show, I'll take over."

"Hey, don't worry. Just think about your test. Do us proud, girl!"

Lucy turned into the alleyway and the small alcove that led to the apartment above Chong Li's. She laughed, fishing in her purse for her keys. "See you tomorrow."

"Yeah! We'll all go out and celebrate."

Just then, Lucy looked down the alley and stood motionless, keys pointed toward the door, as she watched a guy walking away. There was something about his frame, the way he moved as he disappeared down the alley; the tilt of his head strangely familiar.

She shrugged and slipped the key into the lock. Pull, lift and turn the key simultaneously and the old, sticky lock would open. Otherwise, she might as well try abracadabra. It was almost two years now since she'd laid all her money, but for two dollars, on Chong Li's counter in return for the key to the apartment upstairs.

She couldn't get the door open and had to go back to the store to ask him to open it for her. His English getting worse and worse with frustration, he opened the door with an irritated flourish, grumbling his way back to the store. She could have taken over Maisie's apartment after she died. The landlord even offered her the place. She chose this apartment instead for its low rent and proximity to the Manitou. Besides, there was just too much sadness filling every corner at Maisie's place. Lucy didn't often allow thoughts of her. She didn't understand how Maisie could have been so full of despair that she would take her own life. The cops had come to the door, then took Lucy to the morgue to identify her lifeless body. Yes, it was Maisie. Beautiful, brave Maisie. Even though the other girls told Lucy over and over again not to blame herself, she felt sure it was her fault. So she tried not to think of Maisie alone in a corner of the graveyard for the destitute and abandoned.

Lucy pushed the thoughts away and stepped inside the apartment. She changed into her new bell-bottoms and matching paisley blouse and stood in front of the open fridge, barefoot. The ancient linoleum was cool respite for her feet, which were hot and tingling after a long day. Her fridge was empty except for a dozen eggs, a package of toaster tarts and three bottles of pop. The light blazed with so few contents to block the rays of the bulb. She pulled out a bottle of pop, held it against the counter edge and popped the lid off with the base of her hand. She guzzled half the bottle at once, gasping from the fizz of it. She took her place at the kitchen table, placing both palms on the textbook. A familiar nervousness rose in her, constricting her throat. She pushed the textbook away and, instead of studying, emptied every cupboard, the small counter piled with dishes and dry goods. Already spotless, she nonetheless wiped every inch of the cupboard interiors and carefully placed their contents back inside, only to empty the cupboards again and again, each time reordering the contents, this time by size, this time by brand name, this time by shape.

In the evenings, the Manitou's neon sign filled her kitchen with a soft red light. She often sat at her kitchen table, smoking, calm in the red hue, even though it reminded her from time to time of the illuminated exit sign in the dorm. Sometimes she wondered if it was there just to taunt them, to remind them there was no exit, no escape.

Finally, exhausted, she closed the cupboard doors. She gazed out the window at the Manitou. The hookers were just starting to trickle in. They carried their haughty promises in their bearing, swinging their hips, hanging provocatively on the arms of the johns as they headed for the rooms at the Manitou. She would also see them emerge later, more subdued, adjusting their clothes and folding money into their bras or shoes.

Not long after her arrival in Vancouver, Lucy quit her evening ritual of rolling the giant pink curlers in her hair and securing them against her scalp with the bobby pins she had brought with her from the Mission School. She was mesmerized by the hippie girls who sometimes wandered away from Fourth Avenue into the downtown core. She saw their white-pink lipstick, dramatic kohl eyes and long, straight hair, shiny and swaying, unhindered by the brittle freeze of hairspray. In the years since Lucy's departure from the Mission, her hair had grown past her shoulder blades. She thought it grew faster now that it was free of Sister's temper and her well-used razor. She replaced her rat-tail comb with a boar bristle brush, and her hairspray with herb-smelling shampoo. She watched the hippie girls living with a freedom that came naturally without anything or anyone to fear or resist. She wondered if they could even imagine a life without such abandon.

Sometimes Lucy had to remind herself that no one was watching her, waiting to pounce. A turbulent river of exhilaration ran beneath her quiet demeanour with the realization that her choices were now her own.

Lucy sighed and pulled the textbook toward her and read it aloud, in a whisper, as though sound would seal the information in her head.

The next afternoon, Lucy walked into the Manitou parking lot, waving as Clara caught sight of her and raced toward her.

"Well? Come on!" Clara grabbed her elbow. "Tell me! How did it go?"

Lucy hung her head, disappointment heavy in her step. Liz, close on Clara's heels, swallowed her words as Clara turned and whispered to her, "Don't say anything. I don't think she made it." The girls reached out to hug Lucy.

"It's okay, Lucy, you can try again." Clara patted her on the shoulder.

"Psych!" Lucy laughed as she pulled her exam paper from her purse and pointed to the red-circled B+. The girls jumped and shouted their delight at her success. Liz hugged her so hard Lucy could barely breathe, as Clara danced around them, laughing.

"Well, maybe one of us will get out of this hellhole." Clara sighed, not used to laughing so hard sober.

Lucy smiled at her friends. "We'll celebrate tonight. My treat."

"All right!" Clara reached for Lucy's test paper and held it out above her. "You should have this framed." She turned to get Liz's approval and caught Harlan out of the corner of her eye, stepping out of the office door and striding across the parking lot toward them. "Uh-oh. Here comes Hitler."

The girls started toward the linen room, but not fast enough. Harlan cut them off and grabbed Lucy by the wrist. "And where the hell have you been? I'm docking your pay!"

"Fuck you, Harlan. I told you I had to write my test this morning. I told you Clara was going to cover for me."

"I don't know what you think you're trying to prove. You Indian chicks are good for two things, and both of them happen in motel rooms." He grabbed her test and threw it on the ground. "You think this is going to make a difference? Now get the fuck to work."

"Fuck you, Harlan. I quit." The words were out of her mouth before she knew what she was saying.

"You can't quit, you're fired! Ungrateful bitch. Collect your shit and get the fuck out of here."

Lucy stood, unmoving, under the garish neon sign of the Manitou, rage and exhilaration rushing through her like two rivers colliding. "Ungrateful? You should be grateful we don't report you to the health department."

Later, the girls would laugh about what happened next and talk about it for years to come. But in that moment, both Liz and Lucy were left standing, stunned, as Clara, with a raging scream, pounced on Harlan's back, her wiry legs wrapped around his waist, punching him in the back of the head and yelling at the top of her lungs. Everyone knew Clara had a hair-trigger temper in situations like these, when things were just plain wrong. Later, they decided that Harlan should have known better.

"You fucking bastard! You're ruining her best day ever!" Clara rode Harlan like some violent piggyback ride, punching him in the face and head as he swatted at her, hunching and twisting, desperately trying to throw her off his back. He circled and circled, arms flying, as Clara clung to him with one arm and pummelled him with the other. Lucy watched wide-eyed until she and Liz jumped in, prying Clara loose. Harlan then took a swing and Clara flew through the air, landing on her ass on the pavement. The two girls threw themselves between Harlan and Clara as, in a daze, she struggled to stand. Wiping the blood from the corner of his mouth, Harlan waved his fingers at the girls.

"You're all fired! Now get the fuck off the property. And you, Lucy, tell your deadbeat boyfriends to stay the hell away from my lobby."

"You just had to wreck everything like you always do, didn't you?" Clara brushed herself off. "I'm getting my stuff, and if you want to try to stop me, well, go ahead." Head high, Clara limped toward the linen room to get her things. Liz and Lucy walked backwards behind her, watching Harlan twitch in their direction. Clara emerged with her few possessions and the three girls headed down the street, the shadow of the Manitou sign shimmering over them.

"I am so sorry, you guys. I didn't mean for you to lose your jobs," Lucy said, on the verge of tears.

"Aw, to hell with him," Clara muttered. "He needs us more than we need him. Who else would work in that dive? You watch, tomorrow morning he'll be tryin' to track us down to come back to work. Forget him! This is your big day. Let's go party!"

"Well, I'm not going back." Lucy pulled her test paper out again, wrinkled and dirty from the tussle with Harlan. "This will find me something better. Liz, what did he mean? That thing about my boyfriends. I don't even have a boyfriend."

"I was going to tell you, but what with Muhammad Ali over here, I didn't get a chance."

"Tell me what?" Lucy could feel an awful nervousness taking over.

"Some guy came into the Manitou today looking for you. He told Harlan you two were old friends. I guess someone told him you worked here. Harlan told him to take a hike."

"What guy?" Lucy shrugged. "I don't know any guys."

"I didn't see him, I just heard Harlan giving him the boot. Put some lipstick on. Let's go have some fun. You did it!"

Lucy reached into her purse and applied her lipstick as she walked, a little smug, knowing the white-pink frosted tone looked much better on her than on those hippie girls. She didn't give the stranger another thought.

The laughter echoed in Lucy's head as she returned alone to her apartment above Chong Li's. Clara had led the whole bar to the point of hysteria with her story of jumping Harlan in the Manitou parking lot. With each rendition of the story there were a few more punches landed, a few more insults uttered. Lucy laughed under her breath as she reached for the door to manipulate the key.

"Lucy?"

She panicked at the sound of her name coming from the dark alley. "Who is it?" Her chest tightened. She swung around to look and there he was, the man she'd seen before in the alley. "What? What do you want?" She slipped her key in the lock and it stuck, her nervous fingers forgetting how to jostle the door open. Her mouth was sand dry, her voice little more than a squeak. "Who are you?"

"It's me, Kenny."

"Kenny?"

"Yeah."

"What the . . ."

He stepped out of the shadow, and under the light of the Manitou she saw it was indeed him. A man now, but still the same. He walked toward her, his hands in his pockets. She caught a whiff of the alcohol rising from him. She clung to the doorknob, hoping she looked casual, as a light-headed dizziness threatened her balance.

"Can we talk, Lucy?"

"Are you okay?" She ran her hand through her hair, expecting to feel the stubbles and scrapes left by Sister Mary's handiwork.

"Yeah, I'm okay."

She wondered if he thought he would see those scab trails on her head again too. "You been here all this time?" The swirling slowed.

"Naw. Just pulled in a week ago." Kenny ran his fingers through his hair, his face suddenly warm. "I ran into Wilfred down the States. He said you were here." Kenny eyed the now-open door. "Can we talk?"

"You saw my brother?"

"Yeah. Took me a week to know who he was. All grown up."

"I never thought I'd see you again. They told us you were dead."

"Not yet. Give it time." They both laughed, nervous.

"Tomorrow? Can we visit tomorrow?"

Kenny turned to leave. "You don't have to. Just thought I would say hi."

Lucy ran toward him. "No. No! I'm just so surprised. I can't get my thoughts straight. Look, I don't have to work tomorrow. Come have coffee with me in the morning. Okay?"

Kenny smiled. "You're sure all grown up."

Lucy laughed. "You too."

"See you in the morning, then." Kenny turned to leave. Lucy stood there, key in one hand, purse in the other.

"Okay. Knock loud when you get here. Sometimes I don't hear from up there." She looked up at her kitchen window. "I'll watch for you."

"All right." Kenny turned slowly, hands still in his pockets, and made his way down the alley.

She slipped inside and collapsed on the steps, her face in her hands, her head reeling. Images and sounds rattled around her. The nuns' rustling habits and clicking rosary beads; Father and his insidious invitations; the giggling girls and the clatter of meals; the regimental lineups forming before any movement from one place to another. Kenny, with his glances and secreted notes, calming her. Lucy took a deep breath, stood and made her way up the stairs.

Lucy left the lights off and quietly sat at the kitchen table. She watched the usual goings-on outside her window but remained distracted and overwhelmed by the flood of memories she'd worked so hard to keep below the surface. Clara had been there with her at the Mission School, but she was older and they hadn't talked about it much. It was an unspoken agreement between them: the past was the past. It's hard to run from the past, but once stuffed away, they knew it couldn't be allowed to poison the present. They couldn't be who they were now, with their lipstick, paycheques and rooms, if they were also those children, or the children who'd left the other children behind.

Lucy looked at her hands and willed them to stop shaking. *Kenny, the one we believed in.* He was the one who never lost his taste for freedom. The stories of his escapes were legendary, his exploits spiralling into epic accounts in the whispers of the children in their dorms. She laid her head on the table and cried.

The next morning, the patter of gravel on her window woke her.

"Lucy! It's me."

Groggy from too little sleep, exhausted after yesterday's madness, Lucy rubbed her eyes and looked out the window. Kenny stood there looking up at her.

She opened the window and looked down at him. "Hang on, I'll come down."

She splashed cold water on her face and threw on a clean blouse, replacing the paisley one wrinkled from her sleep at the kitchen table.

She walked slowly down the stairs, trying to breathe deeply to calm herself. She turned the deadbolt latch and opened the door.

"Come on up."

He followed her up the stairs. "You live here alone?" He glanced around at the tiny studio, the ancient linoleum sounding like frozen ground, crackling under his boots.

"Yeah, just me. I was working at the Manitou, but I'm not anymore. I quit yesterday. Hey, come on and sit over here. I'll make us some coffee." She put the kettle on the flame and pulled two cups from the cupboard along with the instant coffee. "What do you take?"

"Just sugar." Kenny sat at her table watching her as she slid into her seat, waiting for the water to boil.

"Me too." She smiled. Her happiness at seeing him alive, grown and free, eclipsed the sadness that followed him into her kitchen like a roiling wave. "I never stopped wondering about you, after that last time you ran away. What happened? Father told us you drowned, but we didn't believe him. We knew you made it."

"I stole the new punt, the one they got after I blew out the engine in the old one. Remember that day when they were taking Howie to the hospital after Brother got through with him?"

"Yes. And you walked right past Sister like she was nothing to talk to me. I knew then you would go again."

"I didn't even know I was going again. I just couldn't take it anymore. You should have seen the blood in Howie's bed that day. I thought he was dead. I went down to the dock to see if they were coming back, and I just knew I had to go. But you stopped me. I tried to stay for you. I needed to tell you that. When I finally did leave, all I could think about was you, sitting so quietly in the dining hall with your shaved head."

"It was kind of hopeless without you. Whatever happened to Howie? We heard he escaped to the States with his mom, but he was never talked about again."

"I heard a story, don't know how true it is, that he had to come back to Canada for some government paperwork problem. Had to go all the way back to Arrowhead Bay. All the dumb luck, he ran into Brother and kicked his sorry ass. Been in the can since. But you know, people talk shit."

Lucy smiled. "They sure do. So, where did you go?"

"I didn't stop till I got to Port McNeill. I found someone who knew my uncle. He wanted to bring me back to the Mission. When I told him what was happening, though, he took me home to my mom's place."

Lucy carefully spooned the instant coffee into their cups and added the now-boiling water. She handed Kenny his cup and pointed to the sugar. Kenny reached into the breast pocket of his jacket and pulled out a mickey of rum. He sipped down half his coffee, then filled the cup to the brim. He held the bottle over Lucy's cup, a question. She nodded. He seemed surprised and smiled at her. "Hair of the dog."

"So how did you end up in the States?" The sweet smell of rum in coffee made her nostrils tingle.

"Well, home wasn't home anymore. I hadn't seen or talked to my mom in seven years, and I didn't know that, when they took me away from her, she'd started drinking. It was like we were strangers. But what about you? How did you end up here?"

Lucy sipped her coffee. Her face tightened a little. "Sister put me on a bus to Vancouver on my sixteenth birthday. I was scared to death. Had never even seen a trolley bus, or an elevator, or people just living like people. If I hadn't found Maisie, I would have been done for. She got me my job at the Manitou."

"How is Maisie? What a girl that one was. Took no crap from anyone."

Lucy told him all about Maisie's double life: her strength, her fight to survive, and her suicide. She surprised herself by getting through the story without crying. Kenny exhaled deeply, reached into his jacket and poured another shot into his coffee cup, a slight tremor in his hands. She shook her head at his offer of seconds.

Kenny sipped and looked at her over the rim of his coffee cup. "And now you're not working anymore."

"Well, I've been going to night school after my shifts at the Manitou. Yesterday I passed the last test. I'm going to sign up at the community college. Look at this." She pulled the faded newspaper clipping out of her book and passed it to Kenny. "Look, those Indian girls became nurses. If they can do it, so can I."

Kenny laughed and grasped her hands as she pulled the clipping away. "I always knew you would make something of yourself."

Lucy blushed. "More coffee? Are you hungry? I have toaster tarts."

Kenny laughed again. "No, thanks. I gotta go see a guy about some work. If that doesn't pan out, I might have to go to the Okanagan for a while. Get work in the orchards."

"It's so good to see you, Kenny. Why don't you come back when you're done? I'll do some shopping and make us a meal."

"That would be great, Lucy. I can't remember the last time someone cooked for me."

"Okay, come back around six. Oh, fair warning: I don't know how to cook much. Maisie had to show me how to boil eggs when I first got out."

They laughed and walked toward the door. Lucy reached out and touched Kenny on his shoulder, as if making sure he was real. She felt him shrink into himself.

"I'm all scarred up, Lucy." He shrugged his jacket on and descended the stairs two at a time. He looked up from the bottom and waved. "Later."

Lucy stood by the kitchen window and watched him leave. He seemed so old. He had been an intermediate student when she was a junior, but the age difference between them now seemed far greater than that.

At midnight, Lucy's kitchen was bathed in its usual red glow, but there was no sign of Kenny. She shrugged off her disappointment, wrapped up the roast chicken in waxed paper and slipped it into the fridge next to the toaster tarts. She thought of Maisie and her pauper's funeral, Kenny so ashamed in his purple-flowered dress, and herself, her scalp scraped and bleeding, and sleep resisted her. She turned to her counting game, the one she used to put herself to sleep at night in the dorm, but even that was of no use.

It was the evening of the fourth day before Kenny returned. Lucy and Clara strolled toward her apartment, the arms of their sweaters tied around their necks, too much to wear in the warm fall night. She nudged Clara and whispered something quickly.

"You're late," Lucy said, her face soft with disappointment. "Do you remember Clara? She was an intermediate at the Mission when I was a junior." Clara barely glanced at Kenny, gave him her back and spoke to Lucy alone. "You okay?" Lucy nodded, and Clara turned to Kenny. "You better treat her right, man, or you will have me to deal with."

Kenny took a step back and Lucy laughed, breaking the tension. "And Clara is no one to mess with! Just go ask Harlan." At that the two girls broke into giggles.

Clara recovered first. "But seriously, man. Don't you dare hurt this one."

Kenny blushed and shook his head.

Lucy rolled her eyes and gave Clara a friendly shove. "Okay, bossy!"

The girls laughed and Clara headed off toward her place. "See ya tomorrow, kiddo."

Lucy stood in front of Kenny, the alley so quiet now with Clara's giant presence gone. Kenny uttered the first of a thousand regrets to her as they headed up the creaky stairs.

"Sometimes I'm just no good with people. Just need to be by myself." They walked close, shoulders grazing, the air between them smelling slightly of rum.

"It's okay, Kenny. I'm like that myself sometimes."

They sat together on the threadbare fold-down sofa. Kenny put his arm around her and she placed her hand on his knee. They looked at each other and looked away. He turned to her, took her face in his hands and kissed her. "Can I stay, Lucy? Is it all right?"

Lucy nodded, and rested her face against his chest. She was astonished at the pounding of his heart. The soft red glow from the Manitou reflected against her skin as she sat back from him and removed her blouse. He reached for her and they talked and touched long into the night.

Lucy woke from a quiet sleep, slow to open her eyes, the warmth of the small bed a cocoon. She reached for Kenny, knowing he was gone even before she opened her eyes. She wrapped the blankets tight around herself and turned her eyes to the dank morning outside her kitchen window, the raindrops heavy and even. She lay motionless, her mind turned to her days at the Mission. Not a day without fear. Through it all, she had relied on Kenny. Not just for his encouraging notes and shy smiles, but because he ran and ran and ran. He would not let them beat him. And he believed in her. He even told her so. He was not as hollow then as he was now.

Two months on, she walked to the catalogue outlet store to pick up the nurse's uniform she'd ordered and stopped to buy a pair of proper white shoes at the department store, entering under the giant W. She didn't have much time to think about Kenny now that she was about to begin her training, and as time passed, she thought of him even less, no longer expecting to see him leaning against her door, waiting for her when she turned the corner toward home.

The day before her training started, Lucy headed for the Manitou, hoping to catch up with Clara. She'd been right after all: not only had Harlan pleaded with Liz and Clara to come back to work, he'd even raised their hourly rate to a dollar fifteen.

Clara emerged from the linen room, head down, still in uniform, fatigue in her step.

"Hey girl! You sure had him figured."

Clara laughed as she looked up and saw her friend. "Yeah, for now. You want to go to the Only?"

Lucy waited while Clara changed out of her smock, and the girls walked as they had so many times before through the broken heart of the city. The hookers and addicts and runaway teens, johns and predators scouting their prey, all roamed the core. The hotels had all gone to seed and were nothing more than flophouses rented by the hour and week for those who needed to be within staggering reach of the beer parlours on their main floors. The girls didn't give any of it a second thought; it was their neighbourhood, with dangers and comforts like any other. They slid into their regular booth at the Only, silently devouring their steaming fish soup.

Sighing and satisfied, Lucy turned her attention to Clara, who was opening her fortune cookie. "Hey, it says I will receive good news in four days. I could use some good news."

"So, I start the nursing program tomorrow, up at St. Paul's."

"I knew you would do it. Oh, hey, seen Kenny lately?"

Lucy blushed, looking away from Clara. "Naw."

"He always had a thing for you. Us intermediate girls used to laugh at you guys in the dining hall, looking and not looking at each other. You were just little, and what was he—twelve?"

"You know, he used to pass me notes telling me how brave I was and how pretty I was. He stood up for me. Wouldn't let people laugh at me when Sister shaved my head that time. He made me think I was something special back then. That I could make it."

"Well, he was right."

"Sometimes he would watch me from the boys' side, and when no one was looking, he'd pass me spruce buds to nibble on."

Clara smiled at her friend. "Well, it took him long enough to track you down."

"I guess he just wanted to see what happened to me." Lucy wrapped her sweater around her shoulders and slipped out of the booth. "Walk me home, Clara, you can catch the bus by my place."

The girls wandered into the evening, giggling and talking.

"You should move into my place, Lucy. It's closer to St. Paul's. You don't need to be around the Manitou anymore."

"Maybe, but I like it where I am."

But what she was thinking was: *How will he ever find me way over in the West End?*

6

CLARA

>-------<

Clara sat at the table, oblivious to the empty beer glasses, the overflowing ashtray and the noise of too many conversations straining to be heard above the pounding music. She smouldered alone, her friends now gone after their celebration of Lucy's success. Her anger, a slow, quiet burn, gnawed at her as she thought of Harlan and how he'd tried to make Lucy feel small. She slapped her last five on the table as the barmaid set down two glasses of half-flat draft beer. She downed one without a breath and went slower on the second, the deep drags on her smoke almost calming her.

"Hey baby, you all alone?"

Clara looked up to see the owner of the voice. A tall white guy, bearded, blond hair down to his ass. "If it weren't for the beard, I would swear you were a girl with all that hair. Bugger off."

"Aw, no need for that. Just trying to be friendly. Can I buy you a beer?"

Impatient now, she glared at him. "Do I look friendly to you? You must be new here."

He put his hand on her shoulder, once again offering to buy her a beer.

Clara shrugged his hand away. "Back off, man."

"Man, what's your problem?" Anger rose in his voice as he flopped down at her table. "I heard all you Indian chicks were easy."

Clara leapt from her chair, flew across the round bar table and wrapped her hands around his neck. They tumbled to the floor, Clara pressing her thumbs into his windpipe. They rolled around the floor as the man desperately tried to pry her hands free from his neck. The room was silent to Clara as she straddled him and started bashing his head on the floor. His terrified eyes looked up at her, his mouth forming words, but she heard only a faint, pulsating buzz in her ears. His eyes were rolling into the back of his head when they dragged her off him, the bouncers hauling her to the door, her feet off the ground, kicking at them and the air. They pushed on through the swinging doors and threw her on the pavement. She jumped up and went for the biggest bouncer, wildly punching at his thick frame. He grabbed her by the shoulder, swung and slapped her across the face so hard she collapsed onto the wet pavement. Cars crawled by with their windows rolled down for the show. People on the street gave her a wide berth.

"Stay the fuck outta here. You're banned for a month." The bouncers straightened their clothes and headed back into the bar.

Sound slowly returned to her as her face burned, the imprint of the bouncer's hand pulsing with rage. She slowly got to her feet, slapping away a soggy cigarette butt that had stuck to her jeans. She looked up just as a city cop loomed down at her. She turned her back to him.

"Nothing to see here. I'm leaving. See?" She took a few steps away. "See?"

The cop moved toward her. "I know you. Troublemaker." He put his hand on his baton. "Move along now. If I see you here again tonight, you'll spend the night in the tank."

"Yeah, yeah."

Clara walked away from him. Her legs moved as though independent of her will and she let them take her back in the direction
of the Manitou. The crowds thinned once she got away from East
Hastings. Once there, she leaned against a lamppost, watching the
hookers come and go, hurrying back toward Hastings hoping they
had enough time for another trick. The johns left bedraggled and
shameful, looking this way and that, hoping for no witnesses. Clara
walked a little farther to the bus stop bench and sat, the aches and
pains of the night's brawl starting to set in.

She lost count of the number of buses she waved along as she sat
watching the Manitou sign, its red glow deepening and thinning as
it made its lazy orbit. The fluorescent light of the office blazed as the
night clerk flipped through magazines and drank bottle after bottle
of cola from the machine. At 3 a.m., the clerk locked the front door.
Any late night guests would have to ring the buzzer. He turned
all the lights out except the one illuminating the door; of course,
the big neon sign blazed red all night. With one last look out the
window, the clerk left the lobby and retreated to what Clara knew
was a small bedroom in the back. Harlan had tried to drag her in
there more than once. The night clerk would sleep there, hoping for
no interruptions.

Clara watched the comings and goings of the hookers and their
johns for a while longer. Her swaying foot hit up against the cement
footing of the bench as the idea took shape. What would piss Harlan
off more than not having any chambermaids to work? She scanned
the ground in front of her, stood and circled the bench, looking until
she found a rock the size of a softball. She picked it up and sat back
down on the bench, passing it back and forth from one hand to the
other, thinking about how her mother had always called rocks the
stone people.

She sat until there'd been no movement at the Manitou for a while and then waited a little longer. The rock felt warm in her hand as she sat in the drizzling rain, her clothes now completely soaked through, her hair straggly and wet. Finally she rose, stiff from sitting so long, and looked around carefully. The place was deserted, the hookers sleeping off another rough night. She slowly stepped off the curb and walked toward the office, then turned back and sat on the bench again, her heart pounding. Her mind turned once more to the Mission School, but this time she thought of Lily.

The days passed at school, one like the other, distinguished only by who was caught stealing food or who otherwise met with Sister's wrath. One morning, as thin sunlight poured through the dorm window, Clara lay still, not wanting to leave the warmth of her bed, the dorm too drafty and the linoleum floors too cold for bare feet. She turned to the bed on her left, where Lily had the grey woollen blanket pulled around her head, her face almost completely hidden but for her dark-circled eyes.

"How many days, Clara?"

"Seven. Just six more sleeps. The teacher told me. Three days before Christmas, we go home."

Lily sat up on the side of her bed, tucking her knees under her, the blanket now wrapped around her like a tent. "How do we get home?"

"I don't know. My mom never told me. Maybe we will go in the truck again." Clara shivered.

"We better get up and make our beds before Sister gets here." Lily slipped off her bed, hugging herself for warmth as her feet hit the floor.

"I'll help you." Clara jumped out of bed and helped Lily pull the blankets tight over her cot. Lily in turn helped Clara.

The girls were reaching for their clothes when Sister slipped into the dorm, her whistle in hand, looking left and right for a sleeping girl.

"On your knees, girls. I want to hear your morning prayer." Clara and Lily knelt, their girlish voices rendered dull by their monotone recitation of the Our Father. Clara opened her eyes halfway through the prayer when her friend started coughing again. Sister swooped in and pulled Lily to her feet.

"How many times have I told you to contain yourself during prayer?"

"I'm sorry, Sister, I can't help it."

"Well, you could at least try. Extra chores for you today. After breakfast, report to Mr. Walker in the barn. You can clean the goat enclosure today."

"But Sister, she is sick and it's so cold out there." Clara stepped closer to her friend.

"Then you can help her, since you're so smart. Now get dressed and ready for chapel or there will be no breakfast for you. Let's go, girls." She clapped her hands. "Last one in line will help Clara and Lily with the goats today." The girls scrambled to form the lineup, and Lily got there last. Sister laughed. "You can't even help yourself, can you? Tuck in your blouse." Lily dutifully tucked in her blouse, following close behind Clara as the girls filed to the chapel.

After school, Clara and Lily bundled up as best they could, their legs bare but for their darned and re-darned cotton leotards. Clara set out running across the windy expanse toward the barn but had to slow down for Lily, who barely managed a quick walk. Heads down against the wind, they watched for Mr. Walker, the farmhand. He let it be known to anyone who would listen that he didn't care a whit about God or Queen so long as someone was there to help him with the unending chores at the school. He was neither harsh nor kind, just insistent that chores be done correctly.

"I've been waiting for you, girls. You have to stop pissing off Sister. Now I have to watch out for you. Go over there to the back wall. You'll find the pitchforks. The goats are in the last two box stalls. I'll move 'em and you clean 'em out."

Not five minutes into the job, Lily collapsed on the stall floor, unable to stop coughing. Clara knelt beside her and patted her back. "You'll be okay, Lily, just take a deep breath." Mr. Walker heard the commotion and poked his head over the stall to see Clara wiping her friend's mouth with her sleeve. The pink bubbles formed around Lily's mouth faster than Clara could wipe them. He rushed into the stall.

"Step away, girl." He bent and scooped Lily up in his arms and turned to leave the barn. He looked over his shoulder at Clara. "Stay here and get that work done. I'll be back soon."

Clara shovelled as hard as she cried, praying that Lily would be okay.

That night in the dorm, the lights out, the full moon shining through the window, Clara carried on with her epic prayer for Lily. She looked first to the empty bed beside her and then to the sky.

"Dear Jesus, I know you see everything and must have a lot to do. Did you see Lily fall today? She's so sick, with blood in her mouth. She is like that little sparrow, Jesus, like the one you saw. Please, Jesus, take care of Lily. Make her better with your hands that can make people better. I will even stay here and not go home for Christmas if you make her better, Jesus. Amen."

Clara curled up in her bed. She thought of Lily lying in the white bed in the nurse's room. She closed her eyes, the faint smell of goat rising from her as she drifted off to sleep.

The next morning, Clara chose her seat in chapel carefully, close to the door. At the first "let us pray" and the scuffling sound of the children moving into a kneeling position, Clara slipped out the side door. Careful to avoid the offices of the priests and the classrooms with teachers preparing for their day, she slipped into the nurse's room. The white bed was spotless, neat and empty. Sister Philomena with her white nurse's habit came to Clara.

"Do you need a plaster?"

"Where is Lily?"

"She's gone, child."

"Gone where? Did her mom come and get her? Why didn't she say goodbye?"

"No, child, she is gone to Jesus."

Light-headed, Clara looked at Sister. "Jesus is here?"

"Well, in a way, I suppose." Sister Philomena reached out and took Clara's hands in hers. "She died last night, dear. She is with the Lord."

Lily's pale little face seemed to hover in the air in front of Clara, soaking and shivering on that bench, and once again the rage rose up in her. She leapt from the bench and ran across the parking lot, the rock raised high above her head. With a scream, she threw the rock through the lobby window of the Manitou, and then raced away into the night. She could hear the wailing of the alarm bell as she ran. *Who the hell would think it had an alarm!*

She'd run a couple of blocks when she heard the first siren. She slowed to a walk. *Just a late night party. Just heading home. Manitou? Nope, I wasn't there.* She practised calm replies to imagined interrogations. She made her way back to East Hastings, feeling conspicuous in the thinned-out crowds. She heard the car creeping behind her, and for once she hoped it was just some creep looking for a lay. She looked at the storefront to her right and saw the reflection of the police cruiser creeping behind her then stopping. She walked on, speeding up just a little.

"You!" the cop called after her. "Hold up."

Clara stopped and turned. "What?"

"Yeah, I thought it was you. What did I tell you earlier?"

Clara glared at him. "Just my luck. Look, I'm just heading home. I'm not making trouble."

"Up against the wall. I warned you."

Shaking her head, resigned, Clara put her hands against the brick. The cop cuffed her and put her in the back of the cruiser. Once in the driver's seat, he looked at her in the rear-view mirror. "You didn't have something to do with that mess at the Manitou, did you?"

Clara looked out the window. "What mess?"

"Yeah, woman across the street saw an Indian girl running away from there."

"All Indian girls should run away from there."

They drove the short distance to the police station in silence. The cop escorted her to the drunk tank, its current residents thankfully all asleep. "Next time I tell you I don't want to see you, I mean I don't want to see you."

The cell door clanked closed behind her and she stepped around the others, looking for some space to sit. She pulled the collar of her shirt up over her nose and mouth, nauseated by the stench. Like a small miracle, the only place left to sit was by the tiny slit that passed as a window on the outside world. An old woman with long grey braids sat there, looking out at the street below. Clara sat next to her and nodded a greeting. She wondered why such a beautiful old woman would be in a place like this. As though reading her mind, the woman turned to her.

"Look," she said, pointing out the window with a gnarled brown finger.

Clara looked and shook her head. "What?"

"That little birch tree. Even here they shine."

Clara looked again. A little birch, no taller than Clara herself, stood alone in a small square of dirt carved out of the pavement for it. The rain had stopped and the clouds parted for the muted sunlight of dawn. Clara watched as the leaves of the little tree captured the light, shining silvery and soft. The old woman looked at her with eyes as black as night and placed her hand over Clara's.

"The power of Creation is everywhere. In the tree, in you, in all of them." She gestured to the others. "Never forget." The old lady settled back into the variegated shadows of the cell, her deeply wrinkled hands folded in her lap. Clara gazed at the little birch, blocking out the restless sounds of the cell.

As though no time had passed, Clara found herself back, way back when she was little, walking home from church with her mom. It was a hot, dusty Sunday late in August. Clara walked along the rutted wagon path that ran through the heart of the reserve, creating a direct route home from church. Her favourite part of this road, not much more than a trail, was the few hundred feet that wound through a grove of mature silver birch. She ran her hand over the silky tops of the prairie grasses as she approached the thicket, her Sunday school lessons fresh and at the forefront of her mind. Her mother walked ahead, close enough for Clara to feel safe, far enough for her to feel free. At six, she was old enough to join the rest of the kids at Sunday school in the basement of the church while her mother attended Mass. One of the teenaged daughters of the church ladies read to the children from the oversized blue book of Bible stories, the cover pressed against her chest, the passionate illustrations facing out for the children to see. Clara was amazed each time the fishes fed everyone, railed against the injustice of Barabbas being set free while Jesus was not. She imagined herself in the powder-blue veil that covered Mary's head and shoulders as she rode her mule through Bethlehem. She quietly sang "Jesus Loves Me" without the words, *la la la la la la la*, as the grasshoppers chirped and the wind sent itself rustling through the trees.

Ahead, she saw her mom, Seraphina, veer off the pathway toward their house, the hip-high prairie grasses, as though gracious, bowing in her wake. Clara felt a burst of pride thinking about how all the church ladies gravitated to Seraphina for chit-chat after the service, how they always sought out what she had to say about births and deaths, namings and ceremonial giveaways.

Clara stood for a moment, transfixed by the sunlight reflecting off the shimmering silver-green leaves, and felt the earth's summer heat rising through her feet, seeping into her bones. She stood motionless, thinking she heard something—a tinkling, like tiny bells sounding in the wind. She carried on but heard it again, this time with a whispering sound, almost words, like a quiet chanting rising on the breeze.

"Mom!" She ran to catch up with her, then walked backwards facing her mother. "Did you hear it too?"

"I didn't hear anything, Clara." Her mother turned and stood, holding her daughter's hand, the child's face turned to the sky over the thicket.

"Listen, Mom, listen!"

Smiling and slightly shaking her head at her always-surprising child, her mother squeezed Clara's little hand. "Sorry, honey, I don't hear a thing."

"Mom! I think the angels are playing in the trees!"

Her mother smiled and turned back toward the house, Clara's fingers slipping from hers. "Let's get moving, girl. Your auntie and cousins will be at the house pretty soon."

"Don't you believe me?" Clara looked up at her mom with disappointment.

"Maybe it was not for others to hear. Your grandma used to say the little people played in that thicket. Maybe they were making music just for you."

Clara, confident again, ran ahead of her mom, her braids bouncing against her back.

"Pick some rhubarb!" her mother called after her. "I'll make a pie."

Clara veered off toward the garden.

Clara remembered eating that rhubarb pie, playing with her cousins and finally falling asleep in her mother's bed for what would be the last time. She remembered all the children gathered at the church the next morning, the cattle truck waiting, the priest and the RCMP standing by as the children, Clara too, were loaded into the truck. She remembered the first time she saw Sister Mary. It was long past dark when the children marched up from the dock to the Mission. Sister's black robes were invisible in the night as she stood on the steps looking like a disembodied head in her blazing white cornette. Clara remembered her battle with Sister as she cut her long braids, doused her in green powder and took her clothes away, replacing them with a used brown shift.

Her heart pounding, Clara rose from her reverie and turned to speak to the old woman, but the bench was empty. The hairs on the back of her neck stood stiff and her face flushed hot as she looked around the crowded cell for the woman. But she was nowhere. Clara turned her attention once again to the little birch, trying to calm herself.

>--------------------<

When the time came for the guard to empty the cell of the previous night's captives, Clara made a point of walking next to him. "Um, excuse me. Do you know what happened to that old lady?"

"What old lady?"

"The one with the braids and the long skirt. She was Indian, like me."

"No one like that in last night. You sobered up? Must be the DTs."

Clara collected her belongings and walked out into the morning air, unable to shake the eerie feeling. Outside, she bummed a cigarette and a light, walked down to the little birch tree, pressed her hand against it and smoked.

7

LUCY

Clara placed the swaddled baby into Lucy's arms. Baby-girl's tiny fingers flexed and stretched, reaching into the air. Lucy held her as close as possible, taking in every detail, every chubby wrinkle. Her hair, sleek and thick, lay soft and close to her head; her eyes, blue-obsidian. Hesitating, Lucy placed her pinky finger against Baby-girl's, succumbing to the newborn's grip, tears welling with a rush of love she couldn't have imagined. Relief washed over her, warming her face pink. She leaned and kissed the baby's sweet-smelling forehead, breathing in the intoxicating smell of the newborn, like a doe, imprinting her fawn's scent, forever after recognizable, even at a great distance.

Clara caught Lucy's eye and smiled. "She's gorgeous."

Lucy leaned back against the raised bed, face flushed with fatigued pleasure. "I still feel drugged. C-section is okay, I guess, but man, that anaesthetic. I'm out of it."

"Is that why it took so long to ask for her? The nurses were talking about you when I got here. Said you'd been awake for three hours, still hadn't asked for her."

Lucy looked away. "You're gonna think I'm stupid."

Clara laughed. "I already know you're stupid, so what can it hurt?"

The two giggled, startling Baby-girl. Lucy held her closer and she quit her half-hearted fussing. Lucy looked away again and blushed. "I thought they wouldn't give her to me."

"What? You see? I knew you were stupid." They giggled again, but this time Clara stood up and put her arm around Lucy and the baby.

Lucy whispered, "Were we ever allowed anything good?"

They sat in silence together, lost in a shared truth rarely spoken.

Clara rallied first. "Let me hold her!"

Beaming, Lucy handed Baby-girl over.

The infant cooed and gurgled in Clara's arms. "What will you name her?"

Lucy shrugged. "Not sure yet."

It was about two months after she'd last seen Kenny when the nausea had worsened and become overwhelming. As she accompanied a new doctor on his rounds with the other nurses-in-training, the nausea hit again. Lucy knew she could either puke on the floor or run for the closest bathroom. Lucy ran, hand over mouth, gagging. Barely making it, she leaned over the toilet retching, careful not to splatter her uniform. For the third time that morning, she straightened herself in front of the mirror, checking for any evidence of vomit. She made sure her cap was fastened securely, took a deep breath and felt the nausea rising again. She pulled the door open and Mrs. Reynolds, the matron in charge of the trainees, stood in the hall, arms crossed, waiting for her.

"Come with me, my dear." The head nurse led her toward the staff lounge. Inside, Lucy sat on the edge of her seat while Mrs. Reynolds pulled a straight-backed chair in front of her and sat down. "The other girls are complaining that you are spending too much time in the ladies' room."

"I'm sorry." Lucy longed for the Manitou. She thought about the way Liz was always willing to switch a shift when she had to go to school. If Clara and Liz were in nursing school with her, they would have created a distraction; no one would even have noticed Lucy's morning sickness. These white girls were different. Always quick to exclude her or fault her.

"When are you due?"

"I'm not sure." Lucy closed her eyes, not even trying to deny the obvious. Another wave of nausea passed over her.

"Ginger ale and soda crackers will help with that. Let's get you to a doctor, get you sorted out. You know, of course, you will have to leave the program. At least until the child is born." Mrs. Reynolds stood and put her hand on Lucy's shoulder.

Lucy jumped up from her chair. "But why? I've worked so hard to get here."

"Lucy, you're unmarried. It would be unseemly. You will survive this. You can come back after the baby. Now, head off to the maternity ward and I will send a doctor. There are lots of empty beds up there right now. Just lie down and rest. I'll let the girls know you're coming."

Knowing any protest was hopeless, Lucy focused instead on Mrs. Reynolds's kindness, her desire to ensure she was taken care of. She looked up at the matron, afraid she would cry. "Thank you."

Three days later, Lucy was still holed up alone above Chong Li's. Despite a nearly empty fridge and the last roll of toilet paper, Lucy had not stepped out since coming home from her hospital training class. The sudden sound of pebbles landing against her kitchen window startled her. She jumped up, sure it was Kenny, and ran to the window, peering down to the street below. Clara, sodden with the late fall deluge, stood looking up at Lucy's window. She wiped the rain from her face. "Open the door, for chrissakes, I'm gonna drown!"

"Here." Lucy tossed her key ring out the window to her friend. "Just come up."

Clara bounded up the stairs and burst into her apartment.

"Where the hell have you been? I haven't seen you in days! Is everything okay?"

"Oh, I've just been here. Couldn't handle seeing anyone."

"I was really worried about you. I went to the hospital to meet you and they told me you weren't in the program anymore. What's going on?" Clara leaned against the kitchen wall, looking at her friend, arms crossed, eyebrows furrowed.

"I'm pregnant."

Clara sat down hard on one of the kitchen chairs. "Kenny."

The girls sat, Clara's hands cupped over Lucy's as the news sank in. "Why wouldn't they let you stay in the program?"

"Because I'm not married. It wouldn't look right."

"Well, when the baby comes, you can start again. It will be okay, Lucy. I'll help you. Where the hell is Kenny? I'm gonna kill him."

"I haven't seen him since that night he was waiting by my door. I woke up in the morning and he was gone." Lucy sat with her head in her hands.

"That asshole. He'd better hope I don't get my hands on him."

"What does it matter? What was I thinking, anyway? Harlan was right. It doesn't make a difference."

Clara handed Baby-girl back to Lucy to nurse. With that dreamy nursing-mother look all over her face, Lucy focused only on Baby-girl. "I'm going to name her Kendra."

Clara sighed. "After that bastard?"

"I love that bastard. What can I say?"

Clara sighed again and stood just as a crisply uniformed nurse strode into the room, all business.

"Time for baby's bath demonstration." The nurse's voice was both cheerful and unmistakably instructing Clara to leave. She pulled the privacy curtain closed, the hooks clattering.

Clara shrugged and rolled her eyes in Lucy's direction, then leaned in for a hug and kissed Kendra's sweet-smelling head. "I'll be back later. I'm gonna head to the Indian Centre for a bit." She smiled over her shoulder at Lucy, Mama Lucy, oblivious to all but learning umbilical care and how to cradle a baby's head above the bathwater.

The next afternoon, Clara found Lucy in her room, sitting by the window, clinging to Kendra, her face streaked with partially dried tears. "What's wrong? Don't cry after that Kenny. He's not worth your tears, that one."

Lucy swiped at her dripping nose with the back of her hand. "It's not that. The welfare lady was here today. She said I have to prove I'm a fit mother."

"What the hell? How does she even know who you are?"

Lucy just stared out the window, absently rocking Kendra, watching the cars like toys on the street below.

Clara nudged her. "Lucy, snap out of it. What did she say?"

"Maybe the nurses called her. I don't know. Maybe they do that to all Indians." Lucy started counting out loud. Clara knew of her need to count and order everything when she was having a hard time, but had never seen her do it out loud. "What if they take her? What if she ends up at the Mission?" Lucy's voice rose with panic.

Clara reached for the baby. "Lucy. Get dressed. We're getting outta here."

Lucy stood, looking around the room, stunned. "But they said I had to stay for five days."

"Lucy! Move! Get dressed. What if she comes back? Our grandmothers had babies in the bush. You'll live." She carefully placed Kendra in the bassinet beside Lucy's bed. "I'll be right back."

Careful that no one was watching, Clara walked fast down the hall and slipped into the clearly marked supply room. She stuffed the small knapsack she used as a purse with all the baby supplies she could think Lucy would need and calmly walked back to Lucy's room, smiling at the nurse sitting behind the nurses' station. "Hey, is it okay if I take my friend and the baby out for a little air?"

The nurse nodded absently. "Yes, that would be fine. Use the wheelchair, just in case."

Clara strolled into Lucy's room like nothing was wrong. She pulled her pack open for Lucy to see. She grinned. "Indian School skills."

As terrified as she was, it still made Lucy smile.

Clara pulled the wheelchair from the corner and motioned for Lucy to sit in it. "Just do it!" She took the baby from the bassinet and placed her in Lucy's arms and then covered them with a blanket, placing a hospital gown over Lucy's shoulders so as not to raise questions. Clara wheeled her right by the nurses' station, the nurse smiling at such an attentive friend, down in the elevator, out the front door and all the way home. An hour later, Clara had dumped the wheelchair blocks away and was helping Lucy calm an aggravated and hungry baby.

"What if they find us?" Lucy gently rocked the baby, trying to calm her.

"Pfffft. They don't care enough."

Lucy giggled just a little and placed Kendra in the cot, swaddled tightly and buttressed by the only two pillows in the apartment. "Sometimes I just love how pissed off you always are."

Clara rolled her eyes. "And besides, I gave them a fake address when I signed you into the hospital."

"Why the hell did you do that?"

"Just in case."

They looked at Kendra. Kendra would not become a case.

When she'd been forced to quit the nursing program, Lucy was cut off the meagre training allowance that paid the rent and little more. During her pregnancy, she had no choice but to leave the apartment above Chong Li's and move her few things into Clara's tiny studio suite. Clara slept on a mat on the floor, Lucy on the slightly more comfortable cot. Since getting fired from the Manitou, Clara had found her way into the black market salmon trade, acting as middle-woman between Indian fishers and white buyers. She didn't make much money, but sometimes, if the buyer was stupid enough, as some were, she could grossly inflate the price, and these occasional windfalls kept the wolf away from the door. There were other little perks that came with living under the radar. Someone at the Indian Centre told her she could get welfare, but that white lady with the long nose and that pinched look on her face was more than Clara would put up with. She'd rather make a buck this way or that. There would be no grovelling.

Even though the sun was only a little low on the horizon, the terrifying day took its toll. Lucy lay down next to Kendra, and Clara fell asleep in the armchair before she even knew she was tired.

Through the night, Lucy woke at the slightest mewling from the baby, nursed and changed her, drifting off with Kendra at her breast. Clara had moved to the mat on the floor during the night, but when morning arrived, she was gone. Lucy shook her head, wondering how she had not even heard the door close behind her. She attended to the baby and did a careful scrub of the already-spotless kitchen. She bathed Kendra in the kitchen sink, her one arm resting between baby's neck and the hard porcelain, the other dousing the cooing girl.

Clara returned at midday to find Lucy frantically trying to calm a screaming Kendra. Lucy looked at Clara, panicked. She rocked the baby faster and faster, desperate to calm her.

"What's wrong? Whaddo I do?"

"Jeez, stop rocking her so hard, you're freakin' me out." Clara dug through the basket where she'd dumped all the stuff they'd brought home from the hospital. She grabbed a little booklet with a picture of some rich white lady giving her baby a bottle. *Do's and Don'ts: Feeding Your Bundle of Joy.* "Here," she said, "gimme the baby. You read." Clara started rocking the baby, trying to stay calm.

Lucy flipped the pages, reciting headings: "Formula . . . Breast Milk . . . Bloating . . . Gas . . . Gas! I bet she has gas."

"Okay, genius, but what do we do about it?"

Lucy flipped another page and was visibly relieved by the illustration of a mother burping her baby. "Hand her over." She took the baby from Clara's arms and carefully turned her, laying her against her shoulder, and rubbed her back gently as the baby wailed. And then the baby burped so loud and deep it froze Clara and Lucy in position for a second or two before they both howled with laughter. Lucy continued massaging Kendra's back and she emitted a few more pint-sized burps.

"Holy, she sounded like some big beer-guzzling guy," Clara said, still giggling.

Lucy smiled, shaking her head, relieved to have Kendra finally settled and dozing. "Hey, can you wipe the puke off my shoulder?"

Clara sat down and rustled through her bag. "I have limits, woman."

Once the baby was asleep again, Clara motioned Lucy into the tiny kitchen where they could talk quietly without waking Kendra. Lucy whispered, "What's up?"

Clara reached into her shirt pocket and pulled out two cards: a driver's licence and a Social Insurance Number.

"Who is Carey St. Marie?" Lucy looked at her friend quizzically. "And why do you have her ID?" Clara flipped the driver's licence on top of the SIN and made a face. "That's you!" Lucy grabbed the licence and started at Clara's picture. "What the hell?"

Clara looked skyward with a feigned angelic eye roll. "I told you there are perks to being a criminal."

"You're not a criminal. You just sell fish for people."

"Tell it to the judge."

Lucy grabbed Clara's sleeve and pulled hard. "Anyway, what the hell?"

"I got a set in the works for you too. Should be ready tonight. You're my sister, Bunny St. Marie, with a baby girl I Ioney St. Marie."

"What for? I don't need this. I have ID."

Clara sighed. "Lucy, sometimes you are so damn dense."

Offended, Lucy looked away. "Give me a break. I just had a damn baby."

Clara gently pretended to throttle her. "Look, we're going to the welfare office tomorrow. You're my sister-in-law. Your husband died while you were pregnant. I'm here to help you with the baby. We're going to get on welfare."

"What? You hate those welfare people."

"Yeah, well." Clara motioned to the baby. "I love her more."

They struggled through several meetings with the welfare witch but were eventually approved to each receive welfare. Clara let her landlord know she was moving and found out she was about to be evicted anyway for having Lucy and the baby there. A woman at the Indian

Centre gave Clara her used stroller, and every day Lucy and Clara, with the baby in tow, would head to the library to scour the classifieds for a house to rent. They were often rejected on sight when the landlord saw two Indian girls and a baby. Even when Clara told them the welfare would pay the rent directly, they were brushed aside.

"I don't want any trouble here," one prospective landlord told them.

Clara bristled, tired of rejection after rejection. "What kind of trouble? We have a baby, for chrissakes."

Lucy tugged at Clara's sleeve. "It's okay, um, Carey. Who wants a jerk for a landlord anyway?"

"Yeah, your loss!" Clara spat out her words, and when out of earshot she exclaimed, "What the hell was that?"

"I'm growing a pair. I've got a baby to protect." Lucy raised her chin.

Clara laughed. "Right on, woman, right on."

Finally, two and a half days before they were due to vacate Clara's suite, a landlord agreed to rent them a small two-bedroom house on Frances Street, just sixteen blocks from Hastings and Main. They walked from room to room, Lucy making sure neither the baby nor her clothes touched any surface. They signed the papers and the landlord handed over the keys, reminding them it was rented as is and not to expect him to be running over to fix this and that.

Once the landlord was out the door and down the stairs, Clara looked at Lucy. "Probably couldn't find anyone else who would take it."

The house was filthy. The paint was chipping off the walls and garbage was piled up in the small enclosed porch. The old claw-footed tub was in good shape but for some rust stains, but the rest of the bathroom was filthy and stank. Lucy gagged and headed for the back door to get some air. She looked back into the house at Clara fiddling with the loose knob on the bedroom door. "How the hell can we even clean this with Kendra? I can't even lay her down anywhere."

Clara looked up, smiling, and spread her arms wide. "Hey, it's our palace, our home sweet home. We'll figure it out."

The next day, they packed up their meagre possessions in Clara's suite, leaving everything there in boxes, and headed for the Indian Centre. They made it for lunch and enjoyed soup and fry bread washed down with strong tea. Lucy watched Clara chatting with her friends who volunteered at the Centre as well as the friends she'd made with the people who dropped in for a meal, some advice or just the company of other Indians. For a moment she was jealous of Clara's confidence and ease with other people, but then she looked at Kendra, asleep in the ratty old stroller, and everything else seemed trivial.

Clara straddled the chair next to Lucy and smiled. "I got a whole gang together who are gonna help us with the house. I promised them a few beers and some Chinese food in return for their help." She pointed out a young man with shiny black braids and a buckskin vest. "That's George. He's the one I told you about. He has a car."

George must have caught the women looking at him and immediately walked over to them. "You must be Lucy." He leaned over and peered at Kendra. "Beautiful baby there."

"Yeah, she's something else." Lucy reached down and took off the baby's knitted hat, and her thick black hair leapt out as though held captive by the little hat.

The next day, George's car was parked outside the Frances Street house, loaded up with Clara and Lucy's stuff. Half a dozen young men and women came and went from the house, hauling garbage out, carrying cleaning supplies in, and looking around the backyard with its rickety fence and overgrown hedge. The yard was littered with the rotting blossoms from the ornamental cherry trees. Looking at them for the first time, Lucy felt more than relief about getting the house. She cuddled Kendra and held her facing slightly outward.

"Look, Baby-girl. Maybe next year we will be welcoming spring under those trees. You will be such a big girl then." She wandered around the yard, kicking trash toward a pile she was creating with her feet.

"Hey, Lucy, come in." Clara stood on the back porch, waving her in. "We cleaned a spot for Kendra. You can work now too."

Lucy laughed and headed into the house. Inside, the crew from the Indian Centre had cleaned a place in the living room under the corner windows, where an aging baby buggy now stood. It was a beautiful moss green with giant wheels, a retractable bonnet and a removable bed. Wide-eyed with surprise, Lucy turned to Clara. "Where did that come from?"

Clara pointed to George with her chin. "George found it at the Sally Ann yesterday. He brought it over last night."

George, clearly pleased with himself, nodded. "Yup. They wanted twenty bucks for it, but I talked 'em down to nothing."

Lucy walked over to the buggy, delighted with the little bed already made up with flannelette receiving blankets and a small pink crocheted throw.

George blushed. "Yeah, they threw that stuff in when I told them about you."

Lucy hugged him and gently laid Kendra down in the buggy, hoping she wouldn't fuss. As though reading her mama's mind, the baby lay there, her peaceful blue-black eyes following Lucy's every move.

Lucy rolled up her sleeves and headed to the kitchen and filled a cleaning bucket with water. Clara was already scrubbing the walls. Lucy caught her eye and together they scrubbed the kitchen spotless. "Indian School skills."

Within a week, the little house no longer felt like a stranger's place. Loose doorknobs were tightened, and the bathroom was so clean you could eat off the floor. The kitchen was even cheery, with Clara's tiny table and two lawn chairs scooped up from a laneway giveaway. George's girlfriend, Vera, was handy with a sewing machine and she bought some cheap fabric remnants and fashioned café-style curtains for the living room and the porch window. The curtains were big enough for privacy but used as little fabric as possible. The buggy served as Kendra's crib. Lucy kept the cot, at Clara's insistence, and Clara's room consisted of her mat and a filched Canadian flag hung upside down in the window. The walls were painted with scrounged leftover paint, so no two walls were the same colour. Clara liked the oddness of it. Lucy got used to it.

Life seemed easy. With welfare paying the rent directly, it even came to feel as though the house belonged to them. They never had to deal with the landlord, who was quite satisfied to never hear from them. With Clara's here-and-there black market money they bought Kendra a second-hand crib and furnished the living room with well-worn but comfortable furniture. Soon there were even pictures on the walls. As the months passed, they forgot the house had once been an abandoned, falling-apart mess.

Lucy was head over heels in love with the baby, and with every milestone she was sure Kendra was a genius child, way ahead of the other babies she saw when taking Kendra for walks to the park in the big green buggy. Lucy quickly settled into a comfortable routine with the baby. But she noticed a growing restlessness in her friend, and how she was spending more and more time away from the Frances Street house.

One morning, almost a year to the day after they'd transformed the little house, Lucy woke, splashed water on her face and scooped Kendra from her crib. She settled her into her high chair, and as she turned to make breakfast, she noticed a folded piece of paper with her name scribbled on it, the pen lying across it. She sat at the kitchen table and slowly unfolded it.

Dear Bunny, (ha ha) I gotta take off for a couple weeks.
Love, Carey (ha ha)
P.S. Kiss Honey for me (ha ha)

8

CLARA

Lucy settled into motherhood easily. Clara, on the other hand, was becoming a bit of a ghost, staying away for days on end sometimes. She spent her days at the Friendship Centre, keeping up to date with the protests and demonstrations of the American Indian Movement on both sides of the border. There was a tiny black-and-white TV in one corner of the Centre, and one day over lunch, bored, Clara clicked it on and kicked back in the old recliner that someone had donated. The grainy image of a group of Indians in front of a big old white church zoomed into close-up. There stood a slight brown woman, her fist in the air, microphone pressed toward her face. A detached voice rose above the chatter: "Tell us why you're here, Mae." She looked straight into the camera, fearless, furious, determined. "Who do these white people think they are? Our people saved their raggedy asses when they got off the boat, freezing and starved. They returned the favour with hatred and murder. There weren't so many of them and it changed everything. There ain't so many of us and we will change everything too, and I will lay my life down to take back what's ours." Clara was transfixed by this woman.

How unafraid she was, how ready to fight for a change they all knew had to come. For weeks she couldn't get that woman out of her mind and knew she had to go. She worked out a trade with one of the Friendship Centre regulars and became the proud owner of a one-eyed Falcon.

Clara and John Lennon made it to the border at Osoyoos by dawn. The border guard took one look at her, one look at the broken head-light and one look at John Lennon. Clara knew it would be breakfast before she even made Omak. The guard acted like he'd never seen a ribbon dress before. He tossed the car like it was a jailhouse cell, throwing clothes all over the ground. He ripped open John Lennon's food and turned to Clara with his bug-eye sunglasses, looking like he just walked out of a scene in a Paul Newman jailhouse movie.

"You got your Indian Card?"

Clara gathered up the contents of her purse from the pavement, rooted around in her wallet and handed him her card. "Yeah, I got my Indian Card." He snapped it from her hand like she wasn't going to give it to him or something. John Lennon looked so sad, his kibble scattered around. Looking for contraband, Cool Hand had said, dig-ging it out of the bag by the handful, dropping it on the ground.

"Where did you say you were going?"

"Portland."

"What's your business in Portland?" "None of your business. That card tells you I can come and go as I please. That's what the Jay Treaty says." John Lennon flopped down on the pavement with a huff. Clara clamped her teeth together against a smile. That dog was a fine judge of people.

Lucy had protested loud and fierce the day Clara brought John Lennon home. Just a gangly pup then, all tongue and feet, Lucy was sure he wasn't safe for the baby. Maybe if Clara hadn't been walking through the park at just that time of night, she wouldn't have seen that woman throwing him out of her car. Clara had chased after her, yelling what the hell was she doing? He's no good, the woman said. Some mutt got to her purebred. So Clara took him. Lucy gave up complaining about him when she watched the baby fall in love with him.

"What's this here?" Cool Hand reached for her carefully wrapped eagle feather with his meaty hands.

"Hands off. Law says. Native American Church. You can't touch this." John Lennon huffed again.

Cool Hand swaggered to his booth. But Clara saw him looking at the cars backing up behind the mess of her stuff, trunk thrown open, clothes and camping gear strewn around like a messy autumn.

Clara calmed John Lennon. "It's okay, man. He's just a pig." She scratched the broad, tawny expanse of his head, making her hand look so small. The woman who'd dumped him told Clara half of him was a kind of dog for hunting lions. Ridgeback or something like that. Not pure, she said. The Shepherd got to his mama and ruined the batch. What the hell did she know? "John Lennon, you are perfect."

Cool Hand walked back from his booth, looking through Clara like she was as pink as Doris Day or something.

"Clean this up, ma'am, and move on." He handed her back her Indian Card, dropping it just as she reached to take it. She left it there on the ground until he turned his back to them, then scooped it up and slipped it into her back pocket.

Reaching for her underwear strewn among the dog food, Clara whispered to John Lennon, "He's just tired of us now, boy." John Lennon smiled. She scooped up all the dog food, double handful after double handful. Goddamn if John Lennon was gonna go hungry over this guy. Clara pulled out slow and smooth, the Washington State trooper parked on the other side of the line in Oroville just waiting to pull over some Indian and her dog. Clara didn't look at him as he looked at her, all the way by. She instead jacked up Buffy on the cassette deck and put the pedal to the metal, but not too hard.

Wolf Rider she's a friend of yours
You've seen her opening doors
She's a history turner, she's a sweetgrass burner
and a dog soldier
Ay hey way hey way heya

Clara sang at the top of her lungs, reaching for the same kind of power as Buffy's one-of-a-kind voice.

Lightning Woman, Thunderchild
Star soldiers one and all oh
Sisters, Brothers all together
Aim straight, Stand tall

Clara thought for sure John Lennon raised his eyebrows, sitting there in the passenger seat, trying to look like he really wasn't uncomfortable. She pulled over at the first open area to let John Lennon run and stretch his legs while she put everything back in its place. No room for a mess in a '61 Falcon with a giant dog and pretty much all her worldly possessions. Clara triggered the front passenger seat lever and pushed the seatback down as flat as it would go. Legroom for John Lennon. She laughed to herself thinking about the first time someone heard her calling him. By now she was used to that frozen look people would get on their faces when she'd be callin' around after him. *John Lennon! John Lennon!*

She didn't have to call him this time. With the car back in order after the border pillaging, Clara walked around toward the driver's door and that was enough for him to know. He ran to her through the purple flowering weeds, tongue lolling and happy. Weeds. She remembered George telling her once that Indians were like weeds to the white people. Something to be wiped out so their idea of a garden could grow. He told her weeds were indigenous flowers. "Clara, you're an indigenous flower. Don't ever think of yourself as a weed." That's what he said to her.

John Lennon knocked his head against her hip, his version of hello, and jumped into the driver's seat. He sat there for a minute laughing at her and then crawled over to his side so she could get in.

"You crazy dog." Clara slid into the driver's seat and wiped the drool off the steering wheel. She put the car in gear and eased back onto Route 97 toward Omak. Oliver, Osoyoos, Oroville, Omak, O O O O. She wondered what that was all about. She turned the music down and John Lennon curled into sleep. Buffy and her singers were like a willow broom whisking the ugly feeling from the border cop right out of the air around her. She thought of a fried egg sandwich at Omak. Then she thought of that day George pulled the weeds out of her heart, leaving only wild purple flowers.

It was at the Friendship Centre on Vine Street. Clara was just hanging around there, hoping for a bowl of soup. Harlan had fired her and her friends from their jobs at the Manitou the time Lucy had passed her test. Now she had no food. No money. There were some different Indians there that day. The place was full, and the meeting room was all set up with chairs instead of the usual hodgepodge of tables, some with beading looms, some with papers and half-made posters, some with coffee cups and ashtrays, people hanging around all bright in their ribbon shirts and dresses, bone chokers and long beaded earrings. Clara used to feel nervous when she walked into that room with all that Indian-ness right out in the open. If they'd walked into the Mission School like that, Sister would have had them all black and blue and scrubbing stairs. But anyway, she didn't know what was going on that day with the crowded meeting room, but was really happy to see that there was a whole feast going on for lunch, too. Fry bread, huckleberries, cookies and two big pots of soup: one was salmon chowder and the other was made with deer dry meat. No chicken backs and necks that day. People were milling around, eating, smiling, talking, a layer of blue smoke rising above the group.

The big drum was out and some serious-lookin' Indian men with thick, shiny braids were chewing their bitterroot, getting their voices ready, and laughing with each other as they settled around the drum. The room settled with them. Their voices rose in the AIM song and chills ran up her spine before turning into tears that she didn't understand, caught still behind her eyes. She had to get out. What if the tears fell? What if someone saw? The side door was jammed open with a brick. She walked outside and sat on the bottom step. AIM talked that day at the Indian Centre and she sat there on the step by herself and listened.

The speaker said his name was George and he was there to talk about what was happening at Wounded Knee. He talked about Alcatraz and how the years of protest there had helped Indians feel like they could be heard. How thousands of Indians had marched on DC on the Trail of Broken Treaties. Clara's head felt like it would burst. Indians had taken over Alcatraz? Indians marching on Washington demanding fair treatment? She sat there in sunny Kitsilano, hippies smiling by, the smell of pot wafting after them, the sound of the singing fresh in her ears, and she was terrified. Not scared like she wanted to run away or anything, but scared like this moment might not be true. She thought of Indians taking over the Mission School, and walked back into the room.

John Lennon yawned. Clara pulled off at Omak and headed to the Good Morning Diner, the gravel driveway rumbling under the tires, a signal to John Lennon that he would be able to stretch his legs. Clara walked to his side of the car and opened the window a little.

"I won't be long, boy."

She walked into the diner and Bobbie, her name tag said so, smiled at her. She'd been here before on her trips south. They always talked about the weather and the traffic while she waited for her fried egg sandwich to go and John Lennon's raw hamburger patty. "Coffee on yet?" Clara slid onto the diner stool.

"Just finishing now. Usual?" She was already calling Clara's order into her surly breakfast-cook husband before Clara could nod her assent. She walked back toward Clara, coffee pot in hand, rolling her eyes toward the kitchen. "I swear that guy should just find another job. You'd think morning would kill him or something. I have to get up just as early. You should see him on the way here."

"Yeah." Clara smiled and took a long draw of the hot coffee. "Needed that."

Bobbie laughed and nodded toward the picture window at the front of the café. John Lennon was putting on quite the performance in the parking lot, squeezing his square head through the partially open window, craning his neck to look for Clara.

"He sure doesn't like being without you, does he?" Bobbie shook her head.

"Nope. I feel the same way about him."

"Yeah, sometimes I think I would trade Bert in for a good dog."

"I heard that!" Bert yelled from the kitchen, slapping the order onto the kitchen pass-through. "Make sure she has a coffee to go, my morning queen."

Bobbie smiled, handing off the food and a giant coffee to go. "Men! Can't live with 'em, can't shoot 'em. Where you off to this time?"

"South Dakota."

"You sure do have family all over, don't ya? You drive carefully now, okay?"

"Sure will. See you next time."

She smiled, waving through the window at Clara as she let John Lennon out and tossed him his burger. He wolfed it down as she leaned against the hood, eating her sandwich. Bert made a mean fried egg sandwich. John Lennon headed for the scrub trees that bordered the lot. "Don't go far, man." He wagged his tail without a backward glance. Clara sipped her coffee and watched Bert sideways as he made amends with Bobbie, kissing her cheek and pinching her bum, tying on his Never Trust a Skinny Cook apron just to make her laugh. Clara tossed the waxed paper wrapping into the garbage bin and turned to the car.

"John Lennon! Don't make me wait!" The dog came running around the corner, his paws the size of pork chops kicking up dust and pebbles. Clara opened his door and he jumped in, grinning his sloppy-tongued grin. "Well mister, you think we can make Billings tonight?"

The wind picked up, throwing dust devils around the car, and blew them all the way to Montana.

That day on Vine Street, Clara stood listening as George spoke with a soft fire. She would never forget his words. *Some people naively think they can hijack or control or harness the wind driving this movement forward. Any effort to do this will fail, because the energy behind this awakening, this force, is coming from all directions. Don't just believe me, go outside and, using your own breath, try to blow back the wind in the direction from which it comes. Think of the drum, the heartbeat, the songs, and how all these beautiful sounds roll into an echo carried by that wind from the ancestors through to the lives of our children's children.*

Listening to George, Clara remembered another sunny day, her heart racing. She remembered walking home from church with her mother. The wind in the birch trees. The singing. Clara's heart was racing, and she grew light-headed, almost unable to breathe.

The next thing she knew, she was lying on the floor. Passed right out. George's face loomed over her, the ends of his braids brushing her face.

"Sister, are you okay?"

Clara could feel the tears nudging at her eyes. She jumped up, pushing him out of the way, and headed for the side door, running away, this sudden knowing just too much. But she couldn't make it past the top of the side stairs. He followed, finding her there, arms wrapped around herself, as though only that would hold her all together.

"Sister. It's okay."

Clara felt the shame rise in her at the tears that fell, her weakness right there for anyone to see. She turned away from him and he put his hand on her shoulder.

"The teachings show us that we learn and become strong through suffering. I can see that you are very strong. There is no shame in sadness."

Clara felt the same way she had back then, with those lilting songs dancing among the shimmering birch leaves. Something that had been gone a long time filled her again, like her heart had suddenly started beating again after a long silence.

No matter how long between the times when George and Clara saw each other, it always seemed like no time had passed at all. She and John Lennon pulled up to the rez house just outside Billings. It was long past midnight, but the lights were burning. The headlights cut through the country darkness, exposing the shed, the corral, the front porch. Just as she slid the car into park, George and Vera stepped out onto the porch, waving her in. She opened the door for John Lennon and he was out there like a dart, racing for the porch, a happy swipe of George and Vera with his smiling face and then off to sniff the latest news in that busy yard.

Vera laughed. "That dog is more human than some humans I know!"

Clara climbed the porch stairs and hugged her. "My sister, how are you?"

George put his hand on her shoulder. "You must be tired. Come in, we kept supper for you. Tea?"

"Yeah, long road, Brother. Tea sounds good."

They went into that warm, sage-smelling house and gathered around the table, John Lennon romping outside to his heart's content, his home away from home.

The trio laughed and visited for at least an hour, with no mention of tomorrow's plan. In the small hours, John Lennon snoring on the porch, the talk turned serious.

George put his hand on Clara's. "You sure you want to do this?"

She nodded, a small headache forming at her temples. "Yes. No doubt."

"You know what's at stake, what could happen?"

Clara laughed. "Ah, man, we can do this. Don't worry." She pushed the adrenalin down. No fear. No retreat.

While everyone was glued to their TVs watching the news about the siege at Wounded Knee, no one had even heard of Willow Flats or the countless other reservations where the Bureau of Indian Affairs officials paid off the ones they could buy to do their dirty work on the rez. The showdown between the sellouts and the Traditionals was happening all across Turtle Island, known by the whites as North America. Sometimes the struggle played out in words, and sometimes, like at Willow Flats, too much was at stake on either side. The sellouts were being promised big bucks for getting enough tribal signatures to sell off parts of the reservation lands that were rich in oil and gas reserves. People like George and Clara, in support of AIM, were called in when the old people, who were speaking up for the future, arguing against selling, started getting hurt. No one wanted anyone hurt, but everyone wanted to make sure those old people had someone to stand up for them, someone to protect them.

"When we get to Willow Flats, Vera and I will drive ahead. The tribal police know us, so they will for sure give us grief at the checkpoint. I know they have an FBI agent working with them, collecting information on all the Traditionals. While they are hassling us, you just slide on through and head straight for the church. Our people there sent a message that if you tie a white flag to the antenna, the National Guard will let you through. They are just watching right now, not shooting. Clara, try to look like some sweet young thing."

Everyone laughed.

The next morning, Clara and Vera drank coffee and made breakfast while George bolted the metal box under Clara's car. John Lennon lay under the birch tree, panting, his tongue lolling out as he ignored the goings-on.

"Look at your dog." Vera nodded toward John Lennon. "Does he ever stop looking your way?"

"Only when he's sniffing and running." Clara walked out and sat on the porch with her coffee. John Lennon bounded over, flopped at her feet and huffed. Vera joined her moments later, flipping a piece of bacon to John Lennon.

"Hey!" she called out. "You almost done? Clara, are you going to take John Lennon with you? He can stay here if you want. Celina next door loves him, and she can watch him till you get back."

"No, he comes with me."

George scrambled out from under the car, jumped to his feet, brushed the dirt off the front of his jeans and walked to the shed. He emerged moments later with a coffin-looking box. "Gonna need a hand with this."

Clara and Vera raced to help him. George slid under the car and the women handed him rifle after rifle until he stuck his hand out waving, *no more*. "Hand me that wrench." Clara slipped it into his hand, the two women waiting, the tightening bolts making an angry metallic sound. "Done." George slid out from under the car and they walked back to the porch. Clara concentrated on John Lennon as they walked up the stairs, thankful for how he always sought her out in tense times, filling her with a sense of calm.

"Come and have your breakfast." Vera walked into the house. George lingered as though he was about to say something, but he didn't. Instead, he followed Vera inside. Clara raised her eyebrows at John Lennon and followed them in.

The drive to Willow Flats seemed to go on forever. Clara stroked John Lennon's head, glad for his calming company as the farther they got, the more rattled she felt. It was like a dream, thinking of the guns under her car, the goons they would face, the old people waiting, counting on them. Clara's thoughts turned to Lucy and Kendra and she almost turned the car around. Then she thought of Lily, so small and alone, dying among strangers for no reason at all. Her uncertainty evaporated like it had never been there.

The three of them met up at a rest stop on the outskirts of Rapid City for one last meeting before they headed into Willow Flats.

"I'm gonna take a little walk with John Lennon." Vera scratched his head and he was happy for a companion on his sniff around.

George took Clara by the hand and looked at her. "It's just your car and your new face. We can find someone else they won't know. You don't have to do this."

"Yes, I do. I do. Remember me telling you about Lily?"

"Yeah." He squeezed her hand a little tighter.

"I need to say something for Lily. I think of how many didn't go home. I have to do this." Clara felt the tears rising and shook them off. George hugged her, and they walked back to the cars. John Lennon ran up to her with a tongue-lolling smile so big it was as though she'd been gone for a week.

Clara waited a few minutes, letting George and Vera get ahead of her, before she turned into the reservation. It was almost dark when she pulled up to the checkpoint. As expected, George was spread-eagled against the car, Vera standing by the open trunk arguing with her hands as the tribal police threw their stuff all over the ground. Clara slid the car slowly up to the checkpoint. She rolled down the window and one of the tribal cops rested the butt of his .303 British on the edge of it. Her stomach churned and she thought she would vomit. John Lennon huffed.

She gripped the steering wheel and made herself as small as she could inside, just the way she used to when she didn't want Sister to notice her.

"Where you going?"

"Just want to see the old memorial."

George looked back at the cop talking to Clara and chose his moment. He turned from his spread-eagle position and pushed one of the cops. "Back off, we're just visiting." The guy at Clara's window ran toward George's car. She dropped her car into gear and just slid on by, her heart pounding in a rush of relief.

As soon as the checkpoint was out of sight, Clara pulled over. She couldn't help herself—she clambered over the seat into the back and hugged John Lennon before jumping out, reaching into the glovebox and retrieving the white flag. Hands shaking, she attached it to the antenna. She slid back into the driver's seat and headed for the church.

Clara's heart was still pounding as the church, surrounded by National Guardsmen, came into view. She took a deep breath and approached the perimeter, the one headlight helped a little by the badlands dusk. Two National Guardsmen flagged her down just before the entrance, one motioning for her to roll the window down, the other walking around to the back of the car.

She looked up at the Guardsman. "What's up?"

"You tell me. What's your business here?"

"Oh, my sister's here and she asked me to come pick her up and take her home." She glanced into the rear-view mirror; the second Guardsman was now at the rear of the car.

He motioned to the first one. "Get the keys for the trunk."

"Officer, there's nothing in the trunk. Just the spare and some clothes."

"Give me the keys."

"You have no reason to be searching my car. I told you why I'm here."

Clara glanced into the rear-view mirror again, and when the second Guardsman crouched down to look under the car, she slammed it into gear, spraying gravel as she raced back for the main road. She figured she had only seconds before they would be in pursuit, and she was right. Sirens wailed and the flashing lights weren't far behind. The car was moving faster than she'd ever driven it before, and was up on two wheels as she veered off the main road looking for a place to hide. There was a small thicket not far ahead and she raced for it, making a sharp left onto an almost-indistinguishable access road. The road veered sharply to the left and she missed the corner, careening headlong into a deep ditch surrounded by tall bush.

It was dark when Clara came to. John Lennon lay with his full length against her, keeping her warm against the badlands chill. A searing pain in Clara's shoulder came alive and she cried out loud. John Lennon howled, and she quieted him as best she could, not knowing if they were still searching for her.

The quiet took over the badlands under a small and bitter moon. Clara lay there, not yet able to move, listening to the wind rustling through the pines and the chaparral.

Clara opened her eyes, and for a heart-pounding moment she lay there unmoving, unable to figure out where she was or how she'd gotten there. Panic ran through her like an electric shock. She looked around at the blinding whiteness of the room. The walls, the linens, even the light was white. The smell reminded her of the infirmary at the Mission. She tried to sit up, but the searing pain in her shoulder stopped her dead. She groaned and realized she wasn't alone. "Clara." George's voice caught in his throat as he reached for her hand.

"Where the hell am I?" Her throat hurt, it was so dry. "I need water."

"You're in the hospital." George poured her some ice water from the turquoise plastic jug. "Here."

She guzzled it down and motioned for more, the water easing the painful dryness in her throat. George filled the little plastic cup again, and once more after Clara downed it.

"Help me sit up. Why does my shoulder hurt so much?" Clara looked at the thick bandages wrapped around her left shoulder.

"Don't you remember?"

She dropped her head back down on the pillow, casting around, trying to put it together. The night in the badlands suddenly rolled over her like a nightmare. She sat up straight despite the pain.

"Where's John Lennon?" She remembered the wreck, the torn metal ripping through her shoulder. "George, where is he?" She burst into tears. "Where is John Lennon?"

George jumped out of his chair and wrapped his arms around her. "Be still, Clara. He's fine. He's with Vera. He's pining for you, howling a lot, but he's good. Vera gave him some deer ribs to spoil him."

"What happened? What the hell happened?"

"All we know is we found you the next morning. We went to the meeting place, but they said you two had never shown up. We backtracked, looking for you, but it was so dark it was hopeless.

"We eventually found you just up the canyon from the main road. John Lennon wouldn't let anyone get near you. You were lying there, on your back. I thought you were dead. Vera was eventually able to sweet-talk John Lennon so we could get to you. What the hell happened?"

Clara told him about the Guardsmen and how she'd panicked when they wanted to search under the car. She told him of the chase and how they must not have seen her veer off the main road.

"Those bastards. Why can't they just leave us alone?" George stood up and walked to the window. "We got to your car before the

FBI. We got the box off and the guns to where they were supposed to go, but they're still sniffin' around. They were here earlier, wanting to talk to you."

"I got nothing to say to them."

"The hospital must have called them."

"How did I get here? I don't remember nothing after waking up with John Lennon beside me, keeping me warm."

"We brought you here. Vera's brother hooked a tow to his truck. Went out there last night and took your car and John Lennon back to Billings. It took both of us to wrestle him into the car. Vera called me when she got home. She said he howled for you for over an hour before he wore himself out."

"George. Get me home." Clara tried to sit up again but fell back, dizzy.

"They gave you morphine after they fixed your shoulder."

She lay there quietly, trying to make the dizziness subside. When she just about had it under control, some guy in a white coat, Clara figured him to be the doctor, entered the room, all legs and glasses and papers. He grabbed Clara's wrist and read her name tag. She pulled her arm back, feeling the way she had when they called her number at the Mission.

"Well, Miss, ah, Clara, you've had a rough go of it."

She nodded and looked at George. "Yeah."

"Well, a metal shard went clear through. It missed your shoulder joint but did a lot of damage to the muscle tissue. It will be months before you have full use of that arm again, if ever."

"When can I go home?"

"Oh, well, we will want to keep you for at least a couple of days." The doctor flipped through the chart, clicking his pen and making notes.

Clara looked at George and shook her head.

"How's the pain?" The doctor looked up at Clara again.

"I'm fine."

George interrupted, impatient. "She's not fine. She can't even sit up."

"I'll order some more morphine. The pain should ease in a day or two. You're a lucky girl." The doctor patted Clara's foot and smiled. "You could have lost that arm."

"I don't feel so lucky right now." The conversation left Clara completely exhausted. The doctor retreated, and she lay there looking at George. "My brother, please get me out of here. I can't breathe with all this whiteness."

"Clara, rest."

A nurse bustled into the room with a steel tray in her hands. "Sir, if you will excuse us a moment." She pulled the curtain around Clara's bed. "Roll over now." The injection burned, but soon the warm, floating effect of the morphine replaced all thoughts of the wreck, the cops and even John Lennon. The nurse straightened the linens, opened the curtain and hustled out of the room, busy and efficient. Clara slid into the oblivion of the drug as George sat down again beside the bed, his gentle smile a distraction from his worried eyes.

When she woke again, George was gone. A note left on the bedside table said: *Gone for food. Back soon.* The pain in Clara's shoulder was more of a dull ache now. Risking the possibility of shooting pain, she pulled herself up with her good arm, using the metal triangle suspended over the bed. Taking a few deep breaths first, she mustered her strength and swung her legs over the side of the bed. She exhaled deeply, dissipating the pain. Not so bad this time. The dizziness passed sooner too. Clara wondered how long George had been gone. She looked out the window and watched the dust devils dancing across the gravel parking lot. She scanned the room, wondering where her clothes were, her shoes, the purse Lucy had found for her at the Sally Ann. She tried to stand, but the dizziness was just too much and she eased herself back into bed.

Her thoughts of escape were interrupted by heavy footfalls in the hall outside the room. She knew it was the police even before they crossed the threshold. They flashed their badges and approached the bed.

"I'm Special Agent Frank Yates and this is my partner, Special Agent Arlen Grimes. Can we have a word with you?"

"Yeah, I guess."

"What happened to your arm?"

"I don't know. Don't remember."

"Which is it? You don't know or you don't remember?"

"Ah, both, I guess."

"You want to tell us why you were running away from the National Guard?"

"I don't know what you're talking about."

"We know it was you. You and a big dog in a blue Falcon."

"I was hitchhiking. I don't have a car. I don't know who you're talking about."

Agent Frank leaned in, pulling a picture out of the folder he held under his arm. He flashed it in front of her.

"Maybe this will help refresh your memory."

There was no anger in Agent Frank's voice, he was cooler than that. Power. Certainty. He would get what he wanted from her.

"Now that's a fine-looking car, officer, a little dirty, but it's not mine."

"The officers you ran from say they saw a metal box under your car as you took off. What was in the box?"

Clara shrugged and winced. "How would I know?" She thought of Sister Mary and how she could never make her cry. She had survived Sister Mary. This asshole wouldn't break her. "I can't say I ever seen that car before."

"What happened to your arm, Clara? What was in the box?"

"I told you, I don't remember. Nothing. It's all a blank." The anger started rising in her, and just as she turned to tie into Agent Frank and his silent sidekick, George walked back into the room with a couple of soft drinks and a burger joint bag, grease already marring the logo.

"What the heck is going on here?" He put the drinks by the bed and the bag on the windowsill. He stood between Clara and the officers, forcing them to take a step back. "Have you read her rights to her?"

"Now look here, we just want to know if she might have some information that might be helpful. Lot of strange goings-on around here right now."

"No, *you* look here." George wasn't backing down. "You're just trying to trick her into saying something that will hurt her."

"Now, why would you think that?" Agent Frank leaned in now. "You got something to hide? Don't you want to figure out what happened to your friend here?"

"She's got nothing to say."

"Why don't you let her talk for herself, boy?"

"I told you already, I got nothing to say." Clara smiled at Agent Frank, hoping he didn't see her hands shaking.

"Well, don't go far, girl. We'll be back." Agent Frank and silent Agent Arlen turned on their heels like some kind of nasty ballet and sauntered out of the room.

George grabbed Clara's hand, both of them afraid to speak until the policemen's steps faded at the other end of the hallway. Clara looked at him, desperate. "George, we gotta go."

"I should have never involved you in this."

"Cut it out. It was my choice." She slapped him on the shoulder.

"Still." George looked like he was going to cry.

"Enough! Just get me the hell out of here. Close that door and help me get dressed. Those guys will be back. Who knows, they might want to take me with them next time."

George helped her slip into her jeans and struggled to get her into her socks and shoes. They ripped the neck of her T-shirt wide open to get it over the big bandage and wrapped her coat around her like a cape, doing up the top button to keep it in place. George stuck his head out the door and looked both ways, then came back and helped Clara slide off the edge of the bed. He grabbed the burgers and took her by the hand. "Come on, there's an exit door down this way. We don't have to walk by the nurses' station."

They crept down the hall, Clara's shoulder throbbing, her knees weak beneath her. George left her outside the exit and ran around to the main parking lot to get his car. She heard him gun the engine and then he was there, leaning over, opening the passenger door and jumping out. He helped her into the car and closed the door before running back over to the driver's side.

Clara slid down into the seat below the window so it would look like George was alone in the car. "Don't rev the engine. You'll draw attention. Slowly, now, let's go."

The car crept out of the parking lot and picked up a little speed on the main drag. George drove past the freeway entrance and chose the secondary highway back to Billings, just in case.

Clara fell sound asleep not long after their escape from the Willow Flats hospital. She didn't rouse once until they were pulling into the driveway at George and Vera's place. John Lennon was already on it, running alongside the car on the passenger side barking his high-pitched joy sounds.

"George, let me out! I need to see him."

"Wait, Clara. Let me park and help you. He will knock you over or bash that shoulder of yours."

For all his kindness, Clara couldn't wait for George. She opened the door with her good arm, clambered out and hunkered down with her bad shoulder toward the car, protecting it a little from her big boy. John Lennon ran for her and rammed his nose under her good arm, his massive tail almost invisible, it was moving so fast. "You big beautiful beast you!" She rubbed his head and he backed up a little, the happy whimpers amping up into a big howl that needed some room. "George, if there ever was anyone who loved me, it's this dog." The tears fell. "I would not be alive without him."

"I know, Clara, I know." George decided to break his cardinal rule of no dogs in the house. "Come on inside, Clara. Bring John Lennon. You need rest, and he will be howling for you all night if we try to keep him out here."

Vera was standing by the door, her arms wrapped around herself, eerie-looking in the yellow glow of the porch light. "Clara, thank God you're okay. Come on in."

John Lennon and Clara squeezed through the doorway together, and Clara sat down at the kitchen table, exhausted, her shoulder throbbing.

Vera hugged her gingerly. "Thank God you're here. Every day we hoped you two would show up. Do you need anything? Hungry? Thirsty?"

Clara smiled at her. "Yeah, some water would be good."

George poured himself a cup of coffee and joined Clara at the table with a sigh. Vera brought the water and the three of them and John Lennon sat there silently, not able to even look at each other. How could it have all gone so wrong? They sat, sipping, the wind in the pines the only sound. Finally, John Lennon huffed, freeing them from their despairing silence.

Vera turned to Clara. "We've got to get you home, back across the border."

"Where's my car?" John Lennon pricked his ears up at the sound of the word, game for another road trip. Clara put her hand on his head.

"It's in the old barn," George said. "Vera's brother has been working on it. But the FBI knows your car. You can't take it back across the line. The FBI will be looking for you now."

"I'll go through Saskatchewan instead of BC. The crossing at Climax is a one-man show. He's asleep half the time and there is a way where the border passes through the rez about twenty miles from there. You have to drive through a pasture, but it gets you there."

Vera had that worried, motherly look that everyone loved about her. "But what about your arm? You need care."

"I'll be okay. It's only four and a half hours from Billings to Climax. You've got friends on the rez there, right? Could you call them? Maybe I could stay for a while, rest up a bit before I head back to BC."

"Well, I'm driving you to the border." George gave Clara one of his my-way-or-the-highway looks. "Vera can follow and bring me back home. You're still too weak to be driving that kind of distance, much less running the border."

Clara raised her good arm in protest, but Vera shook her head. "No, Clara, we won't have it any other way. We got you into this. We'll get you out."

A wave of fatigue washed over Clara and she knew they were right. Waiting for death, helpless and alone in the badlands, was not something easily left behind. "Okay. But I need to sleep now."

The next morning, Clara woke with a start, gripping her pillow as though it were the steering wheel, seeing herself careening into the ditch.

"John Lennon!" He jumped up on the bed and lay next to her,

calm and warm. The images passed and the tension eased. Her shoulder throbbed, but it was no longer the sharp, breathtaking pain of a couple of days ago. George and Vera were stirring in the next room. The sun poured in the east-facing window. Clara lay still, wondering what it might feel like to not be afraid all the time. John Lennon nuzzled her.

"Okay, okay, I'll let you out." Clara slipped out of bed and into the robe Vera had left for her and went outside with him. She sat on the veranda and watched him sniffing and peeing and wandering. He kept looking back at Clara as though expecting her to disappear again. "John Lennon, you are the best dog ever."

Vera was rattling around in the kitchen and it wasn't long before she joined Clara with a cup of coffee in each hand. They sat sipping, watching the morning sunlight spread through the birch trees.

Vera turned to Clara like she was reading her mind. "You'll be okay, Clara."

"Yeah. One way or another."

They were on the road by noon, George driving Clara's one-eyed Falcon and Vera bringing up the rear in their pickup. John Lennon snored in the back seat, satisfied, on the road again. They got to the tiny town of Turner, Montana, just before five. George pulled into the grocery store parking lot and waited for Vera to pull up beside him. Then he rolled down his window.

"Hey, is Grimley's Diner still open these days?" He squinted up at her in the truck.

"I think so."

"Well, let's go have a bite to eat there. Kill some time. Clara will have to wait till nightfall."

They sauntered into Grimley's, the one restaurant in town that served Indians without making them pay up front, and slid into a red vinyl booth at the back. George immediately started flipping the pages of the mini table jukebox and dumped in enough quarters to serenade them during their meal.

The waitress, the deeper side of forty, with the most impressive bee-hive hairdo ever, smiled through her busy gum-chewing and tapped her pencil on her order pad. "We got a soup-san special on the back of the menu there for one seventy-five and we got Salisbury steak as the hot special with soup for two ninety-nine. What'll it be, kids?"

Vera smiled and for no reason they all burst out laughing. The waitress scratched her head with her pencil and laughed too. "Just one of those days, huh?"

Clara nodded. "You sure got that right. I'll have a cheeseburger and a chocolate shake."

Vera could hardly stop laughing. "He'll have the hot special and I'll have the soup and sandwich, and bring us a couple of colas."

"Okay, kids, I'll be right back, and do you mind me askin' what the heck happened to your arm? That bandage is almost bigger than you are."

"Oh, I just had to have an operation. Nothin' special."

"Well, I hope it's better soon." The waitress walked off and called out their orders to the cook, never knowing what good medicine her beehive had been for them.

They lingered there, sipping coffee, waiting for darkness. The waitress must have brought them four refills before they finally fig-ured they'd better leave or they'd wear out their welcome. George left her a two-dollar tip and she smiled her thanks to them through the window as they walked back to the car.

George handed Clara the car keys and she let John Lennon out for a quick romp. He looked at her, clearly a little pissed that she'd left him for so long. "Calm yourself, boy. All is well."

"Okay, Clara, we're going to head back. Find yourself someplace to park and play with John Lennon until it's dark. You never know if someone's watching for your plates. Best be sure the border crossing is closed and the agent has gone home before you start."

"Yeah, I will, George." Clara reached over and gave him a one-armed squeeze and stepped back. "Don't worry, we'll be okay." She turned to Vera. "Take care of him, sister."

Tears filled Vera's eyes as she gently put her arms around her friend. "Take care of yourself, little sister. Stay a few days when you get across. Rest up before you head west."

Clara sniffed for fear she would cry too, and turned and called John Lennon. "I will. Don't worry. We'll be fine."

George jumped behind the wheel of the truck and Vera climbed into the passenger seat. She rolled her window down and blew kisses at Clara and John Lennon. Clara waved, turned and opened the passenger door for John Lennon, trying not to look as they drove away, as if that would make it easier. Loneliness and fear descended again, the silence of their absence thundering around her.

Clara took George's advice and found a local park. She closed up the car and sat under a tree, watching John Lennon meander around until it was almost dark. Satisfied no one was watching, Clara stood and headed for the car, and the ever-watchful John Lennon sped by her and waited by the passenger door.

Clara pointed the car out of town and drove along the highway past the entrance to the border crossing at Climax. The road was gated, with a sign showing that the crossing was closed.

"Okay, big guy. It's on." Clara drove for about six miles, watching the odometer carefully. The small dirt road came up as expected with its Dead End sign. She drove to the end of the road and across a shallow ditch into the pasture. She turned the headlights off and slowly crept across the lumpy terrain. She wasn't even a third of the way across when blinding lights from her left suddenly flooded the pasture.

A loudspeaker bellowed: "This is the RCMP. Turn off your ignition and step out of the car."

"Shit, John Lennon, what the hell?" Clara looked frantically around and, without a moment's thought, gunned the engine and floored it. John Lennon fell back hard against the seat and the Falcon bumped and jumped over the stubble and lumps of turf in the pasture. "I'll be damned if they're gonna get me now. Not after all this." She jammed the accelerator as hard as she could, wishing she had a second headlight in the pitch-dark. The beam landed on a small copse of spruce on the other side of the pasture and Clara headed there for cover. She imagined the cops scrambling into their cars, and a few seconds later she heard the sirens wail. "Go! Go! Go!" she pleaded with the Falcon. John Lennon started whining. "John Lennon, no bullshit, when this car stops, you run with me. You hear?" John Lennon whined.

The car came to a screaming halt to the left of the trees and she threw open the door. "John Lennon, let's go!" He was already halfway out the driver's side door. They ran, Clara stumbling over tree roots and slapping branches out of her face. She could see the row of rez houses not a hundred yards away. She looked over her shoulder and the cop cars were stopped at the Falcon. She couldn't tell if they were following her on foot. She stopped for a second, held her breath and listened for following footfalls, but couldn't hear anything over the sound of her pounding heart. Run or hide? She looked desperately around and knew John Lennon wouldn't be quiet enough if they hid. So, they had to run.

About halfway across that endless hundred yards, Clara saw three shadows in the light from the houses running toward her. "Shit!" She turned to avoid them.

She heard a voice. "Keep running! We'll distract them." Three men, their braids flying, ran by her, back toward the cops. "Go!" The closest one frantically waved her toward the line of houses.

Clara ran. Seconds later, she and John Lennon made it to the first house, and she collapsed, her shoulder feeling like it was going to explode.

"Get up. Come on, get up," a woman's voice whispered through the darkness. "Hurry."

Clara dragged herself up and followed the voice. A small black pickup stood waiting, its lights out, the engine running.

"Get in the back."

She rolled in over the tailgate and John Lennon jumped in after her. There was a mattress and a tarp in the truck bed. "Cover up." She lay on the mattress, called John Lennon, and pulled the blanket over herself and the dog. The truck moved slowly away from the house, in the dark, with no headlights or tail lights to follow.

It seemed liked forever, but it might have been an hour later that the truck came to a stop. Clara sat up and looked around. She couldn't see a thing. The driver threw the truck into park, came around back and lowered the tailgate. "Come on." She led them through a thicket of spruce along a narrow trail. "You'll be safe here for now."

"Where are we?" Clara looked around. John Lennon rubbed against her.

"This is Old Mariah's place. She knows you're coming. Vera called and arranged it. She'll doctor you up, take care of you till you're well again. No one comes here but us. No one will know you are here. You're safe."

Clara and John Lennon walked to the front door of the small, weathered cabin, and as they got there, it opened. An old woman stood there, her braids white and down to her hips, a coal oil lantern in her hands.

"*Astamikwa*," she said, beckoning to Clara.

Clara walked through the doorway, and when she turned to thank the driver, she was gone.

9

HOWIE

t was my seventh time before the Parole Board. I didn't even pretend to believe they would hear anything I said. I'd said it all before. It was all there in the thick paper files in front of them. In their expensive suits and shiny shoes, they sat ready to judge me yet again. They explained the way the hearing would work and then started in, asking me questions about how I spent my time inside.

I raised my hand to speak. "Look, I don't want to waste your time. The only reason I am here today is because I need to hold on to my hope that I will get out of here sooner than later. I know what you need me to say. You want to know I'm sorry. That I've been rehabilitated. That I deeply regret my wrongdoing and I will never do such a thing again." I shook my head slightly. "You all know already that I have a clean record in here. Not one disciplinary note. Not a single one. And this is the only crime I ever committed, if you must call it a crime. But I am not sorry. Not at all. You have no idea what that man did to me and a whole lotta other little boys. He deserved what he got and more. Where was the law then when he was beating us, breaking bones, and other, even worse things? That man never saw a day inside, much less inside a courtroom, and yet I am locked in this hell. You've got it all backwards. I am not sorry, and I would rather stay in here till my dying day than tell you a lie, pretending I am. He got what he deserved."

The panel shifted uncomfortably in their seats, not looking at me or each other. The one in the middle who seemed to be in charge finally lifted his pen off the paper and looked up at me.

"Thank you, inmate. I understand this must be difficult for you. You must understand that we are sworn to protect the public safety and so we must."

I looked at my tattered running shoes. "And who was protecting our safety? No one. Not a damn soul."

"We've read over your file carefully, Mr. Brocket. Is there anything else you would like to say?"

"Just that all I wanted was to get out of here before my mother died. She was the only one who fought to get me out of that night-mare. Now it's even too late for that."

"Thank you, Mr. Brocket. You should receive our decision within two weeks."

The guard placed the cuffs back on me—at least it was with my hands in front—and escorted me back to my cell. The guard shook his head as he removed the cuffs again. "Man, why can't you just say you're sorry? We all know you shouldn't be in here, but you got to help yourself. You gotta play the game, say the words."

"I can't. Don't you get it? That would be like saying that it was okay for that monster to do what he did to us. I just can't."

The guard closed me in my cell and turned to leave. "Well, I under-stand that, but nobody gives a shit that you're taking a stand in here. Hell, no one gives a damn that you're even in here."

"I do. I know."

I lay back on my bunk with my hands behind my head, closed my eyes, and took myself out of prison and back to the mountains, back to the only place that left me feeling whole and good since leaving the Mission. I continued with the prison routine, so similar to the one at the Mission, and put freedom out of my mind.

Ten days after the hearing, I came back from my kitchen job to find an official-looking letter in my cell. I sat on the bunk, turning it over and over in my hands before opening it. Parole Board. I knew what it would say. I finally tossed it in the wastebasket unopened. A moment later I fished it out and tore it open.

Your application has been successful . . . complete discharge of your sentence . . . You will be released on . . . you will report to . . . you will be held to these conditions . . .

I sat down hard on the bunk, light-headed and disbelieving. The next ten days felt longer than all the previous years I'd spent behind bars. Each day dragged endlessly, followed by sleepless nights as I thought of the life I would make for myself on the outside.

It was hard to believe the gate was sliding closed with me on the outside.

"Keep your nose clean, Brocket." The release guard couldn't resist getting one more shot in before I walked away from the Mountain.

They offered me a ride to town, but I couldn't take the idea of one more back-seat ride, and besides, I wanted to walk, to feel the air and to see a bigger patch of sky than the stone walls of prison allowed. I didn't remember the landmarks of Cemetery Road from all those years ago when they brought me here, shackled and chained. It was not quite five miles to Mountain Institution from Agassiz back then. Now it was almost eight kilometres from the prison to Agassiz.

Some things change, like the way we measure distance. Some things can never be changed. But my time was done, my debt paid in full. I owed nothing. What was left of my life was mine.

The road from the prison sliced through farmland, and a wave of sadness rolled over me like mist. I was surprised that the once-familiar smells and sounds brought me close to tears. Awash with memories of childhood days in the Southwest, I couldn't help but think of my mother, Sagastis, and how the last time I'd seen her, small and sick, was in the grey visiting room surrounded by killers and low-lifes. My throat tightened and the tears I'd resisted all those years threatened to rise. I pushed her from my mind and thought of my aunt, Laura, and Laura's husband, James. They were our salvation after the nightmare in British Columbia. James loved that woman so much he even learned Cree. He spoke it with the funniest Oklahoma accent, but he spoke it well. He was like a father to me, this Cree-speaking, redneck Okie farmer.

Before I could become lost completely to the feel of freedom and the well of memories, the sound of tires on the gravel shoulder behind me brought me back to earth. An RCMP cruiser pulled up behind me. Irritated, I kept walking, but then decided against it and turned to face him. Who needs trouble on their first day free? The cop stepped out of the car, the yellow stripe of his pants sickeningly familiar.

"Good afternoon." He walked toward me, slipping his hat on, all official.

"Hello." *Nothing's wrong. My time is done.* Still, my heart was pounding and I imagined myself in handcuffs, in the back seat, heading back to the prison.

"Where you headed?"

"Agassiz."

"You from the Mountain?" he asked, knowing full well.

"Yeah."

"You got some ID?"

"Sort of." I hand him my driver's licence.

"This is an expired Oklahoma licence."

"Yeah. Long story. I've been away."

"Why don't you just come with me? I'll run you into town. People around here get nervous about guys walking down from the prison."

"I'd really rather walk."

"Yeah, I bet you would. But this is probably best. Regs say you have to ride in the back."

"And if I say no?"

"Come on, do us both a favour. Don't say no."

"All right."

I felt like puking as I climbed into the rear. One look at the back of his seat and I was small and alone again. I slid over to the other side of the seat and looked out the window.

"You going to the halfway house?"

"No. I'm discharged, not paroled."

"You got a place to stay?"

"Yeah, my cousins are meeting me."

"Where?"

"In town."

He looked over his shoulder at me, determined to know where this ex-con was going to be tonight.

"Holiday Inn."

Blessedly silent, the cop pulled into the Holiday Inn.

"Thanks for the ride." No surprise to me, he sat there watching as I made my way to the desk. I made a big deal of it, taking my time pulling papers out my pack.

"Can I help you, sir?" The clerk, shorter than average, looked like a child behind the huge front desk. I looked straight at her and saw a big spirit in a little body.

"Ah, my cousins made a reservation at a hotel for me and I think it was the Holiday Inn. But I don't seem to have their letter with me. Could you check for me?"

"And the name on the reservation?"

"Brocket."

She flipped through her reservations file, mild consternation on her face. "I'm sorry, sir, we have no such reservation."

"That's okay, Lisa," I said, looking at her name tag. "Would you mind telling me how to get to the Ramada Inn? Maybe the reservation is there."

"I could call over for you if you like."

"No. That's okay."

She pulled out a small coloured map with pictures of parks and streets and stores, and started drawing a route for me. In the mirror behind the desk, I saw the reflection of the cop car pulling away.

"So, you go straight down this main road here"—she pointed out the window—"and you go four blocks, turn right at the McDonald's, and it's about a block and a half down the road from there."

"Thank you for your kindness." I took the map and continued on to my original destination, the bus stop where I could catch a bus into the city. I sat on the bench and waited, the world spinning by at a dizzying pace. Everything felt so fast after the interminable, predictable days of prison.

The bus arrived just as it started to rain. Sprinkling, really, refreshing after years of rarely being outside long enough to feel a raindrop. By the time we got downtown, the bus was full to capacity with drenched, steaming passengers, the shower now a downpour.

I got off, not sure if it was the right stop. I had about an hour before the banks closed, and the guys back at the institution had warned me that it would be hard to cash the cheque issued on my release with no bank account. They suggested a bank in the

Downtown Eastside where they were familiar with situations such as mine. I found it after walking a few blocks, and stepped in dripping and sodden. I stood in line, self-conscious and certain that everyone was staring at me. I tried to block it all out and just stared at the back of the guy's head in front of me. By the time I was in front of the teller, I was so overwhelmed I just pulled my cheque out of my pocket and slapped it on the counter.

"I need this cashed."

She took one look at me and glanced over her shoulder at a man sitting in a glass-walled office. "Do you have an account with us, sir?"

"No."

She looked at the Department of Corrections seal on the cheque. "Oh, um, well, we don't normally cash cheques unless you have an account. Um, but, well, let me see."

She closed and locked her cash tray and headed to the back, to the man in the glass office. She showed him the cheque and I watched, my heart sinking. I'd left the institution with five bus tokens and that cheque. There would be no food and no place to sleep without that cash. I glanced out the window. It was pitch-dark now but for the street lights. The rain was falling even harder now, waves of water from passing cars drenching passersby. I closed my eyes and prayed.

"Sir. My manager says since it is a government cheque, if you've got some identification, we will cash it for you."

My heart sank as I passed her the expired Oklahoma driver's licence. She took one look and headed back to the glass office. Holding my breath, I watched her show it to the man and felt the frustration rise as he looked at me and shook his head. She talked some more to him and I imagined them snickering together about my predicament. Then the man picked up the phone and made a call. My face was flushed hot as I imagined him calling the police. It was all I could do not to just bolt.

"I can help you, sir."

The relief made me heady, almost faint. "Thank you. Thank you so much."

"Well, when you get a chance, get your ID in order. Maybe open an account and you won't have any problems." She counted out the bills in an efficient flurry.

"Yes. Thanks." I gathered up the bills, stuffed them in my pocket and made for the door as fast as I could. I stood under the awning of the building for a while, trying to get my bearings. I hadn't eaten for almost two days, the anticipation of my release deadening my appetite.

The streets were emptying of workers heading home, and a new crowd filtered into the neighbourhood: panhandlers and hookers, dealers and guys trying to sell hot goods. The rain let up a little and I headed down the street looking in windows for a place I could find a cheap meal and not too many people. I finally stopped in front of the Two Jays Café and decided counter service was just the thing.

The bell sounded as I opened the door, but the proprietor and patrons were equally oblivious to me. I knew I'd found the right place. I slid onto the orange vinyl stool and the waitress was pouring coffee before I could say a word. She slid a menu in front of me and walked away, putting the coffee pot back on its burner. I read the menu front and back, and everything from Salisbury steak to the hot turkey sandwich looked like the rarest of delicacies. I was salivating by the time the waitress came back to take my order. I ordered the Salisbury steak with extra gravy, both mashed potatoes and French fries, a side order of fried mushrooms, and a chocolate milkshake. Unable to decide on apple or cherry pie, I ordered one of each with ice cream. The waitress didn't bat an eye.

"Will that be all?"

I laughed for what seemed like the first time in years and caught her eye. "For now."

She shrugged and smiled and kept the coffee coming. I ate as though I hadn't eaten in years.

"You know where a guy could get a room around here?"

She cleared the dishes with practised efficiency. "Yeah, the Balmoral's not far from here and it's cheap. But it's loud from the beer parlour." She slid both pieces of pie in front me along with a clean fork. "You want to head a couple of blocks west of here and see if there's any rooms at the Dufferin. It's a little more, but quiet."

"Well, thanks. I'll check it out." I dug into the pie and was tempted to lick the plates even though the waist of my pants felt considerably tighter than when I first walked in. I took my time over a last cup of coffee and snuck a dollar under the saucer. I paid my bill, pulled my jacket on, lifting the collar against the cooling night, and headed out in search of the Dufferin, satisfied and relaxed for the first time that day.

The sun shone so bright and clear the following morning, it was as though yesterday's deluge had never happened. Even though the bathroom was shared with the other tenants on my floor, my room had a door that locked. For the first time in years I took a shower by myself. I let myself ignore some impatient knocks and let the hot water rain over me, years of tension washing away with it. When the knocks turned to angry voices, I cut the water and headed back to my room, relaxed and ready for the day.

I returned to the Two Jays for breakfast and savoured my coffee while scanning the want ads in the papers left at the counter. After paying for my room for two weeks there was not much left, and I would have to find work soon. Pretty much every ad called for experience. During my time at the Mountain I had worked in the laundry.

Not much call on the outside for that kind of experience, or for ranch hands in the city, the only other work I'd ever done. I downed the last of my coffee and headed out into the warm fall day.

I wandered up and down the six-block stretch of East Hastings, the heart of skid row, the gathering place of the unwanted. It didn't take long to figure out I wouldn't find work there. I jumped a Stanley Park bus, not sure where it would take me, and watched the character of the neighbourhoods change from skid row, to the business core, to department stores, upscale apartment enclaves and, finally, Burrard Inlet and the rich greenery of the park. Stepping off the bus at the park entrance, I felt as though I had been holding my breath all this time and finally, in the sanctuary of the park, I could let go and breathe easy.

I spent the rest of the day exploring the walking trails, and finally the world seemed to stop racing around me. I wandered through the aquarium and sat for over an hour talking to the she-wolf, consoling her, letting her know I knew what it was like to be caged in. As afternoon headed into early evening, I caught the bus back downtown. My heart sank as we moved from paradise to that mile of broken souls I now called home.

I wandered back into the Two Jays for dinner, mentally counting how much I could afford from my dwindling cash. The same girl was behind the counter, pouring coffee and ignoring patrons. I was surprised at how happy I was to see her. I didn't even know her name. I pulled up at the counter and she smiled as she approached with the coffee pot. I ordered a much more modest meal.

"Is that all?" She raised an eyebrow and smiled.

"Yeah." I blushed. "I don't always eat enough for a small family." She laughed and watched as I flipped to the want ads again, thinking maybe I'd missed something that might mean work for me.

"You lookin' for work?"

"Sure am. Got any ideas?"

"What kind of work you lookin' for?"

"Whatever pays."

"The Balmoral sometimes pays cash for guys to help unload and stock the booze in the morning. Talk to Mike behind the bar. It isn't much, but should help keep a roof over your head till you find something else."

"Thanks, ummm . . ."

"Connie." She leaned in a little. "The boss wants me to wear my name tag, but it's easier to ignore the jerks if they don't know my name." She laughed and headed to the till to ring in a customer.

I pushed the paper aside when Connie brought my meal, and once again savoured every flavourful bite. A man grows a deep appreciation for food after years of prison fare. Cheap, bland food chosen for its economy, without a thought for nutritional value or flavour, leaves a man hungry forever. Connie cleared my plate and slid me a piece of cherry pie. I shook my head.

"I didn't order—"

"Sshhh. It was scheduled for the trash tonight anyway. You just out of the can?"

I blushed and looked away. "How did you know?"

Connie shrugged. "I dunno. Just a feeling. Tell you what, I know Mike. I get off here in a couple hours. If you want to meet me here, I'll take you over and introduce you."

"Why would you do that for me?"

"I don't know, uh . . ."

"My friends call me Brocket."

"You seem like a decent guy."

"Well, I don't know what to say. Thanks, Connie."

She ripped the tab off her pad and laid it next to my plate.

I waited for her outside at closing time. She looked different out of her uniform, her long black hair silky and smooth, halfway down her back.

She looked up at me. "What? You'd look different in uniform too!"

We laughed and headed toward the Balmoral. I held the door open and followed her in. The air was thick with the stench of stale beer, cigarette smoke and a faint odour of urine and puke. I looked down at Connie.

"Okay, so the Ritz it ain't. It is what it is."

I laughed as we made our way to the bar, but inside, all the reflexes born of five years in prison jumped up as though I were still there. Instinctively, I had taken Connie's arm as we walked in and she now pulled it away, shaking it slightly.

"Ouch! Geez, lighten up, man."

I took a deep breath. "Sorry. Old habits. I get tense."

We stood at the bar and she waved at the bartender, who nodded in our direction while he filled a tray of draft for his waitress. He wiped his hands on his bar towel as he headed our way.

"What's up, Connie? Haven't seen you in here for a while."

"Yeah, well, no offence, but this is not my favourite place."

Just then a fight broke out by the entrance and the bouncers went to work, grabbing the combatants by the collar and tossing them through the swinging doors.

"Still not as bad as the Cobalt." Mike laughed and nodded his head toward me. "Who's your friend?"

I reached out and shook his hand. "Brocket."

"Yeah, he's new in town and looking for some day work until he can find something permanent. You got anything goin' on?"

Mike checked me out and nodded. "Yeah, sure. I could use a guy in the mornings. I had a guy, but he's a drunk and kept showing up late and sick. You a drunk, Brocket?"

I got the feeling his question was more about Connie than whether or not he would give me a job. I shook my head. "Never touch the stuff."

"Rare in this neighbourhood."

I shrugged, once again wanting to run from the rising decibels of the garrulous drunken chatter and the stink. Connie reached over the bar and tweaked Mike's shirt collar.

"Well, whaddya say, Mike? You know I know how to pick 'em."

Mike shrugged. "Yeah, sure. Ten bucks for four hours in the morning. The swamper unloads the truck and you bring it in and restock the bar and put the rest in the cooler, sweep the floor and clean the bathrooms. All right? Truck gets here at seven. Don't be late."

I shook his hand again. "Thanks, Mike, I won't let you down."

"You better not. And you"—he looked sideways at Connie—"behave yourself."

"Don't I always?" Connie laughed and Mike shook his head, threw the bar towel over his shoulder and headed for the taps to load another tray.

"Come on." I nudged Connie. "Let's get out of here." I couldn't get out of there fast enough and was glad I would be working before the place opened. We walked abreast through the swinging doors into the cool evening air. I turned to Connie.

"Wow! Thank you so much, kid. That will pay for my room easily and I might even get to eat!"

"Don't thank me yet. Wait till after you see those bathrooms." She laughed.

"Come on, let me walk you home. When is your next day off? I want to take you somewhere."

"Well, I take the bus home, but you can walk me to the bus stop. And I'm off day after tomorrow."

I walked her to the bus stop and waited with her. I refused to answer any questions about my plans for her day off.

"I don't like surprises," she protested as she stepped up onto her bus.

"Too bad! You'll like this one. Meet me right here at noon, day after tomorrow." I waved to her once as she took her seat, then I headed back to the Dufferin, amazed at how easily everything was falling into place. After another marathon shower, I sat by the window and watched the world go by.

It was still pitch-black when I woke in a sweat, my heart racing and my head pounding. It was a long time since the dreams had left me sleepless. I sat up and threw the curtains open, looking for anything to distract me and pull me away from the overwhelming dread that was settling into my bones. In my dreams, I was back at the school, hearing voices and footfalls in the night then being lifted from my bed in the darkness.

My heart still racing, I threw my clothes on and headed for the street, taking the stairs two at a time. I walked until dawn laced the North Shore Mountains with the relief of daylight. I was waiting for the truck when it pulled up behind the Balmoral. The swamper jumped out of the cab and threw the back open.

"Well, this is different. Usually it's me waiting on the help."

"Won't be like that anymore. Let me give you a hand with that." Even though it wasn't part of my job, I helped him unload the truck. I waved him off as the truck pulled out, thinking of my uncle James and how he'd always taught me no job is done unless it's done well. I found a dolly in the backroom and hauled the boxes of booze to the front, loaded the coolers and took the rest to the back. Took me a while to find the broom, but I swept like a madman, as though it would sweep my head clean of ugly memories. Then I cleaned the bathrooms. I shook my head, remembering Connie's warning, as I surveyed the wreckage. Two hours later I wouldn't have eaten off the floors or anything, but they were shining clean.

I was just pulling off my rubber gloves and scrubbing my hands at the bar when Mike came in the back door. A cup of coffee in one hand and the newspaper under his arm, he stopped and looked around the room and nodded toward me.

"The johns done yet?"

"Sure are." I put my gloves under the sink and put the broom back where it belonged.

Mike came out of the bathroom, a look of pleased amazement on his face. "Wow. I can't even remember when they looked that good." He reached over, slid the key into the till, hit the No Sale button, fished out two fives and handed them to me. "Thanks, man. Good job."

I took the bills and folded them into my shirt pocket. "Well, thank you. I sure can use it. If you need anything else done around here, just let me know. I got nothin' but time."

"Where you from, man? You kinda talk funny."

I laughed. "I lived in the States for a lotta years when I was a kid. Guess I picked up a bit of a twang."

"Yeah, that would explain it. Sometimes I can use an extra bouncer around here. You look like you'd know how to handle yourself."

"Ah, no thanks, man." I shook my head. "I'm not good in crowds. You got anything needs doing after or before hours, I'm your guy."

"I'll keep that in mind. Things come up from time to time."

I grabbed my jean jacket off the peg and headed for the back door. "Thanks again. Means a lot."

Mike had turned his attention to the bar and waved over his shoulder. "See you tomorrow."

I walked into the brilliant sunlight. Another unusually dry and sunny day. I hoped the weather would hold for tomorrow. I headed back toward the Dufferin, anxious for a shower after cleaning those bathrooms. I avoided the Two Jays, knowing Connie would be starting her shift around now and not wanting to seem too anxious. I stopped by the Army & Navy and picked up some canned goods, instant coffee, crackers, a loaf of bread, a can opener, a newspaper and some shoe polish. I would have to watch my pennies and try to get by on what Mike paid me and leave what was left of my cash stash alone. I wandered back to my room, put my supplies away and, after an undisturbed shower, lay back and scanned the want ads in the newspaper. My eyes burned and I closed them, thinking a short nap wouldn't hurt after a long, wakeful night.

It was full-on dark when I woke up, gasping. I sat on the edge of the bed, letting it sink in where I was and where I wasn't. I walked to the small sink in the corner and splashed cold water on my face. The dreams had faded over the years in prison and I thought for sure, once I was free, I would be free of them too. Why were they back now, when everything was looking up? I made an instant coffee and read the paper, ghosts lurking in the corners.

I rushed through my work the next morning, careful to have everything spotless and finished before Mike rolled in. I was anxious to see Connie and hoped she would be pleased with the day I'd planned for her. Mike surveyed the bar and the backroom and handed me my pay with an appreciative nod.

"This is excellent, man. I can't tell you how shitty it is to come in here not knowing if I'm gonna have to do all this work before my shift."

"Seems simple enough to just do the work." I shrugged, wondering what kind of deadbeats had come before me.

"You'd be surprised."

I washed my hands and grabbed my jacket, eyes on the clock. Eleven forty-five. I walked fast, wanting to be there first, waiting for her, and as luck would have it, I was. But not for long. No sooner had I sat down than a bus rolled up and she slipped through the back door, smiling.

"Hey, Brocket, thought I might see you yesterday for supper."

"Aw, I don't want you to get tired of me, now, do I." I could feel myself blushing and looked away.

"So, what's the big surprise? Come on, give it up."

"All right, let's go." I steered her toward Pender Street. "I'm taking you to the park. Whaddya think of that?"

"Really? I haven't been to the park since last fall. Almost a year."

I was relieved that she seemed to like the idea, and we didn't have to wait long for the bus. We sat together and she chattered on, pointing things out to me, telling me about the city. I slipped my arm around her shoulder and felt encouraged that she didn't seem to mind. We got off at the foot of Denman and walked by Lost Lagoon and into the park.

"Come on!" She grabbed my hand and started running. "Let's go ride the train."

I'd seen the train the last time I was here, its passengers mostly moms and their kids delighted or bored with the exhibits and the fenced-in exotic animals. "Uh, okay." A train had left just as we arrived and so we wandered a little, waiting for the next one. We climbed aboard an open car and settled in, the steam engine sighing and puffing as we meandered through the park.

"I love trains." She looked up and smiled at me.

"Yeah? The last time I was on a train, well . . ." And for some reason I told her the whole story about the time me and my mother took the train to visit her sister, that wonderful summer when the priest came with the cop and took me away. I told her about the school and Kenny and how my mom and her sister's husband helped me escape and how we ran across the border. I stopped short there, regretting having opened my big mouth.

She looked at me and reached for my hand. "I knew you had a story. You know, my dad went to one of those places. He would never talk about it. Not to anyone, not even my mom. She was Metis, so she didn't have to go. My dad gave up his Indian status so they couldn't take me there."

I nudged her to get off the train at the halfway stop, took her hand and led her to the wolf enclosure. It wasn't long before the she-wolf loped out of her enclosure, long-legged and shy. "I think I know how she feels. I spent a lot of time in the high desert mountains in my teens. Wild and peaceful. No people around to mess things up. We had to come back to Canada to take care of some business and that's when I ended up in jail. I would likely be some hermit mountain man by now if I'd been able to stay there."

Connie looked up at me. "Well, you know, if that's what you want, I was reading about people who are setting up homesteads on Crown land up north. It's all legal so long as they make improvements."

I shrugged, wondering how I would stake myself on the little I was making at the Balmoral. "I gotta find real work."

Every passing day with no chance of a job with decent pay weighed on me as though I were being buried alive. Every night now I woke, unable to breathe, choking on memories and the irrational fear that I was back there, a child again, Brother stalking me in my bed. Every night I walked the city for hours before meeting the truck at the Balmoral. My circle widened and soon I no longer felt new to the city. I had a number of routes I would walk, and I'd choose them according to the depth of my mood. One such route cut through the grounds of a huge Catholic cathedral. The gardens were beautiful by moonlight, and on clear nights I would often sit there watching the shadows play against the stained glass windows, a desperation rising in me that I couldn't shake.

It was on one of those nights that it all became too much. I had to get away, back to the mountains. I thought of the she-wolf and imagined her mournful wail to the full moon. As though someone else was in my shoes, I walked to one of the church doors at the side of the building, partially hidden by an alcove entrance. I smashed the side window, reached in and opened the door, not even sure why. I crept inside and found my way to the rows of pews in front of the altar. I walked behind the altar and into the sanctuary. I rummaged through the drawers and closets there, stopping when I found the priest's robes and, dangling from them, a heavy gold crucifix I imagined he wore only when giving Mass. I took a quick look around for any other valuables and ran for the door. Too big to stash in my pocket, I hung the heavy chain around my neck, under my shirt, and all day long it burned.

I finished my work as fast as I could and headed back to the Dufferin. I cradled the piece in my hands, sitting at the edge of the bed, the long, heavy chain wrapped around my fingers. I thought of all the brutality, the indignity. I thought of my mother and how all of this was really what killed her. *Fuck them.* How many lives, besides hers and mine, were broken down like garbage in the name of this cross? I wrapped the cross in one of the hotel towels and stuck it in a paper grocery bag, pulled my jacket on and headed for the pawnshop.

I'm sure I was sweating and shaking when I walked in to pawn that piece of gold, but I tried to distract myself by thinking about whether I would get enough for camping gear, a few tools and a rifle. I could hitch north and maybe I could find some odd jobs, enough to buy me a horse and tack, and a few supplies. I didn't need more than that.

I handed the piece to the man behind the counter. He looked at it, looked at me and shook his head. "We don't deal in things like this."

I knew better than to argue and thought there must be another store that would take it off my hands. Heading for the door, I saw him in the window's reflection picking up the phone. I walked calmly until I was out of his line of vision and then jogged six blocks to the far end of the neighbourhood, where I'd seen another pawnbroker's storefront. No sooner had I walked in and laid the crucifix on the counter than two city cops came in behind me. One sidled up beside me, the other stood behind me, ready.

"Well, what have we here?" He pushed my hand away from the crucifix and dangled it for his partner to see.

Before I knew it, I was turned around, one hand on the wall, the other behind my back, as the handcuffs rattled. No escape. Again. The walls seemed to close in on me and my heart pounded. I leaned in, trying to make sense of what the cop was saying, his words lost in the rushing sounds in my ears. He finished cuffing me and led me to his cruiser.

"It's a small neighbourhood, man. Did you really think you'd get away with it?"

I slid into the back seat, and as I did, I caught sight of Connie, watching as they took me away. I turned away from the confusion in her eyes and tried to think of nothing at all. That night, the moon shone through the small window of my cell and I thought of the she-wolf.

The next morning, along with the other prisoners, I was loaded into a van and taken to the courthouse for my first appearance. My number was called, and I was placed in the prisoner's dock. Just as the judge was asking if I had a lawyer, a young woman in a ribbon skirt and business jacket stood up to face him.

"Your Honour, Ms. Woods. I'm the Courtworker today and will be acting for this man."

"Good day, Ms. Woods, nice to see you." The judge rifled through the file in front of him. "Mr. Brocket, you are fortunate to have drawn this young woman. I will see you again this afternoon."

That afternoon, the Courtworker argued passionately for me. She talked about the school and the nightmare my mother and I had suffered at the hands of the Church. She spoke of how I was a model prisoner and how this was an isolated act of desperation from a man wanting to work and make his way, but without the necessary skills. She requested a conditional release. It was granted. I was to continue living at the Dufferin and report to the Courtworker on a weekly basis. I was to seek training with the help of the Friendship Centre programs, and if I stayed out of trouble for a year, the charges against me would be dropped. I couldn't believe it when they removed the handcuffs and escorted me out. The Courtworker was waiting for me there.

"Now, you meet me at the Friendship Centre tomorrow. Don't be late."

I nodded, embarrassed and thankful. "I'll be there."

10

MARIAH

-->--->--<---<--

Submersed in the kind of darkness one only finds in the country, away from cities and their relentless spray of light, Clara's mind raced to put it together. She had no idea where she was. A furious wind howled through the darkness. It was only when John Lennon's voice, mournful and high, rose above the wind that she remembered. They were at the Old Woman's cabin.

Clara's eyes adjusted slowly, and the outlines of log walls emerged from the pitch-darkness. The sudden movement when she sat up triggered a sharp pain in her shoulder and she remembered her injury. She cradled her arm in front of herself, taking pressure off the shoulder, and slid her bare feet into her boots. She walked as quietly as she could, but when she opened the front door, Clara felt her presence behind her.

"What are you doing?"

"I'm getting John Lennon."

"He's a dog. Dogs live outside."

"Not this dog."

"Yes. Him too."

"I'll go outside and sleep with him, then."

"Fine." She tossed a quilt in Clara's direction. "Go ahead."

Clara walked through the door toward the makeshift shelter where John Lennon was tethered, wiggling with joy now that he could see her.

"It's going to snow, you know."

Clara didn't even look at her, but thought she heard something else, something other than irritation in her voice.

"All right, all right. Light a fire in the porch stove. He can come in there. If it weren't for the weather and that shoulder, I'd let you sleep out there."

Her mumbling faded as she headed back into the cabin. Clara dropped to her knees in front of John Lennon. "Okay, boy. I'm here." She scratched behind both his ears as he contorted himself into almost a complete circle with all that tail wagging and dancing around. She untied him and they made their way back to the porch.

The sky seemed to hum with the spray of stars laid bare of clouds by the wind. Clara thought of another night sky, the full moon, small and cold, a bitter orb above the badlands as she lay there, wounded and certain her death was upon her. John Lennon had put himself between her and death, lying next to Clara against the deep chill that night. Turnaround is fair play. The near-full moon was golden and so bright it cast shadows. Still, there was something so completely unfamiliar about the earth in darkness, no matter how confident Clara walked in the daylight. Storm clouds recaptured the stars as she closed the porch door behind them.

Clara collected bits of bark and dry wood splinters from the woodbox and used them to coax a few small flames. John Lennon sat next to her, resting his bulk against her side, as she slowly added bigger and bigger kindling, the flames growing strong enough to ignite the rounds of poplar from the neatly piled box. Clara left the wood stove open and sat there, the dog's tongue lolling, her arm throbbing. The cabin creaked and, above it all, Clara heard a persistent tinkling, as though the wind was laughing.

"Okay, mister, I got you this far, so no more complaining. Go to sleep."

John Lennon curled up in front of the wood stove and Clara sat in the old, overstuffed chair where the old woman had been sitting the evening before, drinking her tea as the darkness seeped in around the cabin. It wasn't long before the warmth of the wood stove and John Lennon's soft snoring lulled her back to sleep, the thick quilt wrapped around her.

The morning sun slowly filled the porch and Clara could feel John Lennon staring at her in an urgent silence. She opened her eyes and he smiled at her, his ears half down, tail thumping the floor.

"Yeah, yeah, come on."

She wrapped the quilt around her shoulders and opened the door for him. He raced to the tree line, circled three times before lifting his leg, making sure he always had his eyes on her. He'd always been protective, but after Willow Flats he was even more vigilant, and nothing could calm him if he couldn't see her. Clara hoped he would mellow out again.

Clara quickly stuck her head in the cabin door and looked around the neat and organized interior. The Old Woman was not there. Clara wondered how she might have missed her going out before sunrise. She stepped inside and washed her face, wondering if she would be able to wash her clothes. Everything she owned was in the Falcon, which no doubt had been seized by the police. She stood in the porch doorway as John Lennon sniffed around the perimeter of the clearing. She pulled on her boots, trying to ignore the ache in her shoulder.

"Come on, boy." John Lennon dashed toward her, tongue lolling, ears pricked. "Let's check this place out a little." He ran ahead of her, his huge paws tossing up the thin layer of snow from last night's storm.

Clara wandered along the tree line, trying to orient herself. All she remembered from the night before was the rough ride in the back of the truck, her and John Lennon hiding under the tarp, and then the Old Woman in the porch, beckoning her in. Next thing she remembered was waking to John Lennon crying out for her. She put it together that she must have passed out.

Clara came around the corner of the cabin and found herself on a trail that wound through a grove of black poplar, now all but naked of their leaves, their twisted black limbs framed against the sky. The path was slippery with rotting orange-black leaves partially covered in snow. She kept her eyes on her feet, careful not to fall. When she looked up, she found herself in a clearing. At its centre was a dome-shaped structure made of living willows, their boughs woven loosely together to form a ceiling. There was an entrance, a carefully crafted arch, the top no higher than her waist. Inside the structure was a firepit, bare of any remnants of a fire. Over to one side of the clearing was a carefully stacked woodpile, secured under a tarp, and in front of it a clearly well-used firepit. She looked back over her shoulder and saw John Lennon sitting quietly in the middle of the path a few feet from the entrance to the clearing, ears forward, eyes fixed on Clara.

"This way, buddy." She slapped her thigh gently. He didn't move an inch. "What's up with you?" He shook his head and huffed.

A prickle of fear worked its way up her spine, and she walked slowly away from the clearing. John Lennon bounded toward the cabin when he saw Clara heading back up the trail. She looked back over her shoulder at the structure and could have sworn she heard soft singing underneath the tinkling she'd heard well into the night. It was only then, as she wandered back toward the cabin, that she saw them, dozens of small and very old coloured glass bottles hanging from the poplar trees in clutches of two or three. A rainbow against the black, twisted limbs, they swayed in the now-gentle breeze, tinkling as though giving voice to the wind. She wondered how long they had hung there, witness to the changing seasons, and the dark feeling left her. The music of the bottles took her back to those days before Indian School, back to those long walks with her mother though the birch groves, her mother up ahead, Clara transfixed by the songs of angels in the treetops.

When she rounded the front of the small cabin, the Old Woman was back, her small footprints in the snow leading to the front door. Clara looked down at John Lennon.

"I'm okay, man. You stay out here for now."

Clara rekindled a small fire in the porch stove and pointed to where he'd slept the night before. As was his habit, he turned around three times and then flopped down and curled up tight, his eyes following her as she walked through the front door.

The Old Woman was bent over, loading up the wood cookstove with poplar rounds. She straightened up and wiped the wisps of hair off her forehead.

"You're back." She lifted a large black cast iron fry pan off its hook on the wall and set it on the stove.

"You too." Her face burned red at her smart-ass impertinence. *One day*, she thought, *I will learn to just shut up.* "You know, can't remember if they told me your name."

"Mariah."

"Clara."

"That's what they said."

She was a wiry little woman, not more than five feet tall, hair almost completely white in a neat braid that fell below her hips. She wore a calf-length cotton skirt, red with tiny yellow flowers, the hem falling just over the top of her wraparound moccasins. She pushed up the long sleeves of the blue turtleneck sweater and exposed her tightly muscled forearms, her hands obviously accustomed to hard work. She had piercing brown eyes, so dark they seemed black, and the lines around them suggested mirth as well as age.

Clara turned to her again. "Hey, I'm sorry about last night and the dog. I don't want you to think I'm not thankful. I am. I didn't mean to be disrespectful."

Her stern face softened for a moment and she beckoned. "Come on over, I made some bannock. There's jam too, from the last huckleberries of the season. Try some." She put a plate of warm bannock on the small plank table and pushed the Mason jar of jam toward her.

It was a relief to see her soften, and until that first bite of flaky, soft bannock, melted butter and tart huckleberry jam, Clara hadn't realized just how hungry she was. Mariah laughed as Clara reached for a second piece before the first was done.

"I'll make a stew for dinner. Get you fed right." She placed a tin cup of black tea in front of her. "You can help me peel potatoes." Mariah put a large bowl of potatoes and a paring knife next to Clara.

Clara finished the first piece of bannock, and the second tasted even better than the first. Then she turned to her and said, "It's not just words, Mariah. I am so thankful to you. I would be in jail if they hadn't brought me here."

"Well, you wouldn't be the first," she said as she expertly browned the venison that would make their stew. The way she moved around her little kitchen made Clara think of her mom, making something out of nothing, always finding a way to push back the hunger.

"Does someone hunt for you?" Clara wondered if she had dropped the deer herself.

"People come here pretty regular. Some bring meat if they've had a good hunt. I have a trapline, too. Rabbits."

"You don't get afraid living out here all by yourself?"

She tossed Clara a box of wooden matches. "Days are getting shorter. Light those lanterns, would you? This place is home. Nothing for me to fear here."

Clara had never lit a kerosene lamp before, but the room was soon shining with the yellow flames after she figured out the first one. "Have you always lived here?"

"My grandmother raised me here. Hid me. Kept me out of the Indian Schools."

Rolling over her like a dark cloud was the memory of her mom telling Clara why she had to go to school. "I had to go."

"Hmmm. My mother died of the coughing sickness, so my father brought me here, to my grandmother, when I was very small. I saw him a few times after that, but he left me to her. She was a healer."

Clara glanced at Mariah as though she was hearing Sister Mary talk in her head. *Witch doctor.*

"Not many people alive know about this place of hers. Just the ones who keep it safe. This is a healing place, Clara."

Clara peeled as she listened.

"Once we get this stew on, I'll take a look at that shoulder. It doesn't feel good to me."

"It doesn't feel good to me either."

There was something calming about Mariah. She was stern to the point of being gruff, but just as there had been something other than annoyance under her words last night, there was something under her austere exterior that hinted at a gentle kindness.

Mariah relieved Clara of the peeled potatoes and added them to the simmering stew. "I guess your baby out there might like that," she said, pointing to the meat scraps and shin bone.

"Thank you. I know he's hungry." She took the scraps outside for John Lennon and watched him devour them in no time then settle in to gnaw on the bone, working to get at the rich marrow. He would be busy for a while.

Clara walked back into the house. Mariah had cleared off the table, a hide bundle replacing the remains of their meal. She beckoned Clara over as she loosened the rawhide straps that held the bundle together.

"Take your sweater off."

She slipped out of her sweater, self-conscious in her undershirt, and sat down beside the table. Mariah brought a bowl of warm water and placed it beside Clara, then carefully unwound the bandages from around her shoulder. A foul smell filled her nostrils and the bandage was stuck to the wound.

"Infection," Mariah said. "This will hurt a bit, but if we don't do something now, you could lose this arm."

"Should I go to the hospital?" Panic started rising in her. "How can I even contact anyone?" Mariah didn't have electricity, much less a telephone.

"Don't worry. Just be still."

Mariah soaked the dressing with the warm water and soon it fell away, leaving the infected wound exposed.

"Okay, now just sit here and let the air at it. I'm going to mix up a poultice for you."

She opened her bundle and in it were dozens of bags of plants, seeds, teas, tree fungi and long braids of grasses. The air filled with the most pleasant, earthy smell. Sister's damning voice in Clara's head quieted and she felt at peace.

"Mariah, how did I come to be here? This is not chance. Tell me. Please."

"Vera."

Mariah carefully selected the items from her bundle and set a pot to boil on the stove. She pulled a swath of muslin from under the table and laid it out beside the bundle. She then placed layers of her plants on the muslin, wrapped and tied the package carefully, and immersed it in the boiling water. After just a few minutes she pulled it out and wrapped it in a hand towel. She dipped a clean cotton swab in the amber liquid left in the pot, gently cleaned the wound, then placed the hot poultice overtop and re-bandaged the shoulder.

"Vera contacted the woman who drove you up here and told her you were coming. She asked her to bring you to me for a while. None of us imagined it would be like this, running from the cops and all."

Clara shuddered and looked over her shoulder, needing John Lennon. He must have been feeling the same way because, just then, he snuck his head into the doorway between the porch and the main cabin, before scuttling back to his spot by the stove when Mariah turned and saw him.

"Vera is so kind-hearted," Clara said, brushing past John Lennon's effort to join the conversation.

"Like a daughter to me, that one. She's worried about you. Figures you need some good medicine, and not just for that shoulder. Here, drink this tea. I'm going to build up the fire on the porch and you can sit and rest out there with your dog. I can see the medicine between you."

She walked out into the porch and Clara could feel the tears rising. It had been a long time since she'd felt so cared for. She brushed the tears aside and wondered what her mom would say about all this.

Mariah picked up a pile of neatly folded tarps. "Vera sent these up with you. Good thing. I needed new ones. I'll be back in a while. Come on now, go rest by the fire."

Mariah left Clara there, tea in hand, the wood stove open, its warmth comforting body and soul. John Lennon even wagged his tail at Mariah as she left, carrying her mound of tarps.

It was long after dark when she returned, and Clara had dozed off. John Lennon woke her with his thumping tail.

"Come in with me. We need to talk."

They sat again at the table.

"I see you were out by the sweat lodge."

"I've heard of them before. George and Vera talk about it. I grew up in Indian School. I don't know anything about that stuff."

"Hmmm." Mariah crossed her hands in her lap. "Well, it's there for you if you want, Clara."

"For what?"

"Like I said before, this is a healing place."

"My arm will be better soon."

"What about the rest of you? Do you ever think of our ancestors and how we are connected to them? Do you pray, Clara?"

Clara stiffened, the familiar rage rushing through her veins. "Pray? You mean talk to myself and imagine some guy in the sky will make it all better?" Clara stood. "I gotta check on John Lennon."

Mariah put her hand on Clara's arm. "Sit. Talk with me. There is something here for you to learn."

Clara sat back down but looked away from her.

"Clara, the separation between us and all who have come before us, that long line of ancestors, is nothing more than perception. Our teachings, the sweat and other ceremonies, they show us how to open our spirits so we can perceive and be open to the guidance of the ancients. You are so filled with rage. It will eat you alive, child. That is not our way."

Clara's mind flashed back to the Indian School and the echoing silence of the angels as Lily breathed her last breath. Where were the ancients then?

"I think you know more than you let on," Mariah said. "I'll be at the lodge at sunrise."

"John Lennon wouldn't go near it," Clara challenged her. "I trust him."

Mariah looked at John Lennon's nose, barely inside the cabin door. "He's just smart. Knows that dogs aren't supposed to go around the lodge." She tried to hide her smile at John Lennon's trespassing nose. "You're welcome there."

The winter set in, slow and vengeful, sucking all warmth from the air. Within a couple of weeks Mariah and Clara slipped into a comfortable routine. Mariah cooked and was thankful that Clara kept the woodbox full. Sometimes, on clear days, Mariah would take Clara out on her trapline. She showed Clara the fine art of tying snares and dispatching rabbits as kindly as possible. Whenever they found one in a snare, Mariah would reach into the pouch tied around her waist, put down tobacco with soft Cree words, and then knock it over the head, efficiently and even lovingly. She taught Clara the unique way of skinning a rabbit, much like taking off a sweater, once the cuts were made on the extremities. Clara would get dizzy sometimes as she watched Mariah dress the rabbits, thinking back to Indian School and how Sister Mary would've knocked *her* on the head if she saw a return to such savagery. It pleased Clara, thinking of that evil woman and how she would see her Christian mission as failed, seeing Clara in the hands of this pagan.

After a while Clara got used to a group of people who came

to the cabin to join Mariah in the lodge. There was a regular core group, as well as some that came just every now and then. Mariah never extended her invitation to Clara again, but Clara knew the lodge was always open to her. After dark, when the songs, rising into the air, signalled the door was closed, Clara would bundle up as warmly as possible and sneak down toward the lodge. Just before the pathway widened into the clearing, she would huddle halfway behind an old poplar and listen to the singing. It was kind of like the drumming she'd heard in the Friendship Centres, but different at the same time. Sometimes she felt a power rising in those songs that would leave her in a panic she didn't really understand. Mariah was a good woman; that Clara knew without a doubt. But it terrified her anyway, and inevitably it was Sister Mary and her threats of eternal damnation that chased her back up the pathway to the cabin.

One night, breathless from her gallop up the snowy hill, Clara stood outside the porch brushing the snow off her clothes and kicking it off her boots. John Lennon stood with his paws on the sill of the porch window, ears up, smiling at her. As clean of snow as possible, she went into the porch, stripped off her gear and stuffed it in a corner beside the woodbox. She tickled John Lennon behind the ears and went into the cabin to wash in the warm water from the wood stove reservoir, trying to take the chill pink out of her face before Mariah and the rest came back.

Clara was laying out the feast food in the way Mariah had taught her when the first of the group made their way back into the cabin. Mariah looked at her and smiled knowingly. *Damn that woman,* Clara thought. *Can't get anything over on her.*

"Clara, could you please prepare the offering and take it down to the lodge."

Clara could feel her face tightening. "Do I have to?" Everyone in the room was momentarily motionless, aghast but wordless.

Aggie, one of the younger women, walked over to Clara by the feast table and picked up a small plate and handed it to her. "It's an honour to offer the food to the ancestors. Come on, I'll help you."

Clara took a tiny sampling of everything on the feast table, as she had seen others do before. Simple food—bannock, soup, a pie, fruit, dried meat, tea, but always game meat, berries, corn and candy. Aggie added another piece of candy.

"The ancestors love sweets," she said.

Clara walked behind Aggie on the trail to the lodge, the plate of food in her hand. Aggie stood next to the fire in front of the lodge and nodded toward her.

"So, what do I do?" The irritation in Clara rose. How was she supposed to know?

Aggie handed Clara a pinch of tobacco and motioned toward the fire. "Say a prayer of thanks and offer the tobacco and the food to the fire. Things we burn in a sacred fire go to the other side for the ones gone ahead of us."

Clara pressed the plate into her hands, her anger rising. "You give thanks." She turned and walked back to the cabin.

Mariah didn't even look at Clara when she walked in alone. Aggie came in a few minutes later, equally silent.

"Mariah, is it okay if I say the prayer for the feast tonight?" Aggie asked, stepping toward the table and reaching for the braid of sweetgrass.

"Of course."

Clara walked out onto the porch and sat in the big chair, the fire warm. John Lennon lay down on her feet. She could still hear Aggie. She thanked practically everything under the sun, and while Clara wanted to dismiss it as silly, as she heard her say she was thankful for life and the things that give life, she could feel tears rising, but choked them back, thinking of Sister Mary and her handy strap.

The next morning, Clara walked Mariah's trapline alone. It was as though the sun had thrown handfuls of diamonds on the crusty snow. John Lennon romped out of sight and she was left alone in the brilliant sunlight, thankful this day for the empty snares. She stopped, the stillness of the morning making the sound of her feet on the snow unbearable. She looked through the skeletal black boughs of the poplar, so dark against the cloudless blue sky, the tinkling of the bottles filling the air with such a wistful sound that she felt small again. She looked up at the few remaining leaves of those poplar and birch trees, and they were accompanied by a different singing, a singing her childlike spirit knew to be the angels, the ancestors, shining down on her. She hated them. After she had prayed and prayed for Lily, she died anyway, and she hated them for it as much as she hated Sister Mary for making Lily work so hard when she was so sick. How could there be angels or ancestors that would allow little kids to be broken and destroyed?

"Life is a mystery, Clara."

Clara was so startled by the voice, she jumped and ran into the brush beside the trail. "Mariah!" It was as though she was reading her thoughts. "Don't scare me like that!"

John Lennon came running back from his adventure at a full gallop, sliding to a halt at her feet, smiling at the two women.

Mariah laughed. "Didn't you hear me coming?"

"No, I was thinking." Clara flushed with embarrassment.

"I can feel how you suffer."

"My shoulder is almost better. It hardly hurts at all now, thanks to you."

"You know what I mean."

"Leave me alone, Mariah. I survive my own way."

Clara turned and headed back to the cabin, stomping through the snow. She could hear Mariah's voice behind her.

"There is more to life than surviving, child."

"I'm not a child."

Clara immediately felt silly about her childish reply. John Lennon loped behind her as she headed toward the woodpile. She made four trips, each time neatly stacking the wood in the boxes on the porch and by the kitchen stove. Usually, work like this pushed the images of Lily out of her head, but this day her memory persisted, Lily's frail body racked with coughing, the blue of her lips offset by the pink bubbles that formed with every cough. *Lily. I should have stood up for you more. I should have stood between you and her and refused to take you out into the cold. Lily.*

"Who's Lily?"

It was only then that Clara realized she was speaking aloud as she stacked the poplar rounds in the woodbox. "My friend, she was my friend." And then she broke, after years of silent remembrance of her little friend and her lonely death. Clara had never spoken of her, other than briefly to George, and was convinced her death was as much her fault as Sister's. "Where were they then, Mariah? Where were your ancestors when they killed her?"

"Who killed her, Clara?"

"Sister. Sister killed her." Clara told her about Indian School and how Lily had hemorrhaged to the brink of death in front of her. How Sister Mary had let her die, alone and helpless. She told Mariah of her angels, the ones who would sing for her from the highest leaves of the birch trees back home. She told her of how the spirits had touched her in those early days of her childhood, and how they abandoned her completely in the barren halls of the Indian School. Clara cried and cried. For Lily. For herself. For her lost angels. It seemed as though hours had passed, and still she cried, Mariah sitting quietly by her side.

"We were children, me and Lily, and neither of us survived, even though I'm still walking."

That evening, Mariah fed her clear soup and put her to bed as though she were a child, tucking her in warm, and within minutes Clara felt herself fall into a deep, exhausted slumber. She thought she was dreaming when she saw Mariah lead John Lennon to her bedside.

The following morning, there was tea on the stove, but Mariah was nowhere to be seen. Clara sat up in bed and tucked her feet in John Lennon's coat, resting them lightly on his back. He thumped his tail.

Clara was long finished her tea when Mariah returned.

"I've prepared the lodge. Will you come with me?"

They walked together, Mariah and Clara, down the crisp pathway under a pale sun. The fire burned high, and Clara watched as Mariah entered the lodge, seated herself and looked out the doorway, arm extended, welcoming her. Clara crouched, took her hand and crossed the threshold.

There are no English words to describe how one woman walked into that lodge and another walked out. All Clara knew was that it took her back. Back to the birch grove and the angel songs. Back to who she was before Sister Mary, before the school, before they tried to beat her into a little brown white girl. She felt a certainty, from then on, that all the ones who had come before walked with her. Life was no longer just survival. It was about being someone. An Indian someone, with all the truth that was born into her at the moment she was placed in her mother's womb.

After several false starts, spring storms and late freezes, Clara was sure spring was finally here. The green shoots of new grass pressed up through last fall's debris, the lasting light of day and the sound of geese overhead making their way back from the south casting a magical calm over Mariah's clearing. The ever-present twinge of winter anxiety—Was there enough firewood? Would the water freeze? Was the snow building up too high on the roof of the cabin?—melted in the new spring sun. It had been a long winter in the Cypress Hills with Mariah.

"They should be here soon." Mariah sat quietly in the big chair in the porch, a small fire in the wood stove, much like the first night Clara arrived there.

"Yes."

Clara leaned against the door frame and looked out from the porch. John Lennon lay at her feet, waiting and watchful as ever. The winter had been healing for him too. He was no longer quite so anxious if Clara was out of his sight for a moment or two. With Mariah's skilful hands and extensive knowledge of traditional medicine, the infection in Clara's shoulder had disappeared, and slowly the wound healed, leaving her with only the occasional ache and stiffness.

"Did you pack those teas I made for you?"

"Yes, and the other medicines too."

"You remember, that one tea, take it every day, not just when the shoulder hurts."

Mariah seemed so small today.

"Mariah, come with me."

Mariah looked at Clara and laughed. "Don't be crazy. I don't belong in any city. And really not some city way over on the other side of the country. This is my home, here, with the lodge."

"I know. But what about for the winter? I'll get settled and get a place and you can come and stay with me for the winter. I'll worry about you all alone with the storms."

"And who will fix the next broken wing that finds its way here?

This is the life I am blessed with." She pulled the stool closer to her chair. "Come, sit with me before they get here."

Clara perched on the stool. Mariah ran her fingers along the hem of her skirt. "You did a good job on this skirt. It fits you fine."

Mariah had taught Clara the basics of sewing over the long winter, and from her stores of recycled and new bolts of fabric Clara had made herself a beautiful ribbon skirt.

Mariah lifted her eagle feather, struck a wooden match and lit the sage in the abalone shell that she used as her smudge bowl. The gentle Cree words of her prayer resonated in the silence of the morning. Though Clara didn't understand the words, she knew Mariah was sending her prayers up with the sacred smoke, asking the ancestors to watch over Clara on her journey, asking them to help keep her heart and eyes open.

Mariah bathed Clara in the sweet smoke of the smouldering sage, set her bowl back on the table beside her and took Clara's hand in hers, giving it a gentle squeeze.

The sound of the truck engine seemed so foreign as it approached the quiet clearing. John Lennon leapt up and stood at full alert. Mariah and Clara stepped out of the porch just as the truck pulled into the clearing. George was driving, Vera waving madly out of the passenger window. The truck had barely stopped before Vera jumped out and ran over, trying to hug Mariah and Clara at the same time. George parked and walked over, laughing at his wife. John Lennon just about lost his mind running from one person to the next, not sure who to greet first.

Mariah hugged Vera and then George. "How was that road? Lots of mud?"

"Not bad with the four-by-four. We brought you supplies, Mariah. I'll unload this stuff for you."

"Just in time. I'm just about out of flour. No bannock without flour."

"Well, we can't have that." George leaned over and planted a kiss on her forehead.

Vera linked her arm through Mariah's. "Let's have some tea while George takes your supplies in."

They sat around the plank table and sipped Mariah's soothing tea blend. Vera squeezed Clara's hand and smiled. "Woman, you are a sight for sore eyes."

Clara nudged her friend. "Remember that waitress? The one with that giant beehive?" They all laughed. Mariah looked a little mystified but amused. "Seems like so long ago."

"That was a rough forty-eight hours." Vera shook her head. "All we knew was that there were cops at the border when you crossed. We didn't know if you were in jail or hurt or what."

George took a long draw on his tea. "We figured you'd call us if they had you locked up, but when we didn't hear, we were freaked right out that you might be hurt or worse."

"Finally, someone called us. The woman who drove you here."

"Yeah. Your big plan all along. Why not just tell me you wanted me to come here?"

"Like you would have come?"

Clara rolled her eyes. "Maybe. Maybe I would have."

Mariah cleared her throat. "Sure, sure. You who fights everything to the death."

George snorted and Vera giggled, Clara shaking her head, trying not to laugh. She broke down when John Lennon joined in from the porch with his throaty howl. They laughed till it hurt.

Vera passed on the latest news of friends and family as George carried in armloads of supplies followed by three armloads of firewood, refilling the porch and kitchen woodboxes.

"Okay, women, we best hit the road. We have a long drive today."

"Thanks, George." Mariah stood and wiped her hands on her apron.

They all walked out to the truck together. George lifted John Lennon, hesitant to be separated from Clara, into the truck bed. After a nod to him from Clara, he settled into his kennel. George jumped into the driver's seat. Vera stood beside the open passenger door and waited.

Clara put her arms around Mariah and whispered her thanks.

Mariah looked Clara straight in the eye. "Remember, this is a place of healing. I am your family now and this place is yours forever. When things get tough, remember the medicine and never forget, you will always have your angels."

Clara had no more tears. She'd left them in the lodge and faced the world once again with an open heart. She slid into the back seat overwhelmed with hope and sadness as the tinkling sounds faded behind them.

11

KENNY

>-----<

Kendra stood behind her mother, uncertain and shy, grasping onto her just above the knees, sneaking peeks at this stranger. Kenny dropped to one knee.

"You've sure grown, pretty girl." He glanced up at Lucy. "She was just crawling last time."

Lucy couldn't help but smile. "Yeah, she's a handful now. Into everything."

Arms outstretched, Kenny reached out to her. "Come on, Baby-girl. Show Daddy how you can walk."

"She doesn't really walk. She runs full force into things."

Kenny laughed, stood, and the toddler reached up for him. He swept her up over his head and she squealed in delight. Kenny let her down and held her fingertips above her head, steadying her as they walked around the small backyard of Lucy's east side house. Lucy looked on, arms crossed, body tense.

"She looks like you more and more, Lucy, what with those eyes." Kenny passed the girl into Lucy's arms and they headed into the house.

"You're lucky to find us home today. I was just getting ready to take her to the park."

"Glad I didn't miss you."

"You could call." Lucy lowered the toddler into the playpen she had set up in the kitchen.

"Well, the boss gave me a ride from the ferry. Spring breakup."

"Are you going to stay awhile?"

"Of course. I missed my best girls." Kenny wrapped his arms around Lucy and kissed her on the top of her head. "Did you still want to go to the park?"

"Kendra loves it when I feed the squirrels. She just laughs and laughs. You should see her."

"Well, let's go, then." Kenny sat at the kitchen table and watched Lucy get the baby ready, putting together snacks for both them and the squirrels. He was certain he would stay this time. Find work around the city somewhere and just be here with his wife and daughter. It was like this, every time.

"Okay." Lucy scooped up the baby and Kenny carried the stroller down the front step. Juggling the baby, the diaper bag and her purse, she knelt to put the baby in the stroller.

Kenny felt overwhelmed by his affection for them. "Let's get married, Lucy."

Lucy looked up at him, smiling and shaking her head. "Really?"

"Yeah. Really."

The threesome headed down the sidewalk toward the park, Kenny pushing the stroller, Lucy with her arm through his.

"You gonna stick around this time, then?"

"Why not? Other people do it. I can find some kinda job."

"You've taken good care of us, Kenny. I'm thankful I could take time off to be with her."

"Well, don't want strangers raising our baby." He wondered if she was thinking of the Mission too. "I'll get work. We can do it."

Lucy snuggled in closer. "You know she is getting older now. She is going to start wondering who you are. She is not going to be hurt because we can't get our shit together. I won't have it."

Kendra was swinging her legs, the leather heels of her shoes bouncing against the stroller. Her little singsong voice chimed into the conversation. "Dada, Dada."

"You see! She is going to start learning what a daddy is, and where will you be? Either you're her dad or you're not. You can't just drop in when it works for you."

"I haven't had a drink in over a week now. You know I love you."

"Yes. I do know that. But you know how you are, always on the move. That is just not good enough anymore. Either you're her dad for real or you're not. Simple as that."

"I can change. You'll see."

The three spent the rest of the afternoon lazing in the dappled shade of the giant horse chestnut tree that dominated the small neighbourhood park. Kenny fed Kendra her afternoon snack while Lucy sailed higher and higher on the swing, much to the amazement of her daughter. At the high end of her arc she jumped from the swing, landing squarely in the pea gravel. She took a sweeping bow and then flopped back down on the blanket and kissed Kenny on the cheek.

"It's better when you're here."

"We can do this, Lucy. I know we can."

"Let's go. Look at those clouds rolling in. I think it's going to rain." They hustled their way back to the house.

"Well, I smell like a lumberjack, so I'm gonna have a bath."

Lucy bundled a now-sleeping Kendra into her crib in the back bedroom. "Go ahead. You know where the towels are."

Kenny smiled, listening to Lucy rustling around the kitchen. By the time the water in the tub was cooling, good smells were wafting in. It had been a long time since he'd had a home-cooked meal.

The next morning, Lucy poured Kenny a steaming mug of coffee as he held Kendra on his lap and fed her. It seemed like more of the puréed peaches and baby cereal was sticking to her chubby cheeks than finding its way to her stomach.

Kenny looked up at Lucy. "Okay, you better take over, woman. I gotta get ready."

Lucy lifted the baby from his lap. "Where you off to?"

He could hear the tension in her voice. "Work, my girl. Gotta find some work if we're gonna raise this girl right. Who knows, maybe we should get to work on another one. Maybe a little brother?"

Lucy laughed and blushed. "Now don't get carried away. Job first. Then we'll see."

Kenny could tell she liked the idea of a couple of kids rolling around the backyard. "Okay, woman. Job first, baby next." He slapped her butt and hugged her from behind, kissing her on the neck. Then, barely a whisper in her ear, "I love you, woman."

Lucy turned and looked up at him. "I love you too, man."

That evening, Kenny returned, his work clothes dusty and his hands dirty.

Lucy met him at the kitchen door. "Well, that looks promising," she said, pointing at his dirty clothes.

"Yep, got on with a construction crew. Building houses. Under the table for now, but the boss says if I do good, he'll put me on permanent." Kenny reached into his jacket pocket and pulled out a wad of bills. "Cash money. Can't complain about that." He tucked the money into Lucy's hand. "I'll always take care of you."

Lucy smiled and turned as the baby started wailing from the back room. "This is a happier house when you're here."

Kenny smiled all through washing-up and dinner, and over the next few weeks he happily settled into a home life he'd only ever dreamed of. It seemed easier this time. It was just a matter of days when he was home last before those restless urges were on him. It was not for a lack of love, but something inside him that drove him, something he could never explain to Lucy, much less himself. A pressure that only eased up if he was on the move. But this time, things were going well. The foreman put him on the books after only a week, telling him what a hard worker he was. He was always on time, and never showed up drunk.

Kendra seemed to grow every day, calling out for "Daddy" and toddling toward the door as fast as her tiny legs would take her when he came home from work. Kenny always picked her up, swung her over his head and gave her a kiss when he came through the door. It was their summer of love.

They spent Kenny's days off at the beach or the neighbourhood park. Sometimes they would take the bus to North Van and walk the suspension bridge just so Kenny could laugh at Lucy as she inched her way across the swaying span, Kenny carrying the baby so she could hang on with both hands. So it was a surprise to him when fall came and that old restless urge returned.

"What are you doing up so early?" Lucy walked into the kitchen, bleary-eyed. "Thought you'd sleep in a little. It's your last day off."

"Couldn't sleep." Kenny sat at the table and gazed out the window.

"You're leaving, aren't you." Lucy sat down with him.

"No, no. I'm not leaving. Just had a rough night. Those dreams again."

Lucy put her hand on his. "Well, I've been doing some thinking."

Kenny looked at her, the fatigue clear on his face. "And?"

"Well, things are going pretty good here, don't you think?"

"They sure are." Kenny leaned in for a kiss.

"Okay. Then I say yes. Let's drop by City Hall today and do the paperwork. Make some plans."

Kenny jumped up from his chair and lifted Lucy out of hers. "All right! Never thought I'd see the day." He kissed her and held her, the restlessness now barely a hum in the back of his mind.

They bundled Kendra up and headed for City Hall, laughing and teasing all the way on the Broadway bus, Kenny not even minding the crowds that usually prompted him to walk everywhere rather than be sandwiched in with all those strangers.

They told Clara the next day. She bit her lip for the briefest moment and then hugged and congratulated them both.

Lucy smiled at her. "I'm going to need a new dress. You tell Liz. Let's make one."

Clara nodded.

Kenny caught the fiercest look Clara had ever given him while Lucy wasn't looking.

They took their vows in early fall, with Clara and Liz standing as witnesses and Kendra in her stroller, pulling petals off her matching bouquet. They all went out for Chinese food after. Having to work in the morning, Liz volunteered to babysit Kendra so the rest of them could go out dancing. They all ended the night flat on their backs in Queen Elizabeth Park, counting falling stars.

The following Monday morning, Kenny awoke before Kendra and Lucy and, as quietly as possible, slipped into the kitchen and put together the best breakfast he could make. He brought Lucy coffee in bed to entice her to the table, and plopped Kendra in her high chair with her breakfast in front of her.

"Well, we should get married more often," Lucy said as she wandered into the kitchen and sat at her place at the table. Kenny put a plate of food in front of her and sat down with his own. They took turns feeding mouthfuls to Kendra and laughed about the fun they'd had dancing and playing in the park after the wedding. No one would have guessed that the old restlessness was so loud in Kenny that he could barely hear the baby coo or Lucy laugh.

Kenny pulled on his workboots, grabbed his jacket and turned to look at his girls. He leaned in and held Lucy close, turned and walked out the door.

Back in the logging camps on the island, Kenny eased comfortably into his customary solitude. The painful restlessness faded. It hurt to think of Lucy, waiting on him into the night, his departure slowly dawning on her. He tried not to think of her and Kendra. Even he didn't understand why he could only take so much, why he had to be alone. It was a long winter in the logging camp. He didn't dare write her, but he did send her most of his pay and left a general delivery address for whichever tiny town his camp was near. He stopped checking the mail after a few trips came up empty. But one day the postmistress stuck her head out the door of the post office.

"Hello! Hey! You there. I've been trying to track you down. There is a special delivery letter here for you." She waved him into the post office. "You have to sign for it."

Kenny signed the form and she handed over the small white envelope. "You should check your mail more often." Something about the way she looked over her glasses made him think of Sister Mary.

He shuddered as he opened the letter and read Clara's spidery scrawl. *Lucy is in the hospital with bronchitis and strep throat. Her fever was so high she almost died. She didn't want to leave Kendra alone. Get over here and take care of your girls.*

Kenny ran all the way back to camp, grabbed his gear and ran for the foreman's shack. "Boss, I'm sorry, but I have to head back to the Mainland. Need to get paid out today."

"That can be arranged. When will you be back? Everything okay?"

"Uh, family problem. My wife . . ."

"Didn't even know you were married!"

Kenny finished out the day, distracted and silent. Then he headed to the foreman's trailer to pick up his pay.

"I'm giving you a pink slip, but you be sure to come back. You're my best chokerman." The foreman handed over the envelope. "You need a ride to the ferry? I'm headed that way."

"Thanks, man. That would be great."

The two men drove for fifteen minutes along the muddy, precarious logging road to the main highway. Ancient cedars lined the road, which cut through virgin lands for the express purpose of harvesting the huge Douglas firs to feed the pulp mills of Port Alice, Port Mellon and Ocean Falls. The road wove along an almost-vertical precipice on one side, with dense forest on the other. No matter how many times Kenny had seen just how wide the road was, he still held his breath on the ride down to the landing.

It was another hour before the foreman dropped him at the ferry. He regaled Kenny with the birth stories of each of his six children, the travails of marriage and his wife's constant demands for a bigger house. But his voice was just sound to Kenny, whose mind was racing, thinking of Lucy, sick and alone with the baby.

"Well, take care. You got a job with me any time."

Kenny nodded his thanks, grabbed his duffle bag out of the truck box and headed to the ticket kiosk. Once aboard, he settled into a seat next to a window and pulled Clara's letter out of his jacket pocket, the words seeming to scream out at him. The ferry whistle blew, and Kenny wondered what the hell was wrong with him.

It was late when he finally walked up the familiar path on Frances Street, the outside light like a beacon. He had a hard time remembering why it seemed he had to leave the last time. He tried the door, but it was locked. He knocked softly, sure that Kendra would be sleeping. The curtain lifted slightly, and he could hear the deadbolt turning. The door opened and it was Clara, glaring at him, hands on her hips.

"Well, well. Look what the cat dragged in."

Her eyes were so hot with anger he couldn't look at her. "Is she home yet?"

Not moving out of the doorway, Clara replied, "No. They're still keeping her at St. Paul's."

"Kendra?"

"She's sleeping, of course, and you're not going to wake her."

"Aw, for fuck's sakes, Clara, move. Of course I'm not gonna wake her up." Kenny sidled past Clara into the kitchen, took his boots off and headed for Kendra's room. Clara moved to follow. "Back off, Clara. She's mine and I will see her."

Clara sat down at the kitchen table and lit a smoke, muttering under her breath, "Asshole."

Kenny walked softly into the baby's room and stood at her crib. She lay there pudgy and brown, her dark hair longer than he remembered. He stood there for a long time before returning to the kitchen. "Thank you, Clara. I know you're pissed. But thank you for taking care of her."

"I've missed four days of work thanks to you."

Kenny reached into his pocket and fumbled with some bills.

"I don't want your fucking money. Money doesn't make it okay. Not this. Not you runnin' out, either. Why are you such a chicken-shit?"

"I'm going to bed." Kenny rose and headed toward Lucy's room. "I'm sleeping in there."

He headed for Kendra's room instead. Rolling up his jacket for a pillow, he curled up on the floor.

The next morning, he woke first after hearing Kendra talking to herself and then saw her delight when she saw him there.

"Daddy! Daddy!" Kendra clung to the railing of her crib and bounced from chubby foot to foot. "Daddy!"

Kenny rolled over, stiff from his night on the floor. "Baby-girl." He stood and picked her up and snuggled her close. The smell of coffee from the kitchen warned him that Clara was up.

He carried the baby into the kitchen and placed her in the play-pen. "You can go to work if you want, Clara. I'll take care of her."

"No, I took the whole week off. You go see Lucy. You guys gotta figure this out."

Kenny looked away and started opening Lucy's painfully orderly cupboards. He mixed Kendra's breakfast, plopped her in the high chair and started to feed her. Kendra refused the spoon and beat her fists on the high chair tray.

Clara sat down with her coffee. "She feeds herself now. Insists on it."

Kenny handed the baby the spoon and watched with amazement as she fed herself, actually getting most of the cereal in her mouth. "Well, look at you." He ran his fingers through her downy hair.

"How much more you gonna miss? Next thing you know she'll be a teenager."

Kenny poured himself a coffee, downed it in three fast gulps and reached for his jacket. "Give it a rest, Clara." He kissed Kendra, wiped the Pablum from his face and headed for the door. "I'll be back when visiting hours are over."

He stopped at a corner grocery about a block from St. Paul's and picked out a small bouquet of bright flowers. He held them awkwardly as he stood at reception, getting directions before taking the elevator to Lucy's floor. She was sleeping, quiet and small, when he entered the room. He found a vase under the sink and set the flowers next to her. A little colour. She would like that. It wasn't long before she opened her eyes and saw him sitting next to her bed. She shook her head and rolled over, away from him.

"Are you feeling better?"

Lucy didn't reply.

"I'm sorry, Lucy. Really I am." Kenny sat there in the silence for what seemed like forever. The nurse came in and took Lucy's vitals. She didn't say anything to Kenny either, chatting busily with Lucy about how much better her temperature was. An aide eventually brought Lucy's lunch tray and set it on the wheeled table. The aide left and Kenny stood to remove the cover from her meal. "Come on, Lucy. You need to eat to build up your strength."

Finally, she spoke. "I'm not hungry."

Kenny was shocked at her hoarse, gravelly voice. "There's ice cream. It will help your throat."

"So now you're all worried?" She started coughing so hard she had to sit up, gasping for air. Not knowing what to do, Kenny handed her a glass of ice water. She drank and it eased her coughing. "How's the baby?"

"She's beautiful."

"Thank God for Clara."

Kenny lowered his eyes. "Yes. I'm sorry."

Lucy sighed. "You really are a sorry excuse . . ."

"Go ahead, say it."

"What's the point?"

Kenny took her hand. "I don't know why I'm this way. I love you more than anything on earth, but I just . . . I just don't . . . Oh, I don't even know how to explain it."

"One day, mark my words, you will have to explain it to that girl."

Kenny laid his head on the bed. Lucy put her hand on his head and closed her eyes.

The hospital discharged Lucy a week later with a stern warning about not letting things go so far without seeing a doctor. Kenny ordered a taxi to take her home. Kendra squealed with delight when they came home, raising her arms for her mother. Clara gathered her things, looked at Lucy and headed for the door.

"Okay, I'm outta here. You know, that little one, she needs both of you. Figure it out." Clara closed the door behind her.

The days passed, the past unspoken between them. Lucy got stronger every day and Kenny took care of Kendra, making sure Lucy got enough rest. Within a week Lucy was herself again, with no trace of the harsh cough and her energy restored. One morning the three of them sat at the breakfast table. Lucy opened the newspaper, casually turning the pages as though suddenly interested in the workings of city hall.

"You should go back to work." She turned the page.

Kenny turned to her. "What?"

Lucy looked up from the paper. "Maybe if you go before you want to go, you'll come home sooner. I don't understand why you don't want to be with us, but I can feel it sometimes. Like something's pushing you out the door. I guess I can't change that."

"I don't know what to say."

That night, for the first time since Kenny's return, they slept in the same bed, arms wrapped around each other. The next day, they took Kendra to their favourite park and played the day away. Kenny splurged on Chinese food delivery for dinner. They read each other's fortune cookies and laughed.

The next morning, Kenny rose before the baby woke and put his things together. He tiptoed into her room and kissed her on the forehead, closed her door quietly and walked out into the early morning mist.

12

CLARA

They stopped in Hope for burgers after the long drive across the Prairies, through the Rockies and into the rainforest. John Lennon was more than ready for a romp, so they sent George for takeout and Vera and Clara stretched their legs in a riverside park, eventually flopping under a giant cedar tree while John Lennon sniffed and ran, checking out the scents other visitors to the park had left behind.

It wasn't long before George showed up, and the women, ravenous now, rummaged through, looking for their burgers. Clara took a long draw on her root beer, her first soda since leaving Mariah's, and the bubbly fizz tickled her nose. There had been no such thing at Mariah's over the winter, and the soft drink, while a staple in the past, now seemed sickly sweet and foreign. She handed hers to Vera.

"You don't want it?"

"Naw, it's kinda gross."

Vera laughed. "You've turned into a real bush Indian."

"Yeah, I could go for some of Mariah's bannock and rabbit soup right about now." Clara's hand instinctively reached for the medicine bag Mariah had placed around her neck that first time she went into the lodge with her. "I miss her. Everything seems so fast out here in the world."

George put his arm around her. "I know. Me and Vera feel like we are moving in slow motion in a high-speed world when we even spend a weekend with her. Must be wild for you after a whole winter there."

Clara rested her head momentarily on his shoulder. "Man, we been through a lot together, haven't we?"

A peaceful air fell over the trio as they watched John Lennon winding down, making his way back to Clara with his half-sideways long-legged lope. He flopped in front of Clara and nudged her hand.

"Bossy." Clara obliged, running her fingers through his coat. "You too, old man. We've been through a lot." John Lennon huffed.

George sat with his back against the trunk of the tree and Vera lay, her head in his lap, gazing up through the gnarled branches of the old cedar. "I wonder how old this tree is. Imagine all the things it's seen. Maybe it was here even before white people."

Clara turned to George. "Do you still go to the Friendship Centre when you're in town? What's new there?"

"Oh, same old same old. Still helping people. Lots of people from the Indian Schools finding their way to the city."

"I don't know what I'm gonna do when I get there. I sure as hell ain't going back to the Manitou, and I don't want any trouble with the law—no more black market. Who knows if there ain't some warrant floating around after that run across the border?"

Vera stirred first. "Well, I guess we better get moving."

George gathered up the fast-food containers and dropped them in the garbage. "Don't worry, Clara. You'll figure it out. You always do."

Clara shrugged and settled John Lennon into his crate in the back of the truck. "Yeah, I'm not worried. I've got some heavyweights in my corner."

George smiled and slid into the driver's seat, Vera and Clara next to him. "Good thing you're skinny," Clara said to Vera. Laughter filled the cab as they found their way back to the freeway. As George drove, Vera sang along with the radio and Clara fell asleep, her head falling against Vera's shoulder.

A golden light rolled across the sky and over the buildings as the truck approached the city limits. Vera shifted in her seat. "Clara, we're here."

Clara roused herself and stretched. The city seemed so familiar and yet so strange. It was as though she was looking at it with different eyes. George took the Hastings Street exit, the Carnegie Centre rising, stately, above the chaos of the streets. They cruised by the Manitou and Clara shook her head, that thug of a place gearing up for another night. George headed east again and stopped in front of the Frances Street house. George helped Clara unload her few things and took John Lennon's crate into the backyard.

Clara and Vera embraced on the curb. "You want to come in?"

"Naw. You have your reunion. I bet that baby is runnin' around by now."

Clara hugged her again. "Thank you. I'll see you at the Centre in a couple of days."

"Yeah, George is giving a talk this weekend. See you then."

Clara waved from the curbside until she couldn't see the tail lights, then turned toward the house, lamplight, warm and inviting, shining through the drawn curtains. John Lennon nuzzled her hand with his nose, and they headed up the stairs and into the porch. Clara knocked softly just in case the baby was sleeping. Lucy peeked through the curtain, an unmistakable look of delight washing over her face as she pulled the door open and threw her arms around Clara.

"Thank God! I've been waiting all day. I didn't know when to expect you!" Just as Lucy let go of Clara, the baby crawled around the corner, climbed to a standing position, clinging to her mom's leg, and peeked up at Clara from behind Lucy's bell-bottoms.

"Holy, she's grown!" Clara settled John Lennon in the corner and swooped in on Kendra, holding her high in the air and then snuggling her close.

"Well, six months in a baby's life is like forever. She's into everything these days. The pots and pans keep her busy, though."

Clara laughed looking at the blanket laid out in the middle of the kitchen floor with an assortment of pots and pans, wooden spoons and plastic containers strewn about. "I bet they do." Clara wandered through the rooms of the house. "Lucy, the place looks great."

"Kenny was here for a while. He bought the armchairs and a new kitchen table. Well, new to us, anyway."

Clara stiffened. "That jerk."

"Ease up, Clara. He did right by us. He absolutely dotes over Kendra."

"Yeah, sure. Until he takes off again."

"Well, just never mind that. Come on. You want tea? Are you hungry?"

"Tea sounds great."

The two women sat at the kitchen table drinking tea and catching up. Kendra eventually started fussing, and after a quick bath and a cuddle, Lucy placed the sleeping baby in her crib.

"I can't believe how big she's grown. And she's calling you Mama. So cool."

"Yeah, sometimes I feel like I can actually see her growing, it's happening so fast."

Clara laughed and poured the last of the tea. "Welfare still sending my half of the rent?"

"Yeah, no one ever asks any questions. So, what now? You going to hook up with the fishermen again?"

"Naw, I think I'm done with that. Gonna see what's happening at the Friendship Centre. Try to find some work of some kind."

"I hear Harlan's still at the Manitou. Bet he'd give you your old job back." Lucy laughed behind her hand.

Clara burst out laughing. "Yeah. Like that's gonna happen."

The two women talked late into the night, reminiscing and making plans. Lucy rose first and headed for bed, warning Clara that the baby knew how to climb out of her crib and not to be surprised if she crawled into bed with her in the dawn hours. Clara yawned and smiled at the idea.

The next morning, the two women rose early with the baby, packed her bag and stroller, made a picnic lunch, and headed for the neighbourhood park to let the baby wander and explore while they continued to talk about the past and schemed about the future.

On Saturday morning, Clara was antsy to head to the Friendship Centre to help George with his presentation. She caught the bus and jumped off a few blocks early just to wander down Fourth Avenue for a few minutes, mingling among the hippies and street vendors, the musky smell of marijuana floating by from time to time. She turned down Vine Street and her heart swelled with the familiar sight of the Indian Centre, its doors wide open, welcoming all for a chat, some advice, a good bowl of soup, or political organizing. If anyplace was home, this was it.

She saw George sitting on the lawn outside, rifling through a sheaf of papers and handbills. She crossed the street so he wouldn't see her coming and at the last minute leapt in front of him.

"Boo!"

George jumped and burst out laughing. "You crazy woman."

"You all ready?"

"Just about. I'll meet you in there."

"Cool. I'm going to go see who's around."

Clara wandered into the building, the smell of sage and sweet-grass a welcome scent. Visiting around, she had a coffee and read the posters and notices on the bulletin board, each one a story of what was going on in the city for Indians. One in particular caught her eye. The bold heading read: ARE YOU IN TROUBLE WITH THE LAW? Clara pulled the thumbtack out of the poster and took it to her table to read. The poster was for the Native Courtworkers' Society. Clara read on. It described how Native workers would go to court with you and would speak for you and help you so that you didn't go to jail just because you were an Indian. Clara borrowed a pen and wrote down the phone number from the poster and then returned it to the board. She saw George coming in from outside and the men gravitating toward the big drum. She leaned back in her chair and closed her eyes, the voices filling her and reminding her of the lodge.

Monday morning, Clara made a call, and by Wednesday she had an appointment with one of the Courtworkers, Rose. They met outside the courthouse and talked about what it took to become a Courtworker. Clara applied within the week, and three weeks later she was in the six-month training program that would certify her. Part of her training was to observe seasoned Courtworkers speak for Indians who'd been charged and didn't have lawyers. Clara watched Rose every day for a week. During the breaks, the two would head to Chinatown for lunch and, over hot and spicy soup, Clara would pester Rose.

"But I don't get it. Why are you so nice to those bastards? That judge today—what an asshole, looking down his nose at that guy. Geez."

"Clara, get it through your head: your job is not to change the world. Leave that to the politicians. Your job is to keep Indians out of jail."

"How can you take that shit? Kissing ass so they do what they're supposed to do in the first place?"

"That guy today can come and visit me for the next six months and go home to his kids every night. Ask him if he would rather be locked up in Oakalla. Ask him if he cares if I talked nice to the judge." Rose was standing in the middle of the café, her face red and her breath short.

"Aw, sit down!" Clara pulled her arm lightly. "Okay, I get it."

"But seriously, Clara, it's a big deal. It took a lot of talk and a lot of work to get this program up and running. The last thing we need is complaints from the courts that our Courtworkers are a bunch of big-mouth rabble-rousers."

Over the next few months, Clara bit her tongue, listened and watched. She thought of what it was like to lose your freedom. She thought of her helplessness at the Mission and being under the thumb of Harlan and the city cops. She met with court staff, judges and prosecutors during her training and hung on their every word, gleaning everything she could. It wasn't easy to say the words that all of them needed to hear, but Rose was right. This was about those people standing helpless before the law, often for just trying to get by in a world they'd been abandoned to, entirely unprepared.

Lucy was back to nursing now, part-time, and in her spare time, usually when the baby was asleep, she helped Clara study. Clara struggled with some of the words in her reading assignments. At the Mission, her education was no more than darning socks, cleaning and doing endless loads of laundry. But between her and Lucy, they managed, and Clara wasn't shy about asking Rose for help too.

The night before her exam, Clara paced the kitchen, unable to even think of sleep. The baby was sleeping and Lucy, sipping her tea, beckoned Clara to join her.

"Come on, Clara, relax."

"Easy for you to say." Clara pulled up a chair and nervously shuffled an old, worn deck of cards left there from their last game of gin rummy.

"You know your stuff. You'll do just fine."

"I don't know about that."

"Sure you do."

Clara didn't sleep a wink that night and was the first one to show up at the testing room. She sat alone for a good fifteen minutes before the others trickled in. A woman sent to oversee the exam arrived exactly ten minutes in advance of the start time, gave strict instructions and handed out the exam face down on the tables in front of the students. Clara's heart was pounding as she watched the seconds tick away on the big black-and-white clock on the wall.

"Begin!"

Clara flipped her paper over and panic set in as she read the first question and had no clue what the answer was. She kept reading, deep confusion setting in. Halfway down the page she read question five and could almost breathe again. This one she knew. She wrote her answer furiously and returned to the test sheet, looking for something she felt certain about. In the end, she left three questions unanswered, but passed nonetheless.

Three months went by before she was offered work. She did odd jobs, contributing what she could, and minded Kendra when Lucy worked. The two became inseparable, and Kendra cried loud and hard when Lucy or Clara took her to a sitter on days when they both had to work.

Clara pried Kendra's little fingers from around her neck, gave her a quick squeeze, and assured her she would have fun and they would all be home again before she knew it. Kendra sobbed as though the world was ending. One of the Friendship Centre regulars was watching Kendra for them, and she shooed Clara off on her first day, assuring her Kendra would be laughing and playing as soon as Clara was out of sight. Clara quickly left, closing the front-yard gate behind her, and ran for the bus.

Later that night, with the dinner dishes washed and Kendra in bed, Clara told Lucy about her first case. The guy, not much more than a kid, had been caught stealing apples from a corner grocery. Clara leaned back in her chair. "He'd just been let out of Indian School, up north somewhere. They kept him until he was eighteen, then put him on a bus to the city."

Lucy shook her head. "Those people. What was he supposed to do? Starve?"

"Yeah, that's what I said. The judge didn't like it much, but I tried to explain he just didn't know what else to do and had nowhere to go."

"Like us. Just thrown away."

John Lennon stirred from his bed in the corner and sidled up to Clara. She scratched behind his ears. He pressed against her.

"Well, at least he's not in jail tonight, and he's coming to the Centre tomorrow. We're going to try to find him a job. At least he'll have one meal a day until then."

Lucy yawned, stood, planted a soft kiss on Clara's head. "Keep fighting, woman."

John Lennon headed back to his bed, Lucy to hers, and Clara took a pad of paper off the bookshelf and sat down with her pen.

Dear Mariah . . .

13

HOWIE

Howie squirmed a little in his chair. "Hey, do you think you could call me Howie instead of Brocket? I know I told you to call me Brocket before."

Clara nodded. "Sure, why not?"

"It's just that no one's called me Howie since my mom died." He looked intently at his hands. "It's like my own name takes me back to that place, a little boy at Brother's mercy. It's like a part of me died, or I *will* die, if I let myself think about it."

Six months had passed since Howie had stood before the judge, ashamed and full of self-loathing. Thanks to Clara's intervention, he had not been sentenced to jail time, but instead received counselling from her once a week for six months. Today was his last appointment. The two had become close, with a shared history that at first they didn't know they had. Once she got him talking, he told her about the Mission and was amazed when she confided to him that she had been there too.

"You were at the Mission? The one across Arrowhead Bay?" He wasn't completely surprised that they never met at the school, what with boys not allowed to talk to girls, their lives segregated in every respect.

"Yeah, I was there for ten years before they let me go."

They couldn't look at each other, thinking of that place, the air heavy, the silence awkward.

Changing the subject, Howie looked at her, a slow smile spreading across his face. "So, this is our last date, Clara."

"Think you can stay out of trouble?"

"Yeah. Thanks to you. I don't think I could have found a job without your help. My head was still in prison. I was feeling desperate when I really didn't need to."

Clara looked up at him. "Man, we're free. Let's keep it that way. We've spent too much of our lives with other people running them."

"Thank you, Clara. Without you, I'd probably be back in lock-up."

They walked to the front door together and stood there a moment, neither knowing what to say. Clara reached up to put her hand on his shoulder. He reached in to hug her just as she turned to leave, and they ended up bumping noses instead. They laughed, and Howie walked out the door, free again.

He walked down Vine Street toward the ocean, thinking of Clara at the Mission and not wanting to imagine what might have happened to her there. Other than the fact that he'd been there and his hints about Brother, they'd never talked about his time there. Neither had she volunteered any details. He hoped she'd escaped the worst of it. He sat down on a log and watched the giant ships anchored in English Bay, sailboats flitting around them like colourful butterflies.

The next day, after work, Howie made his way back to the Friendship Centre on Vine Street where Clara worked. She was making herself a cup of tea, the tea bag held suspended above the cup, a look of surprise on her face to see him walking through the door. The look of surprise quickly turned to concern.

"Everything okay?"

"Yeah, sure." He pulled a small bouquet of flowers from behind his back that he'd selected from a Fourth Avenue grocery, and smiled. "Well, I'm not required to see you anymore, but I sure would like to." He handed her the flowers. "Would you like to have a meal with me after work?"

Clara laughed nervously. "Well, sure, why not. I just have a few things to finish up here." She finally let the tea bag drop into the cup. "And I'd like to go home first."

"Okay. Well, why not meet me at the Only. It's pretty close to your place, isn't it?"

"Best soup ever. See you there. Six okay?"

"Six it is." Howie left, smiling at the sight of her with tea in one hand, flowers in the other, and a slightly puzzled look on her face.

She looked so pretty that night as she walked into the Only. Her long black hair was neatly braided, her work clothes replaced with jeans and a peasant blouse under a thick knitted sweater. He smiled and waved. She slid into the booth across from him and smiled back. "Made it."

"Yeah, looks like we did."

They ordered and talked about the deep chill in the air, so unusual for the city, how Howie's job was going, how Clara came to work at the Friendship Centre, and finally they spoke of the Mission. The fact that this was a personal conversation, not one ordered by the court, freed them both, and an air of relaxation settled around them.

"What I don't understand is how you, a Cree, ended up in a school on the BC coast."

Howie gazed out the window onto East Hastings. "That, my friend, is a long story."

Clara reached out for his hand. "I'm all ears."

Howie took a long draw of tea, settled into his chair and started in.

The summer my mother and I took the train out west was the best summer of my life. I was five years old, almost six. It was my first train ride, and in the weeks prior to our departure I pestered my poor mother to death with questions: Where will we sleep? Will we have to take food? How long will it take to get there? What if I have to pee? My mother took it in stride as she always did, answering the same questions over and over again, steadying me on the kitchen chair when I wanted to mark the days off on the calendar, tucking me in numerous times a night when I couldn't sleep for the excitement.

We were going to see my mother's sister, Mae. My mother had never been out of Saskatchewan and rarely left the reserve. She didn't need to be anywhere else. That was her home, and the home of her parents and grandparents back to when Treaty Six was signed by her great-grandfather, Pihew-kamihkosit, for whom our Red Pheasant reserve was named. The same couldn't be said for her sister. Mae had married a *mooniaw*, and her red-headed husband took her a thousand miles away to a logging town on the central coast of British Columbia. Auntie Mae was often alone while her husband was away for long stretches in the logging camps. Lonely for her sister and her language, she'd talked her husband into sending my mom money for train tickets. We would spend the whole summer there, my last before I started school.

Fully clothed and ready to go, I was at the table at first light the morning of our departure.

My mother laughed, coming through the front door with an armful of poplar rounds for the wood cookstove. "Did you even sleep at all?"

"Is it time to go?" I could hardly sit still, I was so excited.

"Just calm down, *napaysis*. I want you to have a good, hot meal before we go. There won't be anything but bannock, berries and dry meat until we get there."

I loved it when she called me "little man" like that. She dropped the rounds in the woodbox and I opened the stove, setting the kindling just right and putting a match to it the way she'd shown me. I sat back at the table as she nursed the fire alive and set the porridge pot to boil on the cast iron stovetop. "Tell me again, Mom, what's an ocean?"

"Salty water as far as the eye can see. And the moon makes it move deeper and shallower along the shore."

"Really? How does it do that?"

"You will just have to wait and see."

I sat waiting for breakfast, my feet swinging under the table, my mind filled with huge lakes filling and emptying at the behest of a living moon.

After breakfast, we cleaned up and I showed her I had, in fact, made my bed. Then we closed up the house and sat on the front porch with our bags, waiting. My mother had scrubbed me the night before in the galvanized tub, heating the water on the cookstove. My Moshom, my grandfather, was to take us to the train and we didn't wait long before his ancient pickup truck turned into our approach. He stopped about twenty feet from the house to avoid sending a fine layer of dust over us and our best clothes. Moshom loaded up our bags in the back and we headed to town. I knelt on the seat, looking out the back window. For a moment my stomach knotted, and I wanted to stop the truck and go back. Maybe something in me knew that I might never see that house again.

I had never seen a mountain before and hid my face in my mom's neck when the train ran alongside steep cliffs, the raging waters below us. The dense forests left me short of breath and the craggy peaks seemed to be closing in on us. I sat, fascinated, unable to take my eyes off this strange world for very long as it sped by.

Auntie Mae met us when we arrived, the hissing and rollicking sound of the station punctuated by tearful laughter as my mom and Mae hugged each other. Mae cooed over how big I was as we walked through the small town to Mae's house.

The wonders of that train trip fell away as I explored Auntie Mae's house. Running water in her kitchen, electric lights and flush toilets. It was like a strange and exciting new world. She even had a TV. No one at Red Pheasant had a TV.

"Sagastis, he's flushing the toilet again." Auntie Mae laughed at my fascination with the swirling water. If I wasn't flushing the toilet, I was switching the lights on and off.

"My goodness, *napaysis!*" My mother gently pulled my hand from the switch.

"Is it magic?"

My mother laughed, shaking her head. "No, son, it's electricity."

"What's electricity?"

"Like lightning, but in wires."

My eyes widened, imagining lightning flashing in the wires behind Auntie Mae's walls. I sat down at the kitchen table, stunned. "Can I have a drink of water?"

"Howie," my auntie laughed, "you are not thirsty!" She knew. I just wanted to see the water pouring inside the kitchen. No outside water barrel here; no kerosene lamp. Better still, no trips to the outhouse in the middle of the night. At home those trips weren't so bad with the windbreak of caragana and black poplar around our house. Nothing like the huge, swaying cedars circling Mae's house. Their branches, like black wings and claws dancing on my walls at night, scared me as I lay there, certain some *wīhtikōw* was coming to get me.

The warm days of that long summer passed one into the other, and an air of easy satisfaction rolled over us like the tidewaters that were so close to Mae's house, we could see them through the kitchen window. Some part of almost every day was spent at the beach digging for clams and swimming, Mae and my mother chatting up a storm in Cree, me fascinated by exotic seaweeds, hermit crabs and the seagulls dropping molluscs on the rocks to get at the rich morsels within. I finally understood about the ocean when I saw my first high tide roll in under a rising full moon. Risking bears and bobcats, we hiked into dense bush for the reward of tart huckleberries, blueberries and salmonberries. As foreign as the sea and rainforest were, compared to rolling plains and arboreal forests, these were peaceful days. It didn't even bother me that the neighbour kids would have nothing to do with me. Mae told me their parents wouldn't have anything to do with her either, and somehow that just brought all three of us even closer.

The evenings were starting to cool off when my mother told me I only had four days to wait for my birthday. There was no one to invite to my birthday, so Mae and my mother went a little wild and made it into an extravaganza. They bought balloons and colourful banners all blue and green: *Happy Birthday Six-Year-Old!* and *It's Your Day, Birthday Boy!* The whole front of the house was covered in banners and ribbons. The living room was strung with yards and yards of crepe paper streamers, some scalloped around the windows and some criss-crossing the ceiling. Every vantage point boasted balloons, and the icing on the cake was the icing on the cake. I thought I might faint when Mae came out of the bedroom with a store-bought birthday cake. Never in my life had I tasted such a thing, much less had one myself.

"Stand next to Auntie and blow out those candles."

Poised with her Brownie, my mother snapped a picture.

"Mae, take one of us."

Those pictures survived for many years. One with my mother, her arms tight around me, smiling into the camera, me wide-eyed, pointing at the cake. Another with Mae standing behind me, hands on my shoulders, leaning over to put her cheek next to mine, both of us smiling, the wisps of smoke captured as they rose from the candles.

Mae gave me a squeeze. "Did you make a wish?"

I didn't tell her my wish, of course. I wanted it to come true, after all. But I wished that we three could stay like this forever, an endless summer of feeling so close and safe, playing at whatever struck us as a good idea. My birthday gifts might have been school clothes, but they were clothes for a schoolboy now. I was not a little kid anymore. I could see myself walking into school back home looking just like the big kids. Auntie Mae gave me some tiny cars in all different colours. We had a hot dog roast in the backyard for my birthday supper, and by the time we got to that cake, I was stuffed with hot dogs, candy, chips, even pop, which my mother never allowed. I was drunk with food and celebration.

As we were putting our little fire out, a priest ambled by down the laneway behind Mae's house. His black robes looked like a man's dress to me, and I tried not to laugh. I remembered passing the church on our walk from the train station and seeing him on the steps, chatting with a man who was fixing the screen door. Auntie Mae genuflected and bowed her head. My mother looked away.

"Hello, Father." Auntie Mae smiled, wrapping up the leftover marshmallows.

"Hello, Mae. And who is the birthday boy?" I was a little surprised when he tousled my hair.

"Oh, this is my sister's boy. You remember I told you they were coming to visit this summer."

"Oh, that's right. Well, how old are you today, son?"

"Six," I said, proud, but half hiding behind my mother.

"Quite the young man now." He turned to Auntie Mae and my mother. "Good evening, ladies."

"Good night, Father." My auntie Mae smiled. My mother shivered a little. We were not church people.

That spectacular birthday party stayed with me for days, partly thanks to the one piece of cake I was allowed daily from the copious leftovers of the slab Mae had splurged on. I was oblivious to every-thing but playing and being doted on by Auntie and my mother. That fleet of tiny cars kept me busy the rest of the summer, making net-works of sand roads and obstacles at the beach or in the front yard, Auntie's rock garden improvising as precarious mountain roads.

Mae cried as she helped my mother pack our things the night before we were to return home.

"Don't cry, Mae. *Ki sagahitin, niseem.*" Mother hugged her sister.

"I love you too, sister. Sagastis, I will miss you two so much."

"I'll make tea."

"Yes, tea always helps." Mae wiped her tears on her apron.

"*Tapwe chi.* It's true." My mother stood and put the kettle on.

"I'll make a good supper for you two to remember me by. Oh, I will miss you." She hugged me hard.

I fought back tears, unable to imagine our days without Auntie Mae. That evening I stood on a chair beside her at the kitchen sink and helped her wash the dishes while my mom was in the bedroom packing. She showed me how to rinse the glasses properly, so the water wouldn't taste soapy. I was just putting the last plate away when a loud knock on the door made us all jump. Auntie Mae looked at me with a question in her eyes and a shrug. Wiping her hands on her apron, she went to the front door. It was that same priest who had walked by my party. This time he was not alone. Beside him was an RCMP, who towered over my auntie.

My mother came down the hallway. "What's going on?"

"Mae," the priest said, "we're here to take the boy to school. He's six. It's the law."

"Father, the boy doesn't live here. He's going home with his mother tomorrow."

My mother stepped up, pressing my shoulder, signalling me to stand behind her. "We are going home tomorrow. He will go to school at Red Pheasant."

"Sorry, ma'am." The Mountie stepped forward. "He's here now, and how do I know you are going to take him to school? He's coming with us."

The priest gestured to the cop and he reached around Mom for me.

"No! No!" My mother backed me into a corner, shielding me with her body. "This is a mistake. He is going to school in Saskatchewan. Our school already has a place for him."

The cop stepped toward my mother. "Ma'am, just step out of the way."

"No. You can't take him!" My mother grabbed me and made a run for the back door, but then he was on her, pushing her away from me. She screamed as she fell. I ran for the back door, but he picked me up, threw me over his shoulder and walked with me out the door, my mother chasing him and screaming in Cree, my auntie pleading with the priest as he walked away toward the car. I watched my mother pounding at the cop. Her hands, capable and strong, looked so small against his huge back. He put me in the back seat of the car and the priest slid in alongside me, a wall between me and my mother.

The cop turned on her. "Do you want to go to jail? It's the law. I'm here to enforce the law. Now get in the house."

"Just let me hold him. Let me kiss him." My mother was sobbing, choking out the words.

"Get in the house or I'll arrest you." He slid behind the steering wheel, gunned the engine and drove away.

I wheeled around and watched out the rear window as my mother crumpled into a heap in the middle of the road, her face in her hands. Auntie was running after the car, yelling, "Where are you taking him? Where?"

The cop dropped the priest off at his church and carried on with me, his prisoner, in the back seat. I felt sick to my stomach from the crazy curving road. I had no idea where I was going or why the cop wouldn't listen to my mom.

"Where are we going?" The whirring of the tires on the pavement filled the void in the car. "Where is my mother?" The back seat smelled vaguely of puke. I kicked the back of his seat and yelled, "Take me back to my auntie's house! I want my mother!" I kicked the seat again and again. "I want my mom!"

The cop hit the brakes and pulled the car sharply to the side of the road, threw his door open and then mine. He leaned in, grabbed me by the shoulders and shook me. "Do you want something to cry about, you little shit? 'Cause I'll give it to you for sure. Now shut up. And if you kick that seat again, I will really give you something to cry about. You hear?"

"Yes." His holster at eye level, I thought I better quit. I closed my eyes and bit my bottom lip so I wouldn't cry.

The car finally came to a stop after what seemed like forever. The sun was closing in on the horizon and dusk was not far off. The cop stepped out of the car and walked me down to the dock, where a boat was tethered. When we got there, the cop lifted me onto the boat and a man dressed like the priest but in brown, not black, took me from the cop's hands and sat me on a seat in the middle of the boat along with the fifteen or so other kids who were sitting huddled together. Some were crying, most were just staring at the horizon.

They all looked to be my age, girls sitting on one side of the boat, boys on the other.

After sitting me down, the Brother turned to the cop. "Is that it?"

"Yep, that's the last one. Good luck." The cop turned and headed back to his cruiser and the boat engine roared to life.

I turned to the Brother. "Where are we going? I want to go home." This seemed to set the others off, and in a moment or two all of the children in the boat were crying.

"Now look what you've done. Sit down and mind your business." Brother gave me a shove and I sat back down hard on my seat.

By the time we reached our destination, the sun had set. Two nuns were waiting at the dock and Brother handed us over the side to them. One of them clapped her hands together. "Now children, form a line and stand still." She counted us by tapping each of us on the head and then stood facing the line. "All right, let's go."

We walked up the slope of a winding path. As we rounded the bend, a huge red-brick building with a massive steeple at the centre of its roof stood in front of us. Once again, the nun clapped her hands and we all stopped walking. "Children, this is your home now and you will obey like we are your parents."

Frightening as it all was, I felt strangely calm. I knew my mother and I knew she would not stand for this. She would come and get me. So I did as I was told. I was careful to never be first or last, never to speak out, never to cry no matter what. At night I would imagine a calendar in my head, just like the one at home, and counted imaginary days, waiting for my mom.

Fall slipped into winter and winter into spring, and as the months fell away, I began to think something must have happened to my mother. Maybe that cop went back and did put her in jail. There had to be some reason. By the time fall came around again, I was still turning pages in my imaginary calendar, but I wasn't sure why.

I had never once peed the bed at home, but on the first night at the Mission and every night thereafter, I wet the bed. I tried everything. I wouldn't drink all day after breakfast, until I was so parched I thought I would faint. I peed every night before I went to bed. I tried everything, but still, without fail, I would wake up to a cold, wet sheet. And each time, Sister Mary would strip the pissy sheet from my bed and wrap it around my head like a turban. She would walk me through the dorm that way, pointing me and the other offenders down to the laundry room, where we would be given a clean sheet. I always smelled slightly of piss and the kids teased me, called me Peepants and Pissy Face. And there were worse things. Things in the night that I tried never to think of, wiping things from my mind altogether. I just tried to stay out from under foot, to keep to myself, hoping to get through another day, day after day, month after month, year after year.

Kenny slept in the cot next to mine in the dorm and gave the kids hell if they teased me. I don't think I would have survived without him. I used to go hide in the thicket just off the school grounds, just to get a break from the constant fear. I was so hungry, I would eat grass. One time, Kenny startled me there. I thought it was Brother. He scared the shit out of me. I was so embarrassed, wiping the grass from my mouth.

"I thought you were Brother."

Kenny smiled. "Naw, it's just me. Don't eat the grass." He wiped the rest of the bits of grass off my face. "I know you're hungry, but there's something better. Come on. I'll show you."

That afternoon, we filled our bellies on the plants Kenny knew so well. "This is fireweed. Strip the outside. It's tender inside and you can really fill up on it. These curly fiddleheads are really good too. Wilfred and I save them up for when we can sneak away long enough for a fire."

"Kenny, I want my mother. I don't even know where she is. I'm gonna be nine this year. Why doesn't she come get me?"

"Even if she did, they would send her away, maybe even put her in jail."

I tried not to think of my mother in jail. Kenny and I ate and ate and filled our pockets with fiddleheads. Our bellies full for once, we wandered back to the school, long stalks of fireweed hanging from our lips.

The next day, I woke up in the hospital. I had no memory of being taken out of the dorm or the boat ride to the hospital at Orca Bay. The last thing I remembered was Brother coming for me again, lifting me out of my bed and taking me to his room. This time he beat me too. So hard the last thing I remember was falling to the floor in his room. My face was swollen and sore and my bum burned with pain. I pinched my split lip so the pain would make me forget other pains and things.

It felt strange to be away from the school and out from under the watch of Sister. The nurse was nice. She gave me candy, but all I could think of was home and my mom. The piney hills of Red Pheasant were starting to fade from my memory. I even wondered if I would remember my mother if I saw her. I tried not to cry, but I couldn't stop myself. I curled up in the bed, the pillowcase soon damp. The hospital room was warm compared with the drafty dorms at the school. So warm it overtook me, and I fell asleep.

I was roused by that nice nurse. "How are you feeling, Howie? A little better?"

I rubbed my puffy eyes, winced and nodded.

"There is someone here to see you. Are you up for a little visit?"

I nodded again, wondering who it might be. She must have seen the fear rise in my eyes, because she reached out and stroked my hand.

"I think you will enjoy this visit." She turned to leave the room, her crisp white uniform sounding a lot like Sister's habit, rustling as she moved.

I heard muffled voices just outside the door of my room and sat up in the bed, barely breathing, waiting. I heard the nurse's voice now.

"Be careful not to upset him, and you may only stay a short while. He needs to rest and heal."

I closed my eyes and waited until the voices were gone. When I opened them again, Auntie Mae was standing in the doorway. I tried to climb over the bed railings to get to her. She raised her hands to prevent me and ran to the bed, carefully putting her arms around me, holding me as close as she dared. I sobbed against her chest.

"Don't cry," she said, "it's almost over." She let go of me for a minute to look into my face, then wrapped her arms around me again. "Oh, Howie."

"Auntie!"

She held me tighter. We cried and cried.

"Where's my mother?" I looked around anxiously.

She caressed my bruised face, wiping my nose, patting my hair. "They won't let her see you. She has been raising hell, trying to get you back. But they won't agree. They told her she will go to jail if she keeps trying to get you out of that place."

"Where is she?" I couldn't stop crying. "I need my mom."

"Don't worry, sweetheart, she's here in Orca Bay. She's on your uncle Charlie's boat, waiting for me."

"Can I go with you?" Again I reached for the bed railing.

"No, Howie, you have to get better and then go back to the school. The nurses will call the police if we take you from here. But we have a plan. Can you get down to the dock at night?"

"Yes. Kenny knows how to get out at night to steal food. He'll help me."

"Okay, we will know when they take you back. I will be here to visit you every day. The same day that they take you back, come down to the dock once it is good and dark. Uncle Charlie, your mother and me have been boating around that bay. We know what the dock is like and we can get you, so long as you can get to the dock. We saw them bringing you down the dock and followed them here. The RCMP boat stopped us once last week, but your uncle Charlie convinced them we were just fishing and looking for salvage logs. They just wave and smile when they see us now."

For a week I recuperated, soaking in every minute of every visit with Auntie Mae. It was as though the time with her was more medicine than what the nurse brought me in a small paper cup. I sent messages through Mae to my mom, and my mom sent me tender messages, promising me we would see each other soon.

On the eighth day, just after Auntie's visit, they came for me and took me back to the school. He didn't have to, but Brother carried me up to the dorm, not looking at me as he put me to bed. It wasn't long before Kenny snuck in to see me. The sight of him made me cry. He, more than anyone, knew what I had suffered.

"It's okay, Howie. You're going to be all right."

"I know, Kenny, you too. But I need your help." I told him about Uncle Charlie's boat and the plan.

"Okay, I'll be back at bedtime. I gotta get back downstairs before they catch me up here."

I lay there all day, looking out the high windows. Sister brought me a tray of food at suppertime.

"Now don't be thinking this will go on. Tomorrow you will get back into the daily routine with the boys."

"Yes, Sister." The hospital food and the treats Auntie Mae brought me had spoiled me for the slop they called supper. After Sister left, I pushed the tray aside and lay down again, anxious for the bedtime bell to ring.

Soon the boys started trickling into the dorm after brushing their teeth. Even some of the mean kids came by my bed and told me they hoped I was better. Kenny came over and whispered, "Pretend to sleep. I'll get you when the coast is clear."

It seemed like forever, but finally everyone was asleep, and Kenny climbed out of bed and nudged my shoulder. We hurriedly dressed and I slipped into my boots. He walked me to the fire escape door, jimmied the lock as only he could and held it open for me, the red exit light casting an eerie tone, rendering our faces a pale orange. Outside, the moon hung heavy in the sky, round and full.

"Now go. I'll keep watch. If anyone comes, I'll slow them down if I can. Go fast, but not too fast. Watch your feet. Don't trip. Be quiet. Your boots will echo loud on the dock. Take them off when you get there."

I nodded and headed toward the stairs. I looked back at him, my friend.

"Go!" he whispered.

I stepped back, putting my hand on his shoulder. "Kenny."

"Just go before someone wakes up!"

I tiptoed down the fire escape, holding the railing tight, praying no one would see me, exposed as I was against the wall on the outside staircase. I walked under the cedars, close against the tight underbrush that lined the grounds. Fast and careful like Kenny said, I stopped just before I got to the opening of the trail to the dock and looked around. My heart sounded like a drum in my ears. I held my breath and listened. Nothing. It was dark and quiet, the moon casting enough light to help me on my way.

I ran down the path to the dock, and there it was at the end of the dock, no lights, no engine running, a boat. *Mother!* I ran. The hard plastic soles of my boots hit the dock with a noise sure to be ringing through the trees and into Brother's bedroom. I stopped so fast I almost lost my balance. My eyes never left that dark, brooding boat bobbing silent at the end of the dock. I crouched and removed my boots. Then I ran as fast as my feet would carry me, coming along-side the boat, looking for someone, a ladder, a stool, a way on board. A hand grabbed me and dragged me over the side. The engine roared to life. Taking the controls from my auntie Mae, my uncle Charlie handed me off to my mother below deck. We fell down the last two stairs, tumbling into each other's arms.

"*Napaysis, napaysis,* my little man!" My mother wept, holding me so tight I couldn't breathe.

We sped across the bay to a waiting car and a tight plan. My mother and I hugged Auntie Mae and hustled toward the unspectacular '61 Valiant that would run us to freedom. Mae pressed something into my palm and looked at me and my mother, her eyes filling up.

"You be a good boy now. Help your mom. We'll come see you as soon as we can." She kissed me and hugged me one last time.

"Charlie, how can I ever thank you?" My mother wiped her tears on her sleeve, throwing her arms around my uncle. "You're a good man."

"Sagastis, he is your boy. Only you have a right to him. Now go. They probably won't notice he's gone till morning, but you have a long trip and you want to be across the border before they sound the alarm. Call us collect when you get across the line."

"I will, Charlie. Come see us as soon as you can."

My mother opened the passenger door for me. Running to her side, she threw her purse on the floor in front of the passenger seat. She waved once more to Mae and Charlie, slammed her door shut and drove.

I opened my hand. It was a tiny red car. I slid across the bench seat, clutching that little car, and laid my head in my mother's lap. She drove, one hand on the wheel, one on my shoulder.

Throughout his story, Clara leaned over the table, straining to listen, Howie's voice quiet for fear other patrons would hear. She sighed deeply and rested back against the cushioned booth. "That fucking place."

"Do you think we will ever be free of it?"

"Remind me to tell you about Mariah."

"Tell me now." Howie leaned back, exhausted.

"Naw, maybe not." She motioned to the scowling waiters who'd interrupted them more than once, asking if there would be anything else. Since it was the best Chinese food place in town, a lineup was growing outside the door, a dozen or so people waiting for a table.

"Come on, I'll walk you home." Howie paid the bill and they walked out into the cold evening air. They were strangely silent on the short walk to Clara's place.

When they arrived, Clara smiled at him. "You want to come up for tea or something?"

Howie nodded and they walked up the two flights of stairs to her studio suite. He watched her as she put the kettle on, looking away when she looked to him sitting there at her kitchen table. She placed two cups of tea on the table and sat across from him.

"Remember I told you about my time in the States and how I got hurt?"

Howie nodded. "Yeah. Crazy times."

"Well, after I ran the border, they took me to the Old Woman." Clara sat back and crossed her arms. "Let me tell you about Mariah."

Howie smiled at her. "I got all night."

14

KENNY

>-------><-------<

Kenny awoke in a sweat, the ancient radiator rattling, gurgling and blazing heat. It might have been February in Saskatchewan or something, the way the heat was cranked. The sickly sweet smell of last night's whisky oozed from his pores. His pillow stank so bad that he had to get up, no matter how much his head swam and throbbed. Kenny staggered to the window, holding his head like it might explode at any minute, surprised to make it there in one piece. He threw the window open and it was an immediate, if incomplete, remedy. If nothing else, the late winter Vancouver air, dank and stinking of skid row pavement, was cool. He looked at the moving lump in his bed and realized it was someone, a female someone.

"Kenny?"

"Ah, yeah?"

"Come back to bed," the lump said, emerging from the covers. He had no idea who she was. She was pretty enough, slender shoulders barely under the sheet wrapped tightly around her. But nothing about her rang a bell.

"Uhh, sorry, but I have to go meet someone about some work."

Coy now, she smiled. "Well, can I take a shower first? Will you join me?"

"Go ahead, I gotta make a call." Kenny pulled on his jeans as she smiled over her shoulder at him on the way to the bathroom. Leaning over the sink in what passed for a kitchen in this dive, Kenny splashed cold water on his face and under his arms. The cold water shook some of the whisky from his aching head and he wondered how the hell to get rid of her. He grabbed his shirt off the floor and threw it back down. It smelled. He rummaged through the black garbage bag of clothes slumped in the corner and found a western shirt near the top, clean and barely wrinkled. Kenny threw it on, the only sound in the room other than the complaining radiator the *snap snap snap* as he did up the shirt.

Steamy and stark naked, the woman emerged from the shower. He still had no idea who she was, as she bore down on him like a vulture on roadkill. He squirmed away and headed for the door.

"Ah, sorry, I—"

"It's Louise," she said, all chilly now.

"Louise, I gotta go. Can't miss a chance for work these days."

"Yeah, whatever. Fuck you, Kenny."

Grabbing his jacket, Kenny turned to her. "Sorry, Louise. Really, I am. Just lock the door behind you." There was nothing worth stealing, but in this dump an unlocked door could mean a place to flop.

The three flights of stairs seemed endless. A dungeon, the walls and stairs painted black, with only the cheap metal handrail for relief. The white sky was almost blinding as he stepped out onto the street. Kenny headed to the Two Jays Café for hangover soup and coffee. The bell above the door jangled behind him as he took his place at the end of a long row of orange vinyl counter stools. Penny, the Sunday morning girl, slapped down the cardboard menu and filled the coffee cup in front of him, only spilling a little into the saucer.

"You want the usual?"

"Yeah, but give me a few minutes. Let this coffee work for a bit."

"Rough night?"

"You got today's paper?"

"Sure." She slid a few sections of the *Vancouver Sun* toward him along with a copy of the *Province*, thick from many reads.

Kenny downed the first cup like medicine. The second one went a little slower. His hands were less shaky now with the paper. After coffee, he scanned the pages, not really reading, more just looking at it, like a picture. He turned to page four and the headline was like a kick in the balls: FORMER STUDENTS SUE FEDERAL GOVERNMENT, CLAIM ABUSE. The hair on the back of his neck stood up and a rush of adrenalin pounded through his already-aching head.

Kenny stood and dropped some change on the counter. He tore the article from the paper and stuffed it in his pocket. "You mind?"

"Naw, go ahead. No soup?"

"Nah, not today."

Kenny walked fast to the corner and sat down hard on the bus stop bench, fighting to breathe as images of Brother flashed through his mind. He pulled the article from his pocket but couldn't get past the headline. Raindrops threatened to melt the paper, so he folded it carefully and put it in his shirt pocket. All he could think of was Lucy. Just like those days at school. She made it okay somehow.

He stood and walked, oblivious to the coming deluge. A few blocks on, he took momentary refuge in a phone booth. The coins fell, clinking through its works, and he dialed Lucy's number.

"You home?"

She laughed at the other end. "Well, I'm answering, aren't I? What's going on, stranger?"

"Is Kendra there? Is it okay if I come over?"

"Yeah, she's here. But come anyway. She needs to just chill out."

"I can't blame her."

"No, but she can't blame you either. It is what it is."

"I'll be about an hour. I'm on foot."

"It's pouring out there. Take the bus, for God's sake."

The rain stopped eventually, but he was wet through. He thought about how rough he must look as he stepped up to Lucy's porch and knocked on the door. His heart sank as he saw Kendra through the distorted glass of the back-porch window. She opened the door, standing firm in the middle of the doorway, arms crossed against her chest.

"What the hell do you want?"

That girl never lets up, he thought. "Is your mom home?"

Kenny heard Lucy call out from inside the house, "Is that Kenny?" Lucy came around the corner into view. "Let him in."

Kenny stepped in, slipped out of his jacket and hung it on the one free peg by the door.

"Why don't you just fuck off and leave her alone?" Kendra whispered.

"Kendra! Don't be so rude to your father."

"He's not my father. He's some bum who knocked you up and took off."

Kenny turned to leave, but Lucy touched his shoulder. "Ignore her, Kenny. You're soaked through. Come on in."

"So, Mom, how many times did you rearrange the cupboards this week? How many times did you count the tiles in the bathroom? How many times did you lock and unlock the door this morning before you went out for groceries?" Kendra crossed her arms across her chest again, the anger plain in her face. "And it's always worse after he leaves. And he leaves every time, Mom. And still, whenever he calls, you jump. And every time he leaves, you go back to rearranging your cupboards in the middle of the night."

"Kendra, for chrissake, stop." Lucy stepped between them.

"No, Mom, you stop. What has he ever done for you but build you up, then run off? It's not right."

Kenny sensed the sweat forming on his forehead and felt like he was going to puke. He looked at Kendra. "She's not wrong." He reached for his jacket.

Lucy turned toward him. "Stay. It's not like that, Kenny, and you know it."

Kenny put his jacket back on the peg. Truth be told, he didn't feel strong enough to walk back downtown.

"Kendra, don't you have somewhere to be?" Lucy plucked a raincoat and umbrella from the pegs by the door and handed them to Kendra. "Now, get on with your day. I've got supper planned, so be home by six."

"Mom, I don't know why you go for this."

"That's right, Kendra, you don't. Now go."

"You're looking good, Kendra." Kendra looked at Kenny as though he had slapped her.

"Come on, you're shivering." Lucy walked Kenny down the hall to the bathroom. "Take a hot bath and I'll make some lunch. You're a bit ripe." She handed him a towel and squeezed his hand. "Don't worry about Kendra. She thinks I need protecting."

Kenny lowered the lid on the toilet and sat for a minute. He heard Lucy walking around in the kitchen, the fridge door opening and closing, and somehow it all felt better. He stripped and left his clothes in a puddle by the sink and leaned to fill the old claw-footed tub. It reminded him of the tub at the Mission School, but he didn't mind so much. It was deeper and longer than modern bathtubs and allowed for a real soak, a deep heat to soothe the aches and pains that were harder to ignore lately. Kenny eased in and closed his eyes.

He heard Lucy slip through the door. He listened, eyes still closed, as she stooped and gathered up his clothes. Kenny opened his eyes when he heard the click of the door behind her and saw the fresh set of clothes she'd left sitting on the toilet seat, the ones she'd washed from the last time he was here. Kenny sank farther into the tub, dozing a little.

A half-hour later, he felt like a new man. Lucy was cooking when he headed to the kitchen. Kenny stood behind her and put his arm around her shoulders and leaned in, planting a soft kiss on the top of her head. She turned, looked at him and smiled.

"It's been a while this time, eh Kenny?"

"I haven't been in the city much. Logging on the island, trying to get by."

"They told me I could retire this year. Hard to believe I've been at this for almost twenty-five years. But what would I do? Sit here all day? I think I'll keep working. Maybe part-time. Just till Kendra graduates."

"Do you think she'll ever forgive me?"

"She's only twenty-three. She still thinks she knows everything."

Kenny kissed her on the top of the head again, breathing in her soft, clean smell, noticing the bright white that streaked her hair like thin ribbons. "Yeah." He smiled back. "I remember when I knew everything too. But seriously, it would be nice if she would let me get to know her a little."

"Give her time. You know, you're never here for long. She just gets used to you and you're gone. She makes it about me, but I don't think that's all that's going on. Girl needs a dad, you know." Lucy flipped the grilled cheese onto a plate and handed it to him. "Come on, let's eat."

When they were about halfway done, Kenny pulled the article out of his pocket and put it in front of her.

"So, this is why you're here today."

"I was down at the Two Jays and I just couldn't stop shaking when I read this. Felt like I was right back there."

Lucy pushed the paper away. "Why would they do that? It won't change anything. What's done is done."

"Justice?"

"I don't know. It just stirs up a lot of hurtful memories."

"Is Clara still working at the Friendship Centre? I bet they know what's happening. Why don't we go talk to her? See what's what."

Lucy leaned back in her chair, hands folded in her lap. "They call us survivors."

"Yeah."

"I don't think I survived. Do you?"

"I just don't know. I am so tired, Lucy. Can I lie down somewhere for a while?"

"Of course. Go lie down on my bed. I'll get you a quilt."

Kenny walked down the hall, weary from last night's binge and today's memories of the Indian School. He lay on top of the bed and the smell of fresh linen was like a remedy. His whole body seemed to deflate as the tension eased and he drifted, listening to the sounds of Lucy cleaning up after their lunch. When she was done, she gently covered him with a quilt and lay down beside him. He took her in his arms, and they slept.

It was dark when the pain in his liver woke him up. It had been worse lately and his doctor had scolded Kenny, telling him his liver couldn't take much more. He lay there alone. Typical of her, Lucy hadn't woken him when she got up. He sat on the edge of the bed, waiting for the pain to ease.

"Coffee?" Lucy took her reading glasses off as he stepped into the kitchen.

"Sure, that would be great." The kitchen was pleasingly warm and whatever she had roasting in the oven smelled beyond good.

"I'm just going to run down to the corner. I need some more cream for the gravy."

"You want me to go?"

"Naw. Drink your coffee. I could use the air anyway." She slipped into her jacket, hesitating, resisting the urge to turn the lock back and forth the way she would if Kenny weren't there, counting the clicks before opening the door. It wasn't that Kenny didn't know. It was just that there was nothing he could do about it, so he left her alone about it. She gave him a quick smile and opened the door.

Kenny pulled the article in front of him and this time read the whole thing. He wondered where they went to school, or if he knew any of them from the logging camps or the east side haunts. He sat back, wishing for a drink.

He saw her through the distortions of the old leaded window before Kendra opened the door. He pushed his coffee cup away and rose to go back to Lucy's room. He didn't miss how her face dropped when she saw him.

"You still here?"

"There's coffee." He wasn't sure what else to say.

"Where's Mom?"

"She'll be back soon."

To his surprise, Kendra poured herself a coffee and sat down.

"Still raining?" He fiddled with the handle of his coffee cup.

"Yeah. I was at the Friendship Centre. I've been volunteering there, helping Clara. She told me I shouldn't be so mean to you. She told me some other stuff too."

"Oh?" Kenny had often wondered when she would start asking questions.

"You know, no one talks about it. About the schools. Not even Mom."

"No point in it."

"Clara told me you ran away. They roughed you up pretty bad, eh?"

He could see her struggling to find words after so many years of bad feelings. "Ancient history."

"Look, I've hated you for a long time. Everything wrong in my life was about you. But I didn't know all this. I just didn't know. I can't say anything will change. I still hate how you figure you can just drop in on my mom and then bug out whenever you feel like it. You think she has no feelings? But for what it's worth, I'm sorry for what you went through."

Kenny looked up to see Lucy standing in the open doorway, quietly listening.

"It's okay, Kendra. You have a right to be mad."

Kendra pulled a flyer from her purse. "Clara asked me to give this to you and Mom."

"I'm home." Lucy spoke up as if she had just walked in the door. She put her grocery bag on the counter.

Kendra pushed her chair back. "I'll finish getting supper ready, Mom."

"Thanks, dear." Lucy hung up her jacket and sat with Kenny, reaching for her reading glasses. "What's this?"

She read the flyer and handed it back to Kenny. In large bold type at the top, it said: CALLING ALL SURVIVORS. It was a notice for a meeting of students from the Indian School. A lawyer was going to be there to talk about the lawsuit. Kenny looked at Lucy. She shook her head.

"I think we should go," Kenny said.

"I don't know, Kenny. Why pick at the scab?"

At the Friendship Centre, Kenny held Lucy's hand as they sat listening to the man in the suit explain what was going on in the court case. The usual dirty tricks from the government, saying they had been trying to save Native lives, that it would have been hell anyway, even without the abuse. He looked at Lucy. "No surprises here, eh?"

The lawyer was sure, though, that in the end the survivors would win. He said that anyone who wanted to start a case could talk to him privately after the meeting. Kenny raised his hand.

Lucy looked at him quizzically. "Really?"

The lawyer's helper came over to Kenny and wrote his name on her clipboard. "I'll call your name when it's your turn."

"Yeah, okay."

"Lucy, maybe if I can say what I need to say, things will be better. Maybe this is the way to get it out of me once and for all." He looked at her and took her hand, stuck it in his jacket pocket and held it tight. "Maybe we could have a future if I could get over the past."

She squeezed his hand back. "I don't know, Kenny. I really don't know."

Kenny looked around the room and wondered who these people might have been as children. Had they been his friends? He thought of running into Wilfred at that Wenatchee orchard and wondered who else was here that he might know. So hard to tell. He walked over to the refreshments table and was reaching to pour some coffee when a tall man about his age came up and stood beside him.

"Uh, I heard your lady friend refer to you as Kenny. Is it you?"

"Well, I'm Kenny. Who are you?"

"It's me. Howie."

"Howie?" Kenny couldn't put the two together, this man towering over him and little Howie, always hungry and scared.

Howie threw his arms around Kenny and he could feel the sobs, choked back but convulsing inside him.

"I never would have survived that place without you. You taught me how to find food in the bush. You were our hero, man. You actually escaped."

"Yeah, finally."

Lucy was chatting with Clara, so Kenny beckoned Howie over to a quiet corner. They pulled up a couple of chairs and sat, Howie shaking his head and wiping tears from his eyes.

Howie's face was flushed with embarrassment when he looked at Kenny. "Sorry, man."

"No need to be sorry. We were in hell together. I thought you died, man, when they carried you out that day all wrapped up." Kenny felt sick to his stomach just thinking about it. "I was so glad when you came back."

"I can't thank you enough for showing me the best way to get down to the dock and to Uncle Charlie's boat. I think I would have died there if I had stayed."

"Yeah. Me too. Sometimes I think I did die, I'm just still walking around."

"Well, I just got out of the pen a while back. Clara's been helping me get back on my feet. She told me you might be here today."

"Sorry to hear that. What happened?"

"I beat the crap out of Brother. Ran into him in a parkade when my mom and I had to go back to sort out some government paperwork. I just snapped. If my mom hadn't come running, I would have killed him."

Kenny slapped him on the shoulder. "Right on! He had it coming, that fucking freak."

"He sure did. I almost did my whole bit 'cause I wouldn't tell the Parole Board I was sorry I did it. It was a little weird 'cause just when I'd given up, the Board cut me loose."

"Yeah, fuck saying sorry." Kenny nodded in Lucy's direction. "Do you remember Lucy?"

"Not sure. Oh yeah, was she the one—you two were always passing notes?" Howie smiled.

"That's her over there." Kenny beckoned Lucy over and smiled, thinking of their self-conscious glances back then.

"Ah yes. Lucy."

"Lucy, do you remember Howie?"

"Clara told me you were around. Glad to see you." She shook his hand.

"Glad to see you two together." Howie smiled at her.

"Kenny? Is there a Kenny wanting to speak to the lawyer?"

Kenny grabbed Howie by the shoulder. "Man, it's so good to see you. Why not meet me at the Two Jays tomorrow morning? You know where it is? It's right at the corner of Carrall and Hastings. We'll have breakfast and catch up. Nine, okay?"

"Yeah, sure. That would be great."

Kenny left him chatting with Lucy as he headed for the office to meet with the lawyer.

"I'll wait for you, Kenny," Lucy said, touching his shoulder before he walked away.

A half-hour later, Kenny stepped out of the office and headed for the men's room. He barely made it into the stall before he puked. Why did the lawyer need to know all that? Kenny told him he was abused, but the lawyer said he needed details. More and more details. Kenny leaned over the toilet, his stomach in knots, heart pounding. He could smell Brother, leaning over him, hard against him, grabbing his hair. Kenny knew the pain in his side was his liver, but all he could think of were all those days of shallow breathing, avoiding the pain of broken ribs.

He heard Lucy calling through the bathroom door. "Are you okay, Kenny?"

Kenny left the stall, ran water in the sink and rinsed his face. "Yeah, be right out." He willed his hands to stop shaking, but they wouldn't. He shoved them in the pockets of his jeans so she wouldn't see. "C'mon, Lucy, let's get out of here."

"Are you okay?"

"That was pretty awful, digging into all those memories."

"Yeah. Figured it would be."

They walked down East Hastings and Kenny led her toward the bus stop. "I'm going to go to my room tonight, Lucy. I think I need to be alone. I'll wait for the bus with you."

"Are you sure you want to be alone tonight?"

"Yeah. I gotta meet Howie for breakfast tomorrow at the Two Jays, so I might as well just stay downtown."

They sat on the bench, holding hands, no words between them. Kenny wondered if she knew how much comfort she'd given him over the years. "Lucy."

"Yeah?"

Just then the bus pulled up. "Well, here it is."

The doors slapped open.

Kenny held her. Squeezed her and let her go. "You okay?"

"Yeah. Of course." She looked at him with a question in her eyes.

She got on the bus. Kenny stood there until she found a seat and the bus pulled away. When he couldn't see her anymore, he stepped through the doorway of the bar.

I awake the next morning and immediately something is different. The light. Like nothing I've seen before. I know I drank myself into a hole last night. For some reason, I feel like I am twenty years old. My stomach is calm and the pain in my liver that's been a part of every morning for months now is gone. I can hardly wait to get my day started and to meet Howie for breakfast. But before I can stir, someone is opening my apartment door.

"Hey! What the hell is going on? Get the fuck outta here!"

My voice sounds strange and I am beginning to feel a little light-headed. I can't seem to move, but at the same time I appear to be seeing things from every vantage point at the same time. Two men pull a stretcher into my room and now I am getting really upset, when out of the blue my mother is sitting next to me. Fear shoots through me like cold steel. My mother has been dead for years.

"Sshhhhh, Kenny, my boy, it's okay. You've come to join your ancestors."

"What?"

"Don't look at those men. Look into my eyes."

I try to reach for her, but a thin membrane stops me from touching her.

"Not yet, my son. Four days you must stay with your old form and then you will be free, with me and all the ones who have gone before. Look around us."

As though her words have opened my eyes, I look around and find myself on the outskirts of a village. Men are fishing with their spears and cedar rope nets. Women are working at their fires. The Big Houses are boldly painted with our family crests and I am filled with a peace like I have never known. I look back and start to panic as the men with the stretcher zip the body bag over me.

"Son, just look at the village. Look at your home. See how plentiful it is. Look at the smiles and feel the peacefulness here. Don't look back. Keep your eyes here. When the four days pass, you will be in your own longhouse with family and loved ones. But you have to walk the road of the past before you can fully enter the green grass world."

As soon as she utters these words, I feel myself flying at breakneck speed through images of the Indian School, through the fields of Washington where I survived picking apples, through the coastal fishing grounds, the logging camps, the dish pits and grease pits and flophouses. I am holding Kendra when she is still just so tiny. I see Lucy, glowing and happy beyond words. Me falling in love with that fat baby with the shock of jet-black hair and blue-obsidian eyes. I am holding hands with Lucy in her kitchen, smiling and talking. Finally, I find myself standing in the corner of a room. It settles in. They've brought me here, the ones who took me from my room. There is a body covered in a white sheet, lying on the stretcher, and I know it is me. The fear has left me now. It is no longer me.

The door to the morgue opens and a man in uniform walks through. Lucy is with him. The man lifts the sheet.

"Yes, that's him. That's Kenny." Her voice chokes up. "Can you let me have a minute alone with him, please?"

"Sorry, ma'am, it's a coroner's case, we can't let you touch him or be alone with him."

"Well, can you please just step back? Show me some respect, please." The desperation in her voice pulls at me.

The tears well in her eyes and her breath catches in quiet sobs. "Oh, Kenny, you are leaving me again."

"Lucy!" I stand beside her and try to stroke her hair. "Lucy. Don't cry." She stands as close to the body as the uniformed man will allow, and she speaks to me.

"No one can hurt you now, my love. No more nightmares, no more heartbreak. You are free. Dance away, my love. I will never forget you." She turns to leave.

"Lucy. I'm okay."

She turns and looks at me, and for a moment I am sure she heard me.

As soon as the door closes behind her, I am off again, whizzing through time. Now I am sitting on the pebble beach by my mother's smokehouse and once again she is with me.

"Do you remember, son?"

For a moment the priest with his flowing black robes and the RCMP officer with his yellow-striped pants and spit-polished boots hover near us, and then they are gone. "Yes, Mother, I remember." Now I am in the boat on the open ocean. Then standing at her door when she didn't recognize me after too many days and bottles had passed. Mother.

"Do you know I had no choice?"

"Yes. I know."

"But I let you down, son. When you fought so hard to get home and I couldn't crawl out of the bottle for you. My heart was so broken with you gone. But I should have been stronger."

"I never held it against you, Mother. We all suffered. You, me, all those other children and their parents. I know."

"Can you forgive me, son?"

"Yes, Mother, even though there is nothing to forgive."

"Turn away from it now, son, turn to the village."

I turn to the village again, and this time it seems closer. I can see the faces clearly now and the children are playing and laughing. How it should be. And then I am in the dorm at the Mission School, broken, crying in the night for my mother, but this time she comes for me. She sits on my cot and places my head in her lap and strokes her fingers through my hair. Mom, Mom.

"Son, your friends are calling you. It is the fourth day."

I turn, and they are all gathered in this place, high above a spacious lake. A line of drummers stand and sing a travelling song for me. I know my body is in that casket, but I care nothing for it. Lucy. Sweet Lucy has taken care of everything. My few friends are here, and there is food and coffee for all of them. My casket is draped in a beautiful Pendleton blanket and she is wrapping a set of clothes and a new pair of moccasins to go with me. She hasn't allowed flowers. Just pussy willows and cedar branches. My Lucy always understands. She stands alone, her hands pressed against my casket, and I hear her again.

"My friend, my love, I don't know why you have to leave me yet again, but I guess it's not for me to know. I hope you know that this place in my heart will hold you forever. Dance free. I will join you soon."

I stand next to her, catch her tears and press them to my heart.

I turn and find myself at the hearth, in the longhouse.

15

LUCY

t was a month since the funeral and a week since Lucy and Kendra had scattered Kenny's ashes carefully in the shrubbery of their neighbourhood park, the one where the three of them had spent so many happy days. Lucy sat at the kitchen table, a steaming cup of tea in front of her. Next to it sat a bulging envelope with only a printed return address, no name. Kendra wandered into the kitchen in her pyjamas, yawning. "Good morning."

"'Bout time, it's almost noon."

Kendra plugged in the kettle and then hugged her mom. "Quit being such a badass."

"Quit using that language."

"What's that?" Kendra nodded toward the envelope.

"Not sure. Kinda scared to open it."

"Want me to?"

Lucy nodded. "Yeah. Don't tell me if it's bad. Had enough bad for a while."

Kendra gave her mom a quick hug and reached for the envelope. She sat across from Lucy and quickly slit it open with a butter knife. Kendra placed a thick document on the table, the amazement clear on her face as she read the cover letter. She laid it down on the table as if it were some delicate relic. She looked up at Lucy. "It's about Kenny."

Lucy sat up straight in her chair. "What about him? From who? Don't they know he's gone?"

"It's from his bank. I guess he bought some life insurance and named you to get it if he died."

The shock on Lucy's face was quickly replaced with tears. She held her forehead in her palm. Kendra moved to sit next to her mom and put her arm around her shoulder.

"Ah, Mom. Don't cry."

"I know why you had such hard feelings against him, but this is how he always was. Even as a kid. Always caring for other people. Did you know he sent money home to his mother for years until she died?"

Kendra shook her head. "No, Mom. I didn't."

"I wish you could have seen how kind he was, how good."

"Me too, Mom. I just couldn't stand what he always did to you."

"No, Kendra. No. Don't make this about me. He was good to me. Always. He was the only person in the world who really understood what makes me tick. He loved me. Love doesn't play out like some cake recipe. Who do you think paid for all the work done on this house? That useless landlord?"

Kendra let her arm slip off Lucy's shoulder and shook her head. "I didn't know."

"And those braces you got when all the kids were teasing you at school about your teeth. Who do you think paid for those?"

"I just never had a dad, and every time he took off, I knew how hurt you were. And I was hurt too. Wasn't I enough to make him stay?"

"Child, he loved you more than life. Me too. It was himself he couldn't love. They did that to him. Whatever they didn't break in him, they bent. They beat him and beat him so many times I couldn't even count. He never told me this, but I know Brother was bothering him too. That creep went after so many of those little boys."

"Mom, I didn't know. First time I had any idea was when Clara talked to me about it, just before he died."

"And he never gave up." She told Kendra of all the escape attempts, the times he was caught by Brother or the RCMP and brought back to be humiliated and beaten. "He could have drowned, taking that little punt all the way to the fishing grounds."

"I'm sorry, Mom."

"I know he wasn't the way you needed him to be, but there is no limit to what that man could have done if it weren't for those bastards."

Kendra took a sharp intake of breath. "Mom."

Lucy shook her head just a little. "Just because I choose not to use foul language doesn't mean I don't know the words. And any suffering I felt when he would leave was for him. I knew how much pain he was in every single time he went back to his wandering. He tried to stay. Harder than he tried anything in this life."

Kendra sat a little taller and reached for the thick fold of documents. "Well? Should we look?"

Lucy nodded, folding her hands in her lap.

Kendra read through the papers and then laid them back on the table. "Mom. It's three hundred thousand dollars."

Lucy recoiled in shock, her eyes wide, jaw falling open. "What?"

"Yeah, you heard right."

Lucy stood and turned toward her bedroom. "Call Clara. I need to lie down." She headed toward the bedroom, one hand sliding along the wall as though she might fall without its support. She pulled the curtains open and lay down, gazing out at the now meticulously cared-for backyard. She looked at the yellow blossoms of the forsythia and remembered the time she and Kenny had planted it while celebrating Kendra's fifth birthday. Soft grey pussy willows crowded the branches of the red willow she and Carla had filched from the park as a small seedling. The cherry tree was in full blossom, and she thought of the many times she and Kenny had spread a blanket under its boughs, enjoying warm spring days, sometimes with Kendra, more often not as Kendra grew older and overcome with resentment.

Lucy reached over and pulled open the drawer of the bedside table and reached in for a small folder. She lay back again on the bed and opened it, a handful of photos falling out onto the bed. Their City Hall wedding; one of Kenny outside the Chinatown apartment; one of him cradling Kendra at just a few months old, like she might break. She picked up the one of him outside the apartment. She remembered him standing there that first time he'd come back, the collar of his worn jean jacket pulled up against the chill, his hands stuffed into his pockets. She thought of the first time they'd made love: him, all fumbling and gentle; her, nervous and embarrassed. She thought of the last time he'd been in their bed, their innocent sleep, arms around each other, close and warm. And she wept. Holding the picture against her body, she turned her face into the pillow so Kendra wouldn't hear.

It was late afternoon when she woke to the sound of Kendra's voice.

"Mom. Clara's here."

Lucy quickly returned the pictures to their folder and slipped them back in the drawer. "I'll be right there." She splashed her face with cold water in the bathroom and then headed to the kitchen.

Clara rose from the table and put her arms around her. "Look at your eyes. You've been crying again. You know what Mariah taught me about death? That the only thing our loved ones suffer is when we are suffering here without them. We know he is free, finally, in the green grass world. You know he would not want you to suffer."

"I try. It just hurts so much. He deserved so much better."

"We all did. But I guess the only thing we can do is try to make our own lives better now."

Lucy nodded. "I suppose. Now what about this letter? Is it real?"

Clara nodded at her friend. "Yes, it is most definitely real. What a guy. You're set."

"So, what do we have to do?"

"I don't know for sure, but you probably have to go to that insurance company and sign papers, then they will give you the money."

"Will you call for me?"

Clara nodded, reaching for the phone. "Sure." She made an appointment for the following Tuesday, and hung up the phone. "You'll need to bring all your ID and after you sign their papers, they will give you a cheque."

Lucy smiled for the first time since Clara had arrived. "ID. Remember about the ID right after Kendra was born?"

The two women burst out laughing, Kendra looking at them as if they'd suddenly gone nuts.

Lucy caught her breath and turned to Clara. "Tell her."

Clara, always happy to tell a story, settled back and launched into Kendra's birth story, the attempted apprehension of her by the welfare, the fake ID, the awful state the house had been in and how they'd all pulled together to make her a home.

Kendra took it all in and looked at the two women as though she were seeing them for the first time. "Wow. You two were crazy!"

Clara nodded. "That we were. Crazy for you. But yeah, you don't know the half of it. Well, c'mon, we need to celebrate. How about we go for Chinese food?"

"Well, I'm sure not up to cooking." Lucy turned to Kendra. "You want to?"

The three of them gathered their things and headed out to the Peking Kitchen, a new place just a few blocks from the house. Clara turned to Lucy as they walked. "Too bad they closed down the Only. Best place ever."

Lucy nodded. "Seems everything is changing."

They settled into their booth at the restaurant and ordered their favourites along with a large pot of green tea. Kendra was the only one who ate with chopsticks, and the women smiled at her dexterity. Lucy ordered some ginger beef to go. Kenny's favourite. She would put it out for him when she got home, an offering.

The conversation waned as they finished their meal. Kendra looked at her watch.

"Sorry, Mom, but I am supposed to go to study group tonight." She was in her second year at college, in a sciences program. She had set her sights on becoming a doctor.

Lucy beamed at her. "Yes. Go. I'll see you at home later."

Clara and Lucy watched her head out the door. "She has become quite the young woman," Clara said, the pride clear in her voice.

"That she has." Lucy settled back in the booth, sipping her tea.

"So, what you gonna do with all that dough? I know me and Kenny had our issues, but I never expected he would do something like this. What a guy."

"I've told you all along he was a wonderful man."

"Yeah, well, it's hard to see through all the leaving and boozing and such."

"I know. But he is. Was. Just can't get used to that. Was."

"So?"

"Well, I'm going to put aside enough so Kendra won't want for anything while going to school. Then I think I'll buy a house. A newer one, so she will have something when I go."

"That sounds like a great idea. You must be sick of that old house by now."

"No. Not at all. It was our home, me and Kenny. I feel him there. And it was your home too, remember, during all your adventures."

Clara laughed. "This is true. Still, you deserve something newer."

They paid their bill and wondered out into the evening air. Clouds formed above in billowing patterns and they picked up their pace. They went their separate ways a block before Lucy's house, Clara heading to Hastings to catch the bus.

The money came through just as Clara had said it would, and she, Lucy and Kendra started looking at real estate ads. They eventually hired an agent, an earnest young man new to the business. Lucy was clear she wanted to stay in the neighbourhood even when he pressed her that she might like something on the west side. Something safer.

"No," she said firmly. "I know where everything is here. It's home here."

The agent prepared a list of modest homes within a ten-block radius of Frances Street for Lucy to consider. After a week and a half, Lucy made an offer on a neat postwar bungalow with three bedrooms, a fenced-in yard and a kitchen laid out much like the one at the Frances Street house but bigger, with new appliances and cabinets. She signed the papers and she and Clara went home and waited.

Kendra arrived that evening as the nervous women thought for sure they wouldn't get it at their low offer even though the agent had been confident. By half past eight, they'd still heard nothing.

Lucy shrugged and wrapped her sweater around herself. "Well, I guess that's that. Too bad, I liked that place. Good for grandchildren. Close to the elementary school."

Clara winked at Kendra. "Better get busy, Grandma here's making plans."

Kendra laughed. "Oh no. I can't even imagine being a mom."

The phone interrupted their laughter. Lucy took the receiver off the hook while Clara crossed her fingers and Kendra wiggled in her chair with anticipation.

"Okay. Okay. Yes. Sure. Okay. Yes, that would be fine. See you tomorrow."

"Well?" Kendra was bursting.

Lucy threw her hands in the air. "We got it!"

"That is so fantastic." Clara lifted her teacup in a toast. "To Kenny."

Lucy and Kendra tapped their teacups against Clara's. "To Kenny." The words caught in Lucy's throat and she wiped a runaway tear.

The sale went through without a hitch and once it was finalized, Lucy and Kendra started packing up the house. Lucy insisted that they pack Kendra's things first. They would get her settled and then Lucy would follow. They splurged and bought a new couch, a dining table and some fancy lamps Kendra couldn't keep her eyes off. Lucy told Clara after the big shopping trip how the salesman had tried to shoo her down to the bargain basement and how his attitude changed completely when she pointed out her selections.

The movers arrived on schedule and Clara came by to help.

Lucy sat in the kitchen, tapping her fingers on the table. "It's going so fast."

"That it is, but it's great, right?" Clara glanced over at her old friend, who was looking increasingly distressed.

"I guess so. I've been here so long. Seems like my whole life unfolded in this house."

"I know, but this is a new beginning for you. Do you really want to be reminded of Kenny every day?"

"I do, actually. I don't want to lose these memories."

"You won't, Lucy. How could you? They are a part of you."

"Memories fade. I don't even remember what my mom looked like. Do you? To me the word 'mom' means me. When it comes to my own mom, it's just a word, a sound like a whistle or a bark. No meaning."

Clara nodded. "I know. I don't really remember what my mom looks like either."

The movers returned after unloading Kendra's belongings and delivering the new furniture. The burlier of the two turned to Lucy and asked if the rest of the stuff was to go or if anything was to be left behind.

Clara replied, "Yes, it all goes."

"No," Lucy said quietly. "None of it goes. I'm staying here."

Clara opened her mouth to reply, but one look at her friend and she knew there would be no talking her out of it.

"This is my home. I will stay here with him."

16

HOWIE

Howie stood alone in the deserted cemetery at the foot of his mother's grave. Relatives he'd only met in childhood had left after the new headstone had been placed. It was five years to the day since his mother had succumbed to a heart attack. Working in her small garden, she breathed her last breath, lying amongst the fresh pea shoots, gazing at the brilliant blue prairie sky. Her friend found her that way, flat on her back, eyes closed. For a moment her friend thought she was taking a nap in the garden. Howie was still locked up. He was not there for her funeral, a truth that brought tears to his eyes today, alone in the small cemetery at Red Pheasant.

She'd wanted to come to Vancouver and visit him again, but he'd pleaded with her not to. She was getting on and deserved the peace of home and garden.

"I'll be fine, Mom. I'll get out eventually and get back on my feet and as soon as I can, I'll come home."

"Well, if you think so, son. It will be so good to have you home. We will make a feast and the family can get to know you again."

Now he wished he hadn't talked her out of it. Maybe he would have been with her when she took her journey. Maybe she wouldn't have been alone.

He thought he heard relief in her voice, and the fact that she was getting older sat heavy on his mind. She was always such a hard worker, revealing the stories of her days in painstakingly written letters recounting a much slower life. He had looked forward to the time he could head back here and take care of her. He'd dreamed for years of building a house next to hers on their family land on the rez and starting his own horse ranch. Appaloosas. He'd loved them ever since he was first introduced to the agile, curious breed when he was a boy, growing up in California. Sometimes he was lucky and a horse breeder magazine would show up in the prison library and he would lose himself in it, dreaming of days long ago spent high in the mountains with only a horse, a rifle, a knife and a bedroll. A future, no matter how far out of reach, that was as rich as the past was the dream that had kept him alive.

He knelt and started planting the tiger lily bulbs in front of her headstone, remembering a time, when he was very little, when she would tell him the old stories about Tiger Lily and Weesageechak, and the living stories of her parents and theirs. He knew she would love having a bright-orange spray rising, year after year. The flowers reminded him of her sturdy beauty. He rose and shook the dark earth from his work gloves, picked up his tools, gave his handiwork one last look and headed for his truck.

An emptiness overtook him as he drove back to his mother's little house. The shed out back, grey, weather-beaten and distinctly listing, looked as though it might collapse at any moment. The caragana hedge, whose top leaves he remembered being just able to touch as a small boy, now towered over him and obscured the house from sight from the road. In fact, the day of his arrival, he'd had to ask for directions to the house because it had changed so much from his boyhood memories. The three black poplars that stood guard around the garden had also thrived, their rugged bark like stories written by the elements.

The screen door creaked as he stepped inside. His lunch dishes dry now on the sideboard, he put them away and eased into his mother's armchair, an open cardboard box at his feet. He carried on where he'd left off the night before, sifting through a lifetime of mementoes, letters, birthday cards, recipes and news clippings. He smiled at the array of things she'd chosen to keep.

Inside the box was another, smaller wooden box. Opening it triggered an emotional landslide. Pictures of that summer adventure at Auntie Mae's before the priest brought the cop to take him away. Howie, newly six years old, standing in the wildly decorated living room holding his birthday cake, candles bright, his mother behind him, smiling like there was no tomorrow. Next to the photos was a tiny red car. It disappeared in his hand now, and he smiled remembering how it had not been so tiny in his child-sized hands.

Underneath these memories was a thick file folder. He opened it to see carbon copies of letter after letter penned in his mother's painstaking hand. Letters to the Indian agent, the RCMP detachment at Orca Bay, the Mission School itself, pleading her case, explaining that her son was to go to school at Red Pheasant, even begging them to let him come home. For all her letters, there was not one official letter in reply. Howie thought he might cry looking at her careful printing, her respectful requests for her boy to be returned to her. He carefully replaced the letters in the box and put it away, keeping two pictures, one of him and his mother with that glorious birthday cake and the other of her alone, standing beneath one of the giant cedars around Auntie Mae's home, whose swaying branches had haunted him on those long-ago nights. He placed the tiny red car on the window ledge next to the photos.

It seemed not so long ago that he had stood over the grave of his friend Kenny, not a week after reconnecting with him for the first time since the two had fought for survival together at Indian School. A rage he'd been able to contain for a long time was set free that day, and it would not let go of him. Conversations with Clara helped. She had helped him keep focused on the future, but when Kenny died, the past was like tinder to the rage he had kept bottled up during all those years of confinement. It was that rage that pushed him to make an appointment with the lawyers who had given the presentation that night at the Friendship Centre.

As with everything else, he and Clara had talked about it. "It's not even the money, Clara. It's about telling my story. Having my say after all these years. Not just me, but for the ones who can't speak out. Like Kenny. Like my mom."

"Like Lily."

Howie reached over and held her hand, and Clara sighed. "I mean, think about it. Our childhood memories are about murder and mayhem. How many others can't bear their own thoughts? They need to hear the truth."

He thought of Clara now, and wondered how she was doing. Over the weeks and months he'd spent sharing his progress with her, he'd grown attached to her. She was the first person he'd spoken to in any meaningful way after being arrested again, and it bound him to her. He wondered if she knew. He thought of writing her a letter now, but couldn't think of what to say. Flustered at the idea, he instead went out to the garden.

He'd repaired the greenhouse and put in a garden this year. The idea of looking at a bare patch of ground over the summer and fall was more than he could take. It was almost as though he could see his mother, her hands on her hips, scolding him for not growing food that he could enjoy all winter long. He'd planted following her

pattern: rows of potatoes and corn, beans and squash in their own
mounds, peas reaching for the sun as they crept up their supportive
netting, carrots with their delicate green tops swaying in the prairie
breeze. A calming satisfaction rolled over him, and he turned to the
split-rail corral he'd been working on since he first got here. He'd
been going to auctions every weekend, looking for just the right yearling he could train into a good saddle horse. He figured the right one
would show up when he had a place for her. As the sun bled pink
into the horizon, he headed back to the house.

The next morning, after a quick breakfast, he headed out to his truck,
thinking to head to town, check the mail and pick up a few supplies.
Maggie, his mother's friend and closest neighbour, waved to him as
she hung her laundry out, a line of dancing arms and legs, linens and
bedding. She'd been a wonderful source of information about his
mother's last months of life. He took comfort from her assurances
that his mother was able and independent to her last day. He pulled
the truck up in front of her porch.

"You want me to pick up your mail?"

Maggie took the clothespins out of her mouth. "Sure. That would
be a help, son."

"I'm gonna fix that porch for you, too, Maggie. Lookin' awful rickety."

"Oh, don't worry. I'm sure it'll outlast me."

Howie stopped at the grocery store first and then at the post
office, pleased to see a letter from Clara in the pile of advertisements
and bills, along with a letter from his lawyer. He stopped on the way
home at the old pasture where he and his mom used to walk when
he was little. A fallen tree next to the creek that ran through the pasture provided a place to sit. He turned the letter over in his hand a

couple of times before carefully slitting it open with his pocket knife.

Clara's letter said it was raining as usual in Vancouver. She'd been spending lots of time with Lucy and Kendra. She said she missed their conversations. He read that part three times, a feeling of warmth filling him. She was coming to Saskatchewan to visit Mariah in the fall. Maybe they could have a visit?

For the first time since coming back to Saskatchewan, Howie started to feel alive and purposeful. Over the next months, he completed the new corral and fixed the dilapidated fencing around the old pasture. He would have to build a shelter for the winter if he was going to have horses. He began salvaging lumber from old demo sites in North Battleford. He'd had a little money when he left BC, and his mother had left him her life savings, a little over six thousand dollars. He'd wondered at the time how she could have saved this from her tiny pension. Maggie enlightened him one day.

"She never bought much. Flour, salt, baking powder, tea. Sometimes, for a treat, some bacon. But you know, she was still snaring rabbits and catching fish right up till the day she died."

Howie thought he might cry. "She never mentioned those things in her letters."

"Oh yes. And she raised fryers every year from chicks. Did all her own baking, and then of course there was the garden. She would tell me every pension day, 'That boy of mine will need something to get on his feet.' And she would go to the bank and leave most of it there. For you."

"She never talked about it."

"I know you had to get her a headstone, but now you have to use the rest to get yourself set up. She went without a lot so you could. She even bought her clothes at the thrift store."

"I wish she'd just taken care of herself instead. I'm a man. I can make my own way."

"Oh, she took care of herself. She ate well from her own hard work and she took pride in being able to set that aside for you."

One night, Howie sat down and wrote back to Clara. He told her that he had to meet with his lawyer in Regina in the fall to tell his story of the Mission School. He wondered when she was planning her trip for. He told her about the garden and the fencing work. He rewrote his short note three times. The first time, he signed off *Love, Howie*. The second time, *Yours truly, Howie*. The third time, he just signed it *Howie*. He sealed the envelope and made a note to get to the post office before the day's mail was picked up.

The summer was like heaven to him. It was the hottest summer in years, and he soaked it up, like a man dying of thirst. Even after all the years of cold prison cells, his body remembered the healing heat of his time in the Southwest after his mom had run with him across the border. He spent as many of his waking moments as possible outside. It wasn't hard to do, what with tending the garden and rebuilding the shed bit by bit from the ever-growing pile of reclaimed lumber. He even took his meals outside, often inviting Maggie to join him. She would, never failing to bring an apron full of lemons and some fresh-picked mint from her garden. She made the best lemonade ever and kept him supplied. But other than Maggie, he kept his own company. At first, his aunties, uncles and cousins had come by to visit, curious about this long-lost relation. But that deluge of company soon waned, and it wasn't long before no one dropped by at all. After the initial pleasantries, they found they had little to say to each other, after all the years of separation. Maggie was different, though. She was like a living connection to his mother.

The warm days flew by, not at all like the interminable crawl of life in prison. So, even though the mature garden spelled out the coming days of fall, it was a surprise to Howie when he saw the first shot of deep orange in the leaves of the poplar trees, the silver twinkle of the birch along the creek in the pasture calming into soft fall yellow. Clara had written back quickly, and they had started a summer-long correspondence, which caused his heart to drop whenever there was nothing from her at the post office. He'd understood when she said she wanted to go to Mariah's on her own. The two women had not seen each other in some time.

One morning Howie packed his new jeans, the new matching grey-on-white western shirt with pearl snaps, and a black leather vest, all unworn and bought just for this occasion. He packed up all the lawyer's papers and felt the adrenalin course through him as he thought of sitting in front of some stranger, a judge at that, and telling them about Brother. He picked up the pictures of himself and his mother, slipped the tiny red car in his shirt pocket, closed the door behind him and headed south.

The drive was uneventful, the night at Ida's Motel sleepless, the walls not much thicker than the ancient wallpaper that covered them. Howie checked himself in the mirror and headed for the El Rancho café, where Clara had said she would meet him. No sooner had he slipped into the red leather booth than he felt a light tap on his shoulder. He turned around and there she was.

"Howie, you look fantastic. You're as brown as a bean, man. Lots of time outside, I see."

Howie reached in for a hug, and as soon as he felt her strong arms around his neck, all the nervousness disappeared. She was like coming home. They ordered breakfast and talked like no time had passed at all. Clara caught him up on how Lucy and Kendra were doing, and Howie shared his adventures in rebuilding at Red Pheasant.

"I'd love to see it sometime." Clara pushed her plate out of the way and folded her hands on the table.

"Well, I'd like that too." Howie reached over and took one of her hands in his. "I really would, Clara."

Clara looked at him carefully. "So, you ready for today?"

"As ready as I'll ever be." Howie sat up straight, the adrenalin pushing through his veins again.

Clara held tight when Howie tried to pull his hand away. "Lots of people in Vancouver are going through the process. I've gone as a support person before. It's hard, for real. But listen, you've already survived. This is just letting them know what you survived."

Howie nodded silently.

"You can do this. I know you can."

Howie looked at her. "Will you come with me?"

Clara nodded. "If you want me to."

Howie laid some bills down to cover their breakfast, nodded to the waitress who seemed to be watching them, and they headed out to his truck. "You riding with me?"

"Either that or I'm walking."

Howie shook his head. "Still the same Clara. Always a quick comeback."

"I took the train from the coast, remember? Vera and George picked me up at Mariah's and dropped me here. We're supposed to drop by their place after. It's not that far out of town."

Howie held the truck door open for her, then walked around to the driver's side. The sounds of the city seemed to close in on him. He looked at Clara as he slid into the driver's seat. "Let's get this over with. I'm not much on cities."

He'd been surprised that the hearing was to be at a hotel instead of in a courtroom, and he was even more surprised when he was greeted by the woman who would make decisions about his case, along with a Department of Justice lawyer, casually dressed, sipping coffee around a boardroom table in the hotel meeting room. His lawyer had told him how it would be, but his only other experiences with the legal system had been quite different, so he was still surprised. His lawyer sat on one side of him, with an impressive array of files and document binders in front of him. Clara sat on the other side. The decision-maker introduced herself and explained what was about to happen and how she would make her decisions about his case. She clicked on the recorder, took his oath and asked him to tell her his story.

"My name is Howard James Brocket and when I was five years old, my mother took me on the train to visit my auntie in BC. I was not able to come home until last year . . ."

After the first few gruelling minutes, the day flew by. Howie told her about the birthday party and the cop who dragged him from his mother's arms. He spoke of Brother and the constant fear, hunger and helplessness. And he spoke of Kenny.

"He was my friend. He showed me how to survive, and he died without ever having a chance to share with anyone how he suffered. I am here today for him and for all the others who died far away from home, alone and unprotected. We were just little kids." His voice caught in his throat and Clara reached for his hand under the table and held it tight.

They exited the hotel under the blue Saskatchewan sky. A kind of euphoria filled Howie, even though he felt weak in the knees. It was as if the burden of history had been lifted from his shoulders. He looked down at Clara. "Let's get the hell outta here."

She smiled and held her hand out. "Gimme the keys. I got a surprise for you."

"Oh no." Howie offered a show of resistance and then handed them over.

They drove past the city limits, like a ribbon at the finish line of a long and arduous race. A peaceful air filled the cab of the truck and they held hands as Clara drove.

"Here we are." Clara pulled off the highway onto a dirt approach lined on either side with stately birch trees. The small log house at the end of the road belied the grand entrance. George was tinkering under the hood of his truck. Vera set a basket of vegetables down on the porch and waved a greeting to them as they pulled up. Clara jumped out of the driver's side and the old friends embraced, walking around to the passenger side.

"You must be Howie." Vera reached out for a handshake. "We've sure heard a lot about you." She winked at Clara.

"Aw, cut it out, Vera." Clara looked at Howie and shook her head. George wiped his hands on his overalls and shook Howie's hand before reaching in to give Clara a hug.

"Well, that little girl's been kicking up quite the fuss. You better go tend to her." George nodded toward the barn.

Clara put her arm through Howie's. "Come on. I got something for ya."

"What? You know how I don't like surprises."

"Aw, don't be that way! You'll love this one."

Vera and George headed into the house. "I'll get cleaned up and then I think Vera has something special cooking for supper. Come on in when you're done there."

Howie and Clara headed to the barn. The golden light of late afternoon cut through the dim interior of the barn. "She must be sleeping."

In the back stall, they came to a dog kennel. Clara could no longer contain herself. "She's for you." She knelt, opened the kennel, and scooped out the puppy and stood, handing her to Howie. The puppy, now wide awake, wiggled and writhed in Howie's grip. "I brought her all the way on the train."

Howie set the puppy down and she immediately ran and hid behind Clara. They both laughed, and Clara picked her up and placed her at the heels of Howie's boots. "This is John Lennon's great-granddaughter."

Howie had met John Lennon in the last year of his life and had been there for Clara the day he died and she needed help to get him to his mountain resting spot. It was hard to see the old man in the pup until she turned just so in the light and he saw the trademark ridge along her spine. With that and her outsized paws, he knew he would have a big girl on his hands.

"She was the pick of the litter. Figured you needed some company, out here all by your lonely."

"You are something else, Clara." They put the puppy back in her crate and headed to the house.

"You better name her," Clara said, elbowing him lightly.

"Yeah, well. I'll think on that. Not just any name is gonna do."

They laughed and climbed the stairs to join Vera and George.

17

CLARA

With Howie on his way home, Clara rented a truck to navigate that perilous road. John Lennon was dead and she felt strangely alone in the cab as she made her way south to the Cypress Hills. None of her music choices felt right and she resorted to silence and the hum of the truck. Even though it had been many years since she'd last been there, Clara found the cut-off to Mariah's like she was heading home. The truck rumbled up the crumbling road and pulled up in front of the little cabin. Mariah, smaller, older, stepped through the door and waved at Clara. Clara jumped out of the truck and gently wrapped her arms around Mariah.

"Clara, my girl, you are happiness to my eyes. You look so strong."

"You look just the same."

"Liar."

The women laughed as they headed into the cabin. Clara was amazed by how it looked exactly as it had when she was last there, running from the law, broken and confused. The place was rich with delicious smells.

"I made you a feast. C'mon, sit. I'll feed you." Mariah tied her apron on and busied herself with the final touches to the meal, the women chattering away as though no time had passed. "How's Vera and George doing, now they're moved back this side of the line?"

"So good. Two kids and working on a third."

"Ah, that's good. Kids are good. When you gonna get busy with that? Don't want to leave that too long, you know. I got some medicine for that."

Clara blushed and turned away.

"Ah you, nothing to be embarrassed about. Babies and how we make 'em. Most natural thing in the world." Mariah filled the small table with their feast and they sat, helping themselves and savouring the wild flavours of her pantry.

"And what about you working in the court? Still doing it? Don't you find it hard to be around all those stuffy white people all the time?"

"You get used to it. At the beginning I was harsh with those judges and prosecutors, but then someone reminded me that my job was to keep Indians out of jail. And that is what I do. Some stay out, some don't, but at least they get a chance. It's good honest work."

"I'm proud of you, girl."

Clara reached over and placed her hand on Mariah's. "I would have never been able to do it without you."

"And this man. What about this man?"

"Oh, Mariah, I just don't know. No man has ever really loved me except this one. Most times it's so good, but sometimes I get this feeling, this ugly feeling that he doesn't really know me, and that when he figures it out, he'll want nothing to do with me."

"Hmmm. So, you're still holding on to some of that Indian School garbage, I see."

"You think that's it?"

"Do you?"

Clara lowered her eyes. "Maybe."

The two women rose and cleared the table. They chatted and

laughed while Clara washed and Mariah dried the dishes, then sat down to tea and an evening of catching up.

That night, Clara slept a deep and dreamless sleep, waking in the grainy light of pre-dawn. She lay still, a deep sense of comfort and repose rising in her as she took in the details of this sanctuary of so long ago. She rose and dressed to the sound of Mariah's quiet movements and the smell of coffee. She rustled through her duffle bag and pulled out the package of tobacco and squares of blue, red, white and yellow cotton. She pulled a bill out of her pocket and placed all of it in a small purse made from a patterned wool blanket. She joined Mariah, who had prepared another feast for breakfast, and laughed. "You're going to make me fat!"

"Ah, you're too bony anyway. Gotta get some curves on you for that man."

Clara sighed and shook her head. After breakfast and cleanup, she sat with Mariah and made her offering of the tobacco and the cotton prints. "Will you help me? In the lodge. Help me clear my mind and heart about Howie. Help to understand why, still, inside I feel like dirt."

Mariah held the offering in both hands, closed her eyes and prayed softly in Cree. She opened her eyes, looked at Clara with the wisdom of the ancients in her eyes, and nodded.

The next four nights, Mariah and Clara welcomed the moist, rolling heat of the sweat. Mariah sang the ancient songs and they prayed—for understanding, for clarity, for the weight of the Mission's hatred to be lifted once and for all from Clara's heart. Each night following the sweat, Clara dreamed of the Mission and Sister Mary. She saw her body as a little child covered in bruises, her head shorn, thin to the point of emaciation. Each morning, she was horrified. Desperate, she turned to Mariah the morning of the fourth day, telling her again of the nightmares. "Mariah, this is not working."

"It will be okay, my girl. You know, we think we know what's going on, but we don't. Let the healing come to you in its own way."

That night, they entered the lodge together for the last time. Afterwards, exhausted, they made the food offering and feasted in silence. Clara gave Mariah a hug and went to bed filled with trepidation at what horror her dreams would bring her tonight. She was almost immediately asleep nonetheless. This night, though, it was not Sister Mary who haunted her dreams. It was another who arrived, dressed in an intricately beaded deer-hide dress and moccasins. She was chubby and smiling, her hair tightly braided and decorated with tiny multicoloured shells. Lily. She was sitting under a magnificent birch tree, tall prairie grasses swaying around her. She was glowing, bursting with good health and humour.

"Clara, my friend, your heart is the most beautiful I ever knew. You cared for me, protected me, held me when the sickness was taking me. Clara, your spirit is blameless. Accept your beauty. Accept love. It is your due."

Clara reached for Lily, surprised to see herself too as a child, glowing with the same radiant health. The little girls held each other, and in a moment Clara woke, hugging her pillow, weeping. She lay awake the rest of the night, resisting any urge to sleep, holding fast to the image of Lily and the physical sensation of her presence and her touch. It was not until she heard Mariah's footfalls in the kitchen that she rose, exhausted and exhilarated, and joined her.

Mariah smiled when Clara recounted Lily's visitation. "You see, my girl. The ancestors always know what we need."

For the next two days, the two women rested and relaxed, enjoyed cooking together and taking long, rambling walks through the thick forest of poplar and birch that surrounded Mariah's cabin. On the third day, Mariah packed a lunch for Clara and walked her to the truck. The women held each other and looked into each other's eyes, wordlessly. Then Mariah turned and made her way back to the cabin. She stopped and turned at the doorway and called out to Clara, "And it's not too late for a baby. You can at least have fun trying!"

Clara burst out laughing as she climbed into the truck. "See you soon, woman."

Once back in Vancouver, Clara headed to Lucy's house on Frances Street. The two old friends sat over tea and Clara told her all about fighting her demons at Mariah's and the peace she thought she had a chance at.

Lucy smiled, happy for her friend. "And what about Howie? C'mon. Spill."

Clara laughed and blushed a little. She was reminded of all they'd been through together, she and Lucy. "Well, it's definitely something. Things were pretty intense with his hearing and we got even closer."

"How close?" Lucy waggled her eyebrows at Clara.

"Geez, you and Mariah. Coupla pervs. We held hands. He hugged me. A lot. He's asked me to come be with him."

"You gonna go?"

"I think so. Don't wanna be a fool, but yeah, maybe."

Clara and Lucy visited long into the night, reminiscing, often howling with laughter at some of the antics of their youth, coming close to tears at some of the sadness. Clara spent the night rather than venturing out in the dark and damp. The next morning, they talked over breakfast, last night's gloomy deluge replaced by a brilliant, sunny day.

"I think I'm going to take a leave from work. Take some time to figure out what I want in my life. Might sublet my apartment. I don't know."

"Where will you go? Kendra might know someone who could move into your place."

"I've made up my mind. I'm going to Howie."

Lucy hugged her friend. "You do that."

18

HOWIE

After his reunion with Clara in Regina, the fall seemed to take over at a galloping rate. The leaves fell and the ground froze, with Howie getting the root vegetables out of the garden without a day to spare. With Maggie's patience and help, Howie learned the fine art of preserving vegetables, which he was grateful for during a long, lean winter. His hunting skills were rusty after all those years away, but he soon was able to bag a deer, and his snares regularly yielded rabbits that gave a nice variety to the venison he ate at most meals.

The winter evenings were long, and the puppy, now known as Billie Holiday, in keeping with tradition, was good company. Long and lanky, she would fill out in the spring and had the attitude of her great-grandfather, not to mention his good looks. Howie and Clara maintained their correspondence and closed the year with a promise of a spring visit.

When the letter came from the lawyer, in its large, thick manila envelope, he didn't quite know what to expect. It sat on the kitchen table, unopened, for three days. Finally, the morning of the fourth day, after stoking up the wood stove and making himself some coffee, Howie opened the letter. Good news, the lawyer wrote. Howie set the letter aside and turned to the document included with it: the result of the decision-maker's work. He read it carefully, tears rising as she recounted the horrors that had been his life at the Mission. He turned to the final page and the amount of compensation he would receive. He looked at Billie Holiday and nodded. "Can't give me back my childhood, but maybe we can make a better life with this. Whaddya think, Billie?" Billie Holiday lifted her head and smiled.

The crocuses had just started peeking through the snow, reminders of the small joys his mother had left behind. The purple, yellow and orange made the day feel warmer than it actually was. The quality of light had changed, though, and spring was in the air. Howie was busy scrubbing the residue of the winter's woodsmoke from the windows, washing floors and laundering curtains and bed linens. The place was starting to sparkle. He'd even bought a light fixture at one of the auctions he haunted to cover the bare bulb. As good as it was going to get, Howie cleaned himself up, took one last look at the house, closed the door and headed for the truck. He whistled and pointed, and Billie Holiday jumped into the passenger seat.

"Oh no you don't, get in the back, you. We got company coming." Howie wiped the front seat after Billie Holiday jumped into the back, careful that it was spotless. They drove to pick Clara up from the train in Biggar. Just before town, the same sign that his mother had tried to explain to him when he was a boy still stood in its place: *New York is big . . . but this is Biggar.*

"You get it, Billie Holiday?" She whined. "Okay, girl, we're almost there."

Howie parked the truck at the train station, fifteen minutes early, and stepped out, leaving the driver's side window open just a crack for Billie Holiday. "Now you be good, I won't be long." He walked into the station, checking the schedule on the wall, and then double-checked with the station master to be sure the train was on time. It seemed like forever before the train pulled in, and then there she was, looking tired and dishevelled after her long trip.

Howie walked over and put his arms around her.

"Oh, man, you are a sight for sore eyes. That trip gets longer every time." Clara hugged him back. "Careful, I probably stink."

Howie laughed. "Still tellin' it like it is. Some things never change." They collected her luggage and headed out to the parking lot. Billie Holiday had taken over the driver's seat, her nose sticking out the window, eyes fixed intently on the station door.

Clara burst out laughing. "Yup. Just like her grandfather."

The two climbed into the truck, Howie having to shoosh Billie Holiday into the back again. She eyed Clara suspiciously until Howie leaned over and put his arms around her. "She's on our side, girl." Billie Holiday smiled.

"Woman, I am so happy you are here."

"Me too, man." She scooted up close to him on the bench seat of the truck, Billie Holiday resting her head between theirs on the drive home. They were quiet during that hour-long drive, but not uncomfortably so. Howie placed his hand on her thigh and she placed hers on his.

They pulled into Howie's approach and Clara noted with approval all the hard work he'd done on the corral, which stood empty but for some hay and a grain bucket.

Howie slid on his work gloves. "Well, it's my turn for a surprise." He left Clara standing at the railing of the corral as he entered the old shed that he had renovated into a three-stall barn. He slid the door open wide and from the depths she heard a deep *hyah, hyah*. Seconds later, two yearling Appaloosa fillies trotted out of the barn and into the corral, ears perked, heads tossing in the cool air.

"Wow!" Clara climbed up on the lowest rung of the corral rails. "They are so beautiful. The beginning of your dream."

Howie made his way over to Clara and they stood head to head as she perched a step above him on the rail. He put his arm around her waist. "The one with the black stockings is yours. Picked her out special, just for you."

Clara's face turned sober. "Really?"

Howie lifted her off the railing and stood her in front of him. "Stay with me, Clara. We can make a good life here, you and me."

Clara looked over to the gentle hills, then to Howie, and nodded.

That night, Clara lay still for a long time, her back against his chest, warm. She felt him drift into sleep, his breathing deepening and relaxing. She slipped out of bed, pulled on her nightgown and walked softly into the living room. Billie Holiday observed her but made no move to follow. She opened the kitchen curtains and sat at the table there, watching the angular branches of the poplar trees waving in the night breeze, ghostlike against the bright moonlight. She thought of Mariah, their long winter of discovery and those many evenings, huddled in the snow, leaning against the trees, shivering, the songs rising into the night air. She thought of Lucy, alone and too quiet, incessantly rearranging her cupboards. Maisie, long dead and rarely spoken of. Kenny, who could never seem to stop escaping. But now when she thought of Lily, she saw a chubby girl in the bright sun.

She dug around in her bag and pulled out the package Mariah had given her all those years ago. It was still wrapped in blue fabric with tiny red, yellow and white stars, tied with a red ribbon. She'd known that Mariah had taken three of those ancient glass bottles from the trees around the lodge. All these years later the package remained unopened.

She slipped her jacket and boots on and headed out to three poplars, where she crouched, untied the ribbon and laid the fabric open. Three old glass bottles, one red, one blue, one a golden yellow, complete with the hide ties that had secured them in Mariah's trees. Clara tied them close to each other on one strong branch, as high as she could reach in the middle of the three poplar trees. She stood back, arms folded, watching them glint in the moonlight, the defiant poplars dancing ever so slightly, the wind playing in the new spring leaves as though to say, *we see you, we are with you, dance on.* She slipped back into bed with Howie and lay there, drifting into sleep, the tinkling her song of home.

ACKNOWLEDGEMENTS

To Merilyn Simonds, who so generously and tirelessly worked with me to advance the manuscript. I would give you a kidney. Warm hugs and deep thanks to my champion and unflagging supporter, Michael Glassbourg, who read many drafts and never stopped encouraging me to continue. Love always to my daughter from another mother, Jessica Loyva, who just wants her name in a book. To Buffy Sainte-Marie, love and peace for allowing me the use of lyrics from your anthem, "Starwalker." Dr. Charles Brasfield for being at the forefront of understanding what harm these children suffered. Jennifer Lambert, thank you for getting it, right away. I am deeply grateful for a smooth and rewarding editing experience largely due to the experience and skill of the most wonderful Janice Zawerbny. Diana Davidson, Allan and Mona, Mary Goldie, Kym Gouchie, Judy Mosher, Lisa Riddle, Fiona Scott, Winona Wheeler, dearest friends, my thanks for being there in dark days. Len Marchand, well, you know.

So much love to my father, William Stanley Stiff, who gave me a fascination for language, a drive to understand the power of words and a love of reading

May this be a tribute to my mother, Martha Eliza Soonias Stiff, who lived through the hell of one of these schools. Her tenacity taught me courage; her stories echo here.